THE MAN WITHOUT A FACE

A PETER BLACK THRILLER

DAVID ARCHER

VINCE VOGEL

RIGHTHOUSE

ISBN-13: 978-1-63696-146-0

ISBN-10: 1-63696-146-0

Cover design by: Damonza

Printed in the United States of America

www.righthouse.com

www.instagram.com/righthousebooks

www.facebook.com/righthousebooks

twitter.com/righthousebooks

PRAISE FOR THE PETER BLACK SERIES

PETER BLACK THRILLERS

ONE

LIKE ALWAYS, ST. MARK'S SQUARE WAS CROWDED with tourists. His meeting point, the Café di Biaggio, was nestled in a corner beyond the stone columns of the Procuratie Nuove building. Tables and chairs reached out from the cafés and restaurants that bordered the ancient cobbles. Everywhere thronged with patrons. Waiters weaved in and out of them. The smell of coffee and rich food hung in the air. A three-piece orchestra played Vivaldi on a stage, the music echoing off the tall buildings.

Peter didn't like the position of the café. Sure, it was in a cluttered corner, out the way, but opposite it, at a slight angle, was the Torre dell'Orologio clocktower. Fifty meters across the square, it was the perfect sniper nest, and though he spotted his contact sitting at a table tucked behind a wide column, it was still a little too exposed to the six-hundred-meter-high Renaissance tower.

This was just one of the things that worried Peter as he took a seat opposite a white man in his late fifties, thin face, pale complexion. Dressed like an American tourist in shades and baseball cap, he didn't look much like a man with a gun. More like a man with a desk.

He lowered a pair of Oakleys to reveal a serious expression. To Peter, he looked worried and was trying hard not to let it show. But the leg jogging up and down underneath the table gave it away.

Leaning in, he whispered, "Azrael?"

Peter nodded.

Above the door to the stylish café was a rectangular brass plate. It carried the café's name and had been polished so well it reflected a perfect panoramic view of the whole square behind his seat. This was what Peter's eyes fixed to as he spoke with the contact.

"You look so young," the man commented absentmindedly. "How old are you, son?"

"Twenty-five."

"I've got a daughter close to your age. She's studying medicine at John Hopkins."

"Good for her," Peter said dryly. "Is there a reason I'm here or did you just want to chat about your daughter?"

The man's expression changed. "Of course," he said. Then. "Do you know who I am?"

"You're Walter Smith, deputy director of Central Intelligence. Which is why I find this whole meeting odd."

"Odd how?"

"You're the deputy director. Why are you meeting with an asset your agency officially denies even exists?"

"Good question. I'll answer it. I'm here because there was no one else, son, and because of luck."

"Whose luck," Peter asked, "mine or yours?"

"Yours, son. You see, two hours ago, eight assets in the Fallen Angel program—the same program you are a member of—were terminated whilst awaiting orders at what we thought were secure locations."

As Walter Smith's words washed over him, Peter studied the square through the brass plate. An old man fed pigeons in the center by the fountain, stooped over and scattering seed. The birds kicking up a stink as they clambered for it.

"Who terminated them?"

"GRU."

"How'd the Russians find them—a leak?"

Smith nodded. "A rogue officer that I will do everything in my power to find."

"Okay. So why then is the deputy director of the CIA telling me all of this, rather than, say, another officer?"

"The only reason I'm here is because I happen to be on vacation in Venice with my family. Hence your luck, son. I offered to give you the message in person, because all communication channels are currently corrupted."

Peter took his eyes off the plate. Narrowed them on Smith.

"What about the tracker?"

"That's what's been corrupted. We're sure that the GRU were led to the other assets by their tracker data."

Peter concentrated on the plate, his mind photographing each and every single body around him for any sign that one of them was an enemy asset.

While he did, he asked, "So how in the hell am I going to get it out of my head?"

"You're not. But this will make sure it doesn't work."

Smith slipped a hand in his pocket and brought out a small rectangular device that resembled a USB stick.

"What is it?" Peter asked as he took it and felt around the thing with his fingers. It was heavy, like a paperweight, and bore no other markings except for a single oval button in the center.

"It's an EMP. It lets out a short but very powerful electromagnetic pulse that disables electronics. I need you to place it at your right temple and press the button. It will scramble the tracker."

Peter held it to the side of his head.

"But watch out," Smith cautioned as Peter went to press the button. "I've heard it described as like being hit in the head with a sledgehammer."

With that in mind, Peter thumbed the button.

Pain exploded inside his skull, rushing down his neck and filling his entire body. His teeth clamped shut and his eyelids burst open. His spine arched back with a crack of vertebra. The chair legs scraped the stone as he went into cramping spasms. His face twisting on one side like he was having a stroke.

Right at the moment he thought he was going to faint, it stopped and the pain drained out of him. Sighing loudly through clenched teeth, he was thankful he'd managed to control his bladder in time not to urinate himself.

For a second or two Peter sat panting, limbs weak, sweat dripping down his face.

"It's not fun," Smith remarked.

"No," Peter mumbled. "It isn't."

There was a jug of water on the table. Peter poured himself a glass and drank it down quick. His skull felt like it was slowly shrinking back to normal size.

Smith took his cell phone and checked the tracker. "Good," he said, placing it back in his pocket. "You're no longer on there."

"So what now?"

"Now you come with me, Azrael. The Russians have put their best man on the job. A man they call the Hunter."

Peter had heard of him. A Russian asset who lived just like he did, in the field. The Hunter specialized in the termination of other countries' assets. In the last four years he had personally killed, or was suspected of personally killing, twenty-two active assets. Including five hard assets like Peter.

"Eight angels are already dead," Smith went on. "Killed in a series of attacks. You're to come with me now to a secure location. Once there, I can..."

While he talked, Peter watched the golden reflection of their surroundings. Two children ran in and out of the tables. They almost hit a waiter, who kinked his body into a Z to avoid the tray of food being knocked from his hands.

"The whole program has been jeopardized," Smith droned on.

Peter's eyes scanned the rooftops around the Piazza. For the innumerable time, they stopped on the visage of the ancient clocktower—the Torre dell'Orologio. Something glinted in the sun.

The scope of a rifle.

Peter grabbed Smith by the shoulder. As he yanked him sideways off the chair, a round whipped past and punched a hole through the wooden back of the deputy director's empty chair, penetrating the spot where his heart had been a second ago.

Peter jerked Smith up off the floor and onto his feet as more rounds splintered the table. They needed to move, needed to get away from the X. The shooter was using a high-caliber sniper rifle, at least a .30. The shots came in clear sharp cracks rather than continual pops.

Peter grabbed his rucksack and half dragged Smith through the crowd of people into the café, getting clear of the sniper's vantage. It was at this point, as they entered the throng inside, that everyone outside on the square exploded into a confused stampede and ran blindly into the café.

Peter pulled the deputy director into an alcove as the place descended into screaming, shouting chaos. He removed a Heckler & Koch 45 from the bag, unscrewing the suppressor. He wouldn't be needing stealth for this but accuracy and range.

The front window of the café exploded. A nearby woman took the hit, screaming as the .300 Winchester Magnum round slammed all the way through her back and out her chest.

By the time she landed face first on the floor, she was no longer screaming.

The sniper had moved position and was now firing into the café from an opposite rooftop. A chunk of marble exploded by their feet and Peter used it as a cue to grab Smith once more and run headlong toward the kitchens at the back.

He kept close to the people.

An elderly man tripped and fell under the stampede

rushing for the rear of the building. The surge of bodies carried on like a wave, and the fallen man cried out as he was trampled into the floor.

It was then that Peter spotted something. Or someone.

Over the torrent, one man stood out as the only person not hurrying to escape. Instead, he was standing like a rock in the middle of a rapid river. His eyes pierced at them and he raised a hand: a gun fitted tightly inside. The muzzle flashed. Peter tugged Smith to the left. A man running across them shrieked and spun around, a spray of crimson shooting from his neck.

The explosion of the gun signaled total chaos. The crowd surged behind Peter and Smith, pushing them toward the shooter. Peter threw Smith to the ground and, as a second flash exploded, ducked through the stampede.

The bustle pushed into the shooter, his arm shoved upwards, held aloft by the press of bodies. When he finally managed to lower it, he'd lost sight of Peter, and it was only when the assassin burst at him through the scrum that he finally got a look.

By then it was too late.

Peter swung a chop into the guy's wrist, hitting the tendons and nerves, making the fingers involuntarily snap open. It knocked the gun out of his hand. As he straightened, Peter brought an elbow angling sharply back, catching the guy in the nose and flattening it to his face with a crunch. His opponent tried to change his feet, get a better stance, but the close proximity of rushing bodies made it impossible. His fighting style, the one he was trying to use, needed more space.

Peter didn't need any.

Avoiding the stifled punches and kicks that came his way, he got in several well-aimed blows, finishing with a flurry of palm strikes to the guy's throat—all the way until he heard the larynx crack as the guy dropped to his knees.

While he writhed on the floor, gasping for air that refused to come, Peter found Smith and they continued on their way out of the building.

"Not that way!" Peter shouted when the deputy director went to follow the others out of a back door fire exit. "He'll have the alley covered."

They entered the kitchen instead. The chefs gone, the place empty.

"It's a dead end," Smith complained as he followed Peter to a walk-in fridge.

The assassin ignored him as he hauled the sliding door to the side and ushered the deputy director into the frigid air before getting in himself and slamming the door shut behind them.

Shelves of produce lined the walls. In the frigid light of a low-wattage bulb, Peter went to the rear and began hauling buckets of sauces away from that end of the fridge. It was at this moment that Smith spotted the drainage hatch.

Peter wrenched it open and signaled for him to go down.

A minute later they were walking the Venetian sewers.

Smith asked, "How did you know this would lead us out?"

"You recall the Afrid Hassani assassination?"

"The official thing for me to say is that I have no knowledge of any such assassination."

"Well it happened. And how it happened was that myself and a four-man wet team used the sewers to gain access to the suite he and his twelve-man security detail were stationed in. We got up through a hatch right underneath the hotel's kitchen. During recon I had to remember every detail of the sewage plans in case things went wrong and we needed another way out. I remember that at the Piazza San Marco every café has access to the sewer from the kitchens. Di Biaggio's is in the refrigerator."

They came to a ladder. Peter went up first. Reaching the top, he opened the hatch and cautiously poked his head out, gazing between the running feet that tore past.

"We're as safe as we'll ever be," he said down to Smith.

Having lifted himself out of the sewer, Peter leaned down and called, "Come on."

Smith began making his way up. In the meantime Peter scanned the narrow alleyway the manhole had led to, the HK45 gripped in his hand. Ancient stone buildings towering over him on both sides.

The rooftops. They'll be on the rooftops.

The sun shone in razors of light at the edge of a chimneystack. It was momentarily blocked by the profile of a man. Peter aimed his pistol as the guy rounded the chimney, grasping the stock of an assault rifle.

This wasn't the sniper.

The shooter showed too much of himself as he knelt on the terracotta tiles. A single bullet from Peter's HK45 struck him in the throat and sent him rolling like a rag doll down the roof, long before he could pull the trigger on his AK.

The body toppled off the eaves, landing right at the feet of a runner. It made a resounding slap, bouncing at least a foot, and covered the woman in a spray of blood.

Peter didn't see it. Only heard the woman's scream. He

was too busy pulling Smith out of the sewer. The moment the deputy director was free, a bullet smashed the cobbles close by. The impact sent chips of flint everywhere. Peter spotted the outline of the sniper. He was silhouetted by the sun. Standing on a rooftop about a hundred, a hundred twenty meters away. Beyond his pistol's effective range.

"Come on!" Peter shouted at Smith.

The two of them set off, running toward the mouth of the alley, zigzagging as more shots struck the buildings and ground around them.

At the end, the alley opened out onto the lagoon. A small dock lined its edge. Several motorboats tied to it bobbed along the choppy waves. One of them was occupied, the motor ticking over. Peter jumped onto it, quickly flung the pilot into the water, and, with Smith onboard and the Italians all shouting curses at him, tore out of there, heading into open water.

The runabout had a rearview mirror. As they cut across the lagoon, Peter checked it. At the exact moment he did, a bullet whistled past his head, striking the water a few meters in front of the bow.

When he turned over his shoulder, he saw the silhouette of the sniper standing proudly on the roof.

He was watching them. And not just that. The bastard appeared to be waving.

This, Peter thought, *must be the Hunter.*

TWO

CALIFORNIA, 2021

SIX YEARS LATER, HEADLIGHT BEAMS ILLUMINATE the edges of curtains, waking Peter from his reverie. He cocks the silenced HK45 and stays perfectly still in the darkness of the trailer.

Sitting opposite the door disguised one last time as Paul Adams, he has spent the last six hours waiting patiently for this moment like a snake that has infiltrated the warren while the rabbits are away.

The doors of a pickup creak open and two sets of feet crunch down on gravel. One of the men moves with a wide, confident gait. The other shuffles behind like the condemned.

They reach the door. The key scratches in the latch. Next, it is opening and a hand is reaching inside and flipping the light switch.

Jimmy Palmer doesn't notice at first. As he steps into the

trailer, he is looking back over his shoulder at his son Danny. It is only when he is standing right in the middle that he realizes, first, the plastic sheeting covering everything inside his trailer—the floor, furniture, sideboards, ceiling. Second, that his former neighbor Paul Adams is sitting in a chair aiming a pistol at him.

Jimmy goes to speak but the two bullets that hit his kneecaps, one after the other, turn any speech he may have had into a hollow shriek as he collapses to the floor.

Danny Palmer, the man's teenage son, stands on the threshold, wide-eyed and scared. He doesn't have to be. Peter is doing this for him.

During the fall, Jimmy had flung his car keys across the trailer. They'd landed at Peter's feet. He picks them up, rises from the chair, and steps over the squirming Jimmy. At the door he holds them out to Danny. The teenager is still staring at him, unsure.

"Here," Peter says. "Take them."

The teen reaches a trembling hand out and cautiously accepts the keys.

"Tell them what happened," Peter says. "Tell them Paul Adams did it. Tell exactly the truth. *Do not* lie."

Danny nods.

"Take the pickup and go home to your sister," Peter concludes.

"Boy!" Jimmy screams from the floor. "Get my pistol from the truck. Shoot this son-of-a-bitch."

Danny does no such thing. He walks away from the trailer, gets in the pickup, and drives out of there.

Peter closes the door after him. The trailer is in a secluded area of woodland in the middle of Monterey

County. Just as Jimmy does when he brings his son out here in the middle of the night, Peter has all the time in the world.

But Peter is not a sadist.

So the second he can no longer hear the sound of the pickup's engine, he faces Jimmy, locks eyes, and unloads the clip of the HK into the child molester's head. Then he pulls all the plastic down, wraps it around the body, leaves. He fetches a drum of hydrochloric acid from the back of his own pickup and uses a sack-bearer to wheel it to the trailer.

The body of Jimmy Palmer, or any sign of it, will never be found.

THREE

ALASKA, 2021

OVER TWO THOUSAND MILES NORTH OF MONTEREY, in the wilds of Alaska, a thirteen-year-old boy is busy smashing his fists into the well-beaten wall of a barn. The strapping around his knuckles is pink with blood and sweat. Pain burns all the way up to his elbows, which he does his best not to show to the birdlike, elderly woman who stands behind him.

She leans heavily on a black cane, shouting instructions at him. "Right jab to ten. Left hook to fourteen. Left kick to two," and so on as the kid strikes the thick wood slats with rapid punches and kicks, hitting the numbers that dot the outline of a man with precision. "Now, follow pattern while repeating rules."

"Rule one," the kid says breathlessly as he beats the wood: "Never, huh, drop your guard. Rule two, huh, never underestimate, huh, your opponent. Rule three: don't stand out. Rule four, huh, never assume, only, huh, plan. Rule five: never, huh, hurt an innocent. Rule— Ah!"

His wrist makes a distinct crack that reaches the rafters of the old barn, unsettling the watching birds. The kid buckles over, holding the throbbing limb, whining until the whip of her cane across the backs of his calves straightens him up.

The old woman is in her seventies, withered and senile. But, man, can she hit hard with that fucking cane.

"You must be tougher, boy!"

"I'm sorry. I—"

She whips him again. "Don't whine that you're sorry. You want to be assassin, Peter?"

She's still calling him Peter. No matter how many times they tell her his name is Michael. Lately, they don't even bother. Michael is Peter. And Peter is something else altogether.

"Of course I do," Michael says.

"Then stand up straight and stop whining."

The day is bright, yet cold. Winter has ended and it is now spring. Out here that means little more than longer days and less snowfall. Outside, the frozen drift is yet to melt and it sheets everything.

Michael pulls himself into fighting stance. Faces the wall again. The man's outline. The pummeled, blood-smeared wood. Mother raises her cane, is about to recommence with instructions, when a certain thought comes to her.

"Actually," she says, lowering the stick. "I have an idea. Do you know what it is like to be shot?"

The kid slowly shakes his head.

INSIDE THE FARMHOUSE, Mother's oldest friend and fellow former trainer of child assassins, Magda, is vacuuming the floors. She is six-five and built as well as any man. Long gray hair, once black, flows down the back of the blue boiler suit she wears and a troubled expression hangs on her wind parched face.

It is only when she is finished that she realizes Mother and the boy are no longer in the barn. She can't hear them. To make sure, she checks.

Standing in the open doorway of the outbuilding and staring at its deserted internals, a thought bites Magda, twisting her stomach. It makes her run to the weapons shed. And when she spots that the small-sized body armor is missing from its peg, the knot in her guts threatens to consume her.

It is enough to make Magda dash into the woods as fast as her thick old legs will carry her, hollering: "Katya, no!"

TOO FAR TO HEAR HER cries, Mother and Michael stand in the middle of the icy trees, the missing body armor strapped to the teenager. They stand approximately ten meters apart in a clearing.

"Today," the old woman says, "we will be performing a shooting test different from what you have done so far."

Michael realizes that the main difference is him being unarmed.

"One day," she goes on, "you will be shot, Peter.

Nothing will prepare you for it, but at least this will give you some idea."

Mother lifts a SIG Sauer P226 from her hip holster and aims it at him. The gun trembles in her hand, looking far more heavy than it is in her feeble grip.

Michael flinches.

But Mother doesn't shoot. Instead, she smiles, shakes her head, lowers the gun.

"No. You're expecting it," she says. "Are prepared for it. I can tell you now that when a bullet finally does bore its way into your flesh, it will come without anticipation."

"So you're *not* going to shoot me?"

"Not me."

"Not you?"

"No."

"Then who?"

Mother says nothing. She just remains stock still, the pistol hanging at her side, her steely eyes searching the wide trunk of an Alaskan cedar about twenty meters behind Michael. She stares for so long that he feels obliged to look himself.

When nothing emerges from behind the tree, he turns back to her. It is at this point that Michael begins to hear the faraway sound of Magda calling to them.

"Where is she?" Mother asks no one in particular.

Michael answers anyway. "Who—Magda?"

"Yes. She was supposed to come from that tree."

"I think she's coming now."

"Not enough time."

"Why? What's going to—"

The blast echoes in the forest. The birds scatter. By the

time Magda arrives at the scene, Michael is on his back, twisting about in the frozen dirt, trying desperately to breathe, terrible pain filling his entire left side where the bullet struck the armor.

Magda swoops down and lifts him up. "Breathe, Michael," she yells. "Breathe!"

But the boy is going pale.

FOUR

HAVING COMPLETED THE LAST FIVE HOURS OF THE journey in a Sno-Cat nicknamed Kitten, Peter arrives at the farm.

Driving slowly past the front of the house, he spots Magda's trepidatious expression haunting a downstairs window. He parks Kitten at the far end of the barn and is busy covering it over with tarp when she joins him.

"Where's Michael?" he asks without turning from the work.

"I'm so sorry, Peter," she mutters.

She looks apologetic. Her shoulders slumped, her face forlorn.

"Where is he?" Peter repeats.

"In the house."

Peter marches past her and out of the barn. He already knows what has happened. It is written all over Magda. In her dark eyes and pensive expression.

In the house, he carries on straight upstairs and bursts

into Michael's room. The kid is sitting in bed, propped up on a stack of pillows. Mother is in a chair beside him, both hands rested on a black cane, her chin rested on top. She eyes Peter's entrance through narrowed slits.

"Hi, Peter," Michael says in a hoarse whisper.

"What happened?"

"Live fire training," Mother says. "Nothing out of the ordinary. Just two cracked ribs and a little winded. He'll be back in training by end of week."

"I don't want him back in training. I don't want him in training *period*."

"Nonsense. The boy is getting along fine."

"I don't want him doing anything except studying with Magda. If you can teach him geometry or something else that he'll actually need in the real world, then go ahead and teach him. But do not hollow him out like you hollowed me out."

Her pierced eyes study him curiously. As a boy, this look would have filled him with foreboding fear. But Peter isn't a boy anymore. He is what this woman made him: a stone-cold killer. So he returns the look until *she* turns away with a shiver burrowing its way up *her* spine for once.

"You talk such nonsense," she mutters, eyes now on Michael. "The boy wants to learn the way of the assassin, don't you?"

"Yes," Michael croaks, before turning to Peter and adding, "You won't teach me. So I had to ask her."

"You should stick to your books. Ready for when—"

"I'm not going back to the normal world. I told you before. There's nothing left there for me."

FIVE

THE MORNING AFTER PETER'S ARRIVAL, MICHAEL IS fit enough to leave the house for the first time in three days. Wincing from pain, he helps Peter empty and reset the rat traps, placing the stiff bodies in a bag ready for the freezer. This way they'll have the option of rat meat in winter when everything else is hibernating.

"Where did you go?" Michael finally plucks up the courage to ask.

The two of them are kneeling at the back of the barn, Peter opening up the hammer of a heavy trap.

"Unfinished business."

"That's what Magda said. But what business?"

Peter decides to tell the truth. He tells him that he went back to Monterey to kill Jimmy Palmer.

"Why?"

Peter continues with honesty. He tells him what he learned about Jimmy abusing his son.

"You think that's why Danny beat on me all those years?"

"Partly, I guess."

Michael thinks about it. Then he says, "His old man deserved it."

"Maybe."

Peter had risked so much going back to Monterey. Had tried so hard to leave it alone, to let the itch settle, the thought of retribution die. But it had burned a hole through his brain. In the end, it was unavoidable. Jimmy Palmer's fate had been sealed six months ago, during that period of time Peter had sat in his basement listening in on the horrors of the Palmer household.

It just *had* to be done.

Peter and Michael leave the trap, a smudge of peanut butter on the plate, and go on to the next. It is situated inside the barn itself, in a corn cellar under the floor.

Within the shadow of a torn punch bag, a hatch opens out and they climb down a set of wooden steps worn smooth at the edges. There are two traps. Both hold fat specimens crushed beneath the bars of their hammers.

"How are your ribs?" Peter asks when he catches Michael wincing.

"Real sore."

"It'll teach you not to trust her."

"Who—Mother?"

"Yes."

"All she wants is to teach me the ways."

Peter rolls his eyes and gently shakes his head. "You don't need to learn *the ways*. Especially the *ways* that she has to teach."

"But she's teaching me how to survive," the kid insists.

"You're thirteen years old. You should be enjoying your youth. Not learning how to crush a man's windpipe with the heel of your palm."

"I *was* enjoying my youth before you came along and ended it."

Guilt floods Peter. The song comes to mind.

What'll I do, when you, are far away...

"Anyway," Michael adds, "not everything she's taught me is bad. What about this?"

Michael holds something up to him. When Peter looks, he sees his Heckler & Koch HK45 in the kid's hand. Checking his underarm holster, he finds it empty.

He hadn't felt a thing.

"I took it while you were arming the trap."

"So she's been teaching you pickpocketing," Peter points out.

"Isn't it cool?"

"No, it's not," Peter snaps, snatching the pistol back. "It is not cool."

SIX

In the afternoon, Peter takes Michael hunting.

The kid is a natural at crawling stealthily through bracken. Using the compacted snow, he slides silently along his front, keeping level with Peter, the two slipping through the tight gaps side by side. When they reach the edge of the rough vegetation, they stay within the shade, their all-white hooded coveralls blending them in with the icy brambles.

Caribou dot a vast valley of frozen grassland. Michael reaches over his shoulder and pulls a Steyr SSG 69 bolt-action rifle from his back. Soon the scope is lined up with his right eye, Michael easing his breathing, just like Peter taught.

A herd numbering around fifty mill around the edge of a frozen stream. It is early spring and sunlight melts the edges of the ice, allowing the deer to drink.

"You have your target?" Peter whispers.

"Uh-huh."

A large female stands aloof from the others. Michael

settles his crosshairs on her. He prefers the does to the bucks. Their meat is more tender, less sinewy. Peter tells him to target the older ones. He picks a caribou that doesn't appear to be nursing young. After all, he knows what it is like to lose a mother.

"You got it lined up?"

Michael doesn't answer. Instead, he breathes in, settles his finger snugly over the trigger. His heartbeat is slow and regular. There are no nerves. He squeezes.

The shot echoes throughout the valley and scatters the herd. All except the female. She lets out a desperate cry that almost sounds human. She flails about on the icy grass where she has fallen, trying to lift herself, thrashing limbs, slips and trips, blood dribbling down the gray fur of her neck, dropping onto the white ground, her movements spreading it about like some demonic snow angel.

Michael goes to take a second shot, the deer's head moving in and out of the crosshairs, but before he can take it, Peter covers the end of his scope with a hand.

The kid glances sideways at him.

"We need to preserve ammunition," Peter whispers.

"But she's suffering."

Peter removes a hunting knife from his belt and hands it over.

"Like I taught you," he tells Michael as the teen takes it.

The kid looks at the knife. Then at the bleating caribou trying to lift itself from the ice.

"I can't," he breathes.

"You have to. She's in pain."

"I just can't."

"You could shoot her, but you can't use a knife to ease her into death?"

"Please don't make me."

The kid has gone red. He looks ashamed.

I'm not like her, Peter tells himself.

He takes back the knife and Michael watches him leave the bushes and venture toward the crying caribou. Reaching the animal, Peter grabs its waving antlers, steadies its head, and thrusts the knife through the front of the caribou's chest straight into the heart, before twisting. A jet of blood comes out with the knife and the animal drops to the ice.

In the bushes, Michael is trembling.

SEVEN

MOSCOW, 2021

IT IS RAINING WHEN HIS PLANE TOUCHES DOWN. All the apartment buildings and monuments look gray and drab in the overcast afternoon, the sun no more than a ball of light in the bruised clouds.

Semyon Mikhailovich takes the train from Belorussky station to Tverskaya Zastava Square. From there he gets a Metro to the outskirts of the Kuzminki district and walks home in the pattering rain. His apartment block is at the top of a steep hill, all on its own. Just like the men and women who live in it.

The floor he lives on is almost exclusively made up of assets working for either the FSB or the GRU. None of them speak. They simply ignore each another when passing in the hallways or standing in the lift. Semyon recognizes a few of them from jobs they've done together. Not that there's any reminiscing. Merely a nod of respect.

Entering his lonely apartment, he is greeted by a fat tabby, who rubs its soft flank against his leg. He would have preferred a dog, but with him being away so much it would be cruel. A dog is a companion. A cat no more than an occasional friend who doesn't mind you dropping in from time to time.

Semyon feeds the animal, then prepares a meal for himself out of freeze-dried food powder that he pours into a bowl from a foil packet before adding hot water to it. After all, what's the point of filling the place with fresh food if you spend ten months of the year away from it?

The food done, he switches the television on and sits down to eat the tasteless slop in front of it. Soon, he is idly watching some cheap reality show about clairvoyants and soothsayers, the cat purring on the arm of the chair.

It has been four months since he has been here. The mission he had undertaken in Kyiv had taken far longer than initially planned. In that time, someone else has visited the apartment daily to feed the cat, water his plants, and generally keep the place in order. That person probably spends more time in his home than Semyon does.

While he ponders this, his phone rings.

"Semyon," a familiar voice says on the other end.

"*Dah?*"

"There is a car waiting outside for you. Get into it and I will see you soon, *Hunter*."

EIGHT

ALASKA, 2021

IT IS A PALE MORNING. THE EAVES OF THE OLD farmhouse drip incessantly, the ice's retreat somewhat underway. Emerging from the bathroom, Peter hears whispered voices coming from Mother's room. It lies at the opposite end of the landing. The door wide open, he can see Michael, the kid's back turned to him.

Mother he can't see.

He creeps like a cat to the doorway to get a better view.

Mother sits in an armchair. The kid standing before her. She is handing him something. Noticing Peter in the periphery, she looks sharply his way. Michael follows the direction of her gaze, twisting around to see, a guilty look across his face the second he spots Peter.

The kid's fist closes around something.

Peter steps into the room. "What's that?"

"Nothing," Michael replies sheepishly.

"I saw it. She handed you something. What did she give you?"

"Nothing."

"Michael, don't lie. I saw it. Now show me."

Michael comes listlessly forward. Opens the hand.

She has given him a mini garrote. A loop of razor-sharp steel flex with two tiny wooden handles, one each end, that fit neatly within the fingers of a thirteen-year-old boy.

She had gifted one similar to Peter when he was twelve.

Peter turns to Mother. Asks why she would give such a thing to a child.

"To protect him."

"From who?"

"Men like you."

Peter sighs.

"I'm not a child," Michael says.

"You think so?"

"I've seen a lot for someone my age."

Holding out a hand, Peter says, "Give it to me."

The kid is cautious.

"Now," Peter insists.

Michael holds the tiny garrote out to him and Peter takes it.

With a whip-crack movement, he flexes the razor-sharp wire right in front of Michael's face and asks, "You think you can loop this around another person's neck and pull tight?"

Michael looks back over his shoulder at the steely face of Mother for support. She nods and the kid turns back.

"Yeah. I do," he says firmly.

Peter goes on. "You think you can hold him there until he either bleeds out or chokes to death? The guy kicking and struggling and ramming you into things. Doing everything he can to live."

"I do."

"Pull the handles back and forth like you're sawing a tree stump?"

"Yeah."

"For a quick kill, I once sawed two thirds through an ISIS commander's neck before he stopped struggling. By the time I had finished, his head was hanging halfway off and I was drenched in his blood." Leaning in so that he's real close to the kid, he adds in a whisper, "I could smell the bastard on me for days and days afterwards. Are you prepared for that?"

Swallowing, the kid nods. He's almost green.

Peter steps back. Shakes his head. "Michael, you couldn't even finish the deer with the knife. I don't see you—"

"Stop criticizing the boy," Mother snaps.

Peter gives her a hard look before returning his attention to Michael. "Look, I didn't come here to upset you. I was going to ask if you'd like to come fishing."

Michael's face brightens. "You mean the ice has melted enough?"

"I wouldn't be asking if it wasn't."

"Awesome."

"Go get packed. I want the fishing gear ready for departure in ten minutes. No longer."

The kid runs off and Peter watches him skip across the landing and throw himself headlong down the stairs. He can't remember ever having been that carefree inside this dark place during the seven formative years he'd called it home.

He closes the door. Her eyes are pierced when he turns

to her, closing to mere slits by the time he's walked across and is standing over her.

"What about *you*?" he says ominously. "Do *you* think he's capable?"

"You were. Weren't you?"

His eyes match hers. Two slits in a white mask. "So you recognize me today?"

She stares at him. There is a sudden, unexpected lucidity to her when she speaks. "Why did you come back?"

"This is the only home I've ever known."

"Men like you don't have homes."

"Men like me?"

"Yes. Men without faces."

NINE

MOSCOW, 2021

THE CAR LEAVES SEMYON AT THE BACK ENTRANCE
to a large gloomy-looking house that sits in a cluster of tree-
hidden mansions on the northern edge of Sokolniki Park. A
gigantic stone structure, without the slightest claim to architectural beauty, it is a dirty green color. Built toward the end
of the sixties to home the very highest members of the old
communist party, there are a few of these old Soviet-era
houses still standing in this part of Moscow. Showing little
change from their original form and color, they are solidly
built, and remarkable for the thickness of their walls, as well
as for the fewness of their windows, many of which are
covered by gratings.

The house always makes an inhospitable and mysterious
impression on Semyon—one that is difficult to explain,
unless it has something to do with the actual architectural
style.

At the door, he looks up at the legend over it, which runs:

HOUSE OF ROGOZHIN, hereditary and honorable citizen of his beloved Russia.

HE HESITATES NO LONGER. Opens the door at the bottom of the rear staircase, the old servants' entrance, and makes his way up to the second story. The place is dark and dreary; the walls of the staircase are painted a dull red. A sour-faced housekeeper meets him at the top, says nothing, merely nods, and leads him onwards through several rooms, up and down many steps, until they arrive at a large door, where the housekeeper knocks. The echo of feet approach from the other side and it is soon creaking open.

A room unlike any of the others Semyon has traveled through presents itself. A large bedroom where the vaulted ceiling is so high it is almost unseeable in the tepid light of a stone fireplace.

Semyon's eyes study something on the other side of the room. The remains of a man, reduced to no more than skin, bone and the organs inside. He lies in a giant four-poster bed that has been carved from dark mahogany. Medical machines sit idly churning away beside it, tubes and wires looping out and feeding into the limp body.

In a lonely corner, a long-legged doctor sits on standby, reading a book, and resembling a security guard at a gallery.

The man in the bed—this great leader and organizer, this great commander, and, long ago, the KGB's greatest asset—this man is the closest to a father that Semyon Mikhailovich has ever known. As a teenager he had lived with Parfyon Rogozhin until he was eighteen. Trained one on one as his protégé. Never a father and a son were closer than these.

This is the first time Semyon has seen his old mentor since the beginning of his illness, and it causes him to linger in the doorway a little longer than he should.

"I know, I know," the old man's hollow voice echoes across the spacious chamber. "It's not nice. Even the president's usual stoicism was tested when he came to see me yesterday. I noticed a twitch in his cheek. But, I tell you now," the sick man rouses himself to sit up a little, "it's still me inside this pale sarcophagus of skin and bone. Now come, my boy. Don't be afraid. Cancer isn't contagious."

Semyon makes his way across what seems like an endless marble floor. He takes a seat at the side of the bed and holds the old man's cold and frail hand. It feels so delicate in Semyon's paw. Like the bones of a sparrow.

What light is left in Parfyon Rogozhin's eyes shines at his former protégé when he says, "How is your life, Semyon Mikhailovich? Are you satisfied with it?"

"Yes, Parfyon."

The old man cocks an eye at him. "You're not lying?"

Semyon grins. "No. I am being sincere. I am satisfied."

The old man squeezes his hand as best he can. "That's all we can hope for in this life. All we can hope for."

Semyon lets go the hand and it struggles to retract to the bed where it rests beside the half-corpse. Parfyon turns to the ceiling, and for a moment the only sound in the room apart from the machines is his labored breathing.

"You recall when we first met?" he eventually asks.

"Yes."

"When you came to live with me."

"Those were good days," Semyon says with some joy.

"I wasn't too strict?"

"Only as much as you needed to be."

"And that wasn't often. You were such a good pupil. So determined to succeed. Especially when it came to stagecraft. I hear because of your skill as a chameleon the Motherland has one less enemy tonight."

"I'm afraid that as you are an *ex*-commander, I cannot divulge state secrets."

This automatic answer makes the old man smile.

"Then thank God I have other sources," he says. "I was told that you had spent four months playing the role of an American journalist to get close to your target."

"It was an easy role to play. Americans are all the same."

"Did you enjoy living this *other* life?"

"It was a means to an end."

"But did you enjoy it? After all, you lived as another human being for four months. This person had their own life in Kyiv. Their own identity. Do you miss this person?"

Semyon narrows his eyes at his old mentor.

"This isn't a test of your loyalty, Semyon," the old man says. "I really want to know."

"You always taught me that we must keep our distance. Compartmentalize. Live the role but don't let it become your life."

Parfyon turns to him. His old, sunken eyes shimmering in the dull light of the room. "As you know, I spent most of my career out in the cold pretending to be other people."

"You are a legend for it."

"Yes. But it was difficult. At times I played characters for whole years. I had friends. Girlfriends. Homes. Pets. Even boyfriends when the need was necessary. I created whole worlds. Whole personas."

"And I will always be grateful that you passed this skill on to me."

"Getting close to a target is the hardest part of our work. To do so, we must lose a little of ourselves. I remember when I came back to Russia in 1990. It took me a long time to get used to being called Parfyon again." He pauses. His eyes shimmering. "I hope that you always remember who you are, Semyon."

"I will, Parfyon. I will."

A proud smile bends the sick man's emaciated face.

"I never had a son," he says. "Something I regret. But if I did, I would have wanted him to be like you."

Light illuminates the soul of Semyon Mikhailovich.

"That is why I have called you here today," Parfyon goes on, his expression becoming serious. "You are not just my proudest achievement: you are my greatest pupil. Therefore, it is *you*, Semyon, who I wish to entrust my dying request to."

"Anything, Parfyon."

"Before I die, there are things I need done in order to lie down in peace with my ancestors."

"What things?"

"I need you to go to America."

TEN

ALASKA, 2021

A GIANT LAKE SPREADS OUT FROM THE HIGH BANK Peter and Michael are perched on. They sit within a gap in the trees, gazes fixed to a pair of floats that bob a few meters beyond a fallen Sitka spruce that lies half submerged in the water.

"It's such a nice place," Michael remarks.

"It is," Peter agrees, gripping his rod as he spots bubbles closing in on his float. "I used to come fishing here all the time when I was growing up."

"With Tommy?"

The name stuns Peter and he turns to the kid.

Michael explains, "I read it under my bed. It was scratched there by a knife. Yours says Peter. Mine says Tommy."

Peter smiles at a certain recollection. "Yeah," he says joyfully. "We wanted to put our names on them, to make them officially ours, I guess, but she'd told us not to. So we scratched them underneath where she couldn't find them."

"Who is he?" Michael asks.

Peter's expression darkens. "He was my brother."

"*Was?*"

"Yeah."

"What happened to him?"

"He died."

"How?"

"He was killed."

"By who?"

Peter swallows. Then he answers. "Me. I killed him."

ELEVEN

ALASKA, 2004

IT WAS PETER'S FOURTH SUMMER ON THE FARM when Tommy arrived. Fourteen years old, he was busy chopping wood and ignoring the incessant flies when he heard the echo of a jeep's approach. Out here it was an odd thing to hear. Wolves: yes. Bears: uh-huh. A fourteen-year-old boy being shot at by two grown women: obviously. But a motor engine? This was something that caused Peter to instantly lay down the axe and gaze in the direction of the yard.

It wasn't long before the grumble of the engine was followed by the appearance of an olive green Hummer emerging from the trees. It was military issue but without insignia. Two people sat in the front. An insipid-looking man wearing aviator shades, whose bleached skin shone in the bright sun. And a young boy with big eyes, who sat in the passenger seat gripping a rucksack to himself.

Peter crept closer as the Hummer parked in front of the farmhouse, staying out of sight within the shadows of the tall pine that surrounded the farm.

Rule One: Never drop your guard. Always suspect a stranger to be an enemy in waiting. Never reveal yourself until vitally essential.

Hidden amongst the trees, but within earshot, Peter listened as the Hummer was met by Magda and Mother, the two women strolling out of the farmhouse to greet their visitors.

The man got out the jeep while the boy stayed inside.

The stranger was tall, slight, and athletic. Scrawny, but you could tell there was muscle under his clothing due to his shape. He took the shades off and Peter couldn't decide if he had a face or not. It seemed like it was flat, all the features and ends smoothed out. He looked like the beginnings of every white man's face that has ever been. The starting point before character and features are added. A blank canvas.

Little did Peter know back then, but one day he would wear such a face.

"What is this?" Mother barked, her voice resounding over the buzz of the insects.

"I need a favor, Katya," the man said in a voice as insipid as his featureless face. "I need you to train this boy for me."

She looked past the stranger at the Hummer. Then her eyes were back on him. "I already have boy. Three-and-a-half years left until he is ready for field. So you can take this one somewhere else."

She pointed at the boy when she said this last sentence.

Up until then, the boy had faced forward, away from the

scene happening to his left. But when she pointed, he appeared to sense it and turned to meet her bony finger.

The stranger began, "This boy has potential," but she cut him off.

"Then get other to train him. I tell you, I already have boy. Good boy. One who will prove very efficient asset. Why do I need to exchange him when we are already so far in his training?"

"Not an exchange."

"No one can train two."

"He's already failed three farms."

"Why?"

"Injured one of the training assistants the first time. Last two times it was running away."

"Then he doesn't want to be trained."

"But that's the thing. One of the times he ran away, he managed to survive in the woods on his own wits for six whole months. We were sure he was dead. Couple of rangers happened to come across him living in an observation shack. Hunting rabbits with a homemade spear. He damn near killed the pair of them with his bare hands before they subdued him. You tell me if that isn't potential."

Once more she gazed past him at the boy.

"His name is Tommy," the stranger added, trying to make the boy more human to her. "I thought perhaps being as you've seen so much success with asset 92, you could perhaps use him to control this one's behavior. Another boy may get him to stop resisting the training. Let himself be shaped for a future. Because otherwise," his voice went ominously quiet, "he'll have to be let go."

Mother sighed. She knew *exactly* what this meant.

TOMMY WAS SLIGHTLY SHORTER and a year younger than Peter. Like Peter, he looked sinewy and tough. It was clear that he too had been hardened like a piece of oak soaked in salt water. Vulcanized by hard work. His hands sported the callouses and dried cuts that came with it. Each knuckle capped with thick scar tissue.

Peter was sure that a barn wall was the culprit.

After their introduction, Peter was told to take the boy upstairs. To unpack his things into the only other piece of furniture in his bedroom besides his bed: an old chest of drawers he and Magda had made last autumn to replace the metal footlocker he'd originally been given.

"Shirts go in the second drawer down," Peter said, taking the clothing from Tommy's rucksack, which sat on top.

The boy remained reticent.

Still, he made quite the impression on Peter.

He had these sad brown eyes, Roman nose and jet-black hair that reminded Peter of a crow. His skin, like Peter's, was a washed-out white.

Tommy was what Peter was. And for the first time in his life, the latter felt that he had a confidant. Someone who could relate to him. A brother. A real brother.

It made Peter feel like he wasn't alone.

"Peter?" Magda's deep voice called from downstairs.

Peter went to leave when Tommy, with lightning speed, caught his arm and stopped him. Upon facing the boy, Peter found those two lamp-like eyes staring right into him.

"Are they like the others?" Tommy asked in a whisper.

"I don't know who the others are."

"People like them. Training kids like us."

"What are the others like?"

The kid sighed a breath out. "Bad," he told Peter in an ominous tone. "Real bad."

"Peter, come on!" Magda bawled up the stairs.

IN TRAINING, Tommy was exceptional. On the farms he had been at before, he had shown himself capable. That was obvious by the fact that he wasn't far behind Peter. Certainly less than the year that denoted their difference in age.

Over the following months, the competition pushed both boys. Like two elite athletes or sports teams, they egged each other on to better performances through their rivalry. Like Ali-Frazier. Lakers-Celtics. Red Socks-Yankees. Nadal-Federer.

Mother never openly encouraged this competitiveness, but it certainly didn't escape her shrewd notice that both boys were pushing each other to new heights.

This initial bliss wasn't to last, however. It was in Tommy's fourth month that something happened.

It had begun like any normal morning. Both boys were standing beside their beds when Mother entered the room at five a.m. like a drill sergeant. The gray sheets and blankets were neatly made up on both beds, and each boy was impeccably dressed. Everything ready for inspection.

Walking down the middle of the room, she eyed each bed disdainfully before turning sharply on Tommy's and sniffing the air like a bear sensing prey.

Her stare fastened on the bed. Then on the flushed face of Tommy.

"What is this?" she wanted to know.

Tommy said nothing, staying perfectly still, arms behind his back.

In a whip-snap movement she clasped a corner of his sheets and ripped his bed apart. Only then, with the flowing sheets kicking up the air, did Peter smell it.

Urine.

On the gray sheet of the bed there was a dark circle of it where Tommy had slept. Mother let go the blankets and rushed at him, fury burning in her eyes, Tommy recoiling back from her until he hit the wall. Then she was over him. Pressing him into the cold plaster.

She sniffed the air above his head and the fury erupted further on her face.

Magda stood in the doorway. Mother turned to her and barked, "Get him undressed. Today, he will train without clothing, and from now on he will sleep without sheets and blankets."

Magda stooped into the room, her huge frame filling it up with the four of them crammed in there. She took ahold of Tommy's thin wrist and guided him out, marching the boy quickly across the landing to the bathroom, the door slamming shut.

Following that, she was true to her word. She made that boy spend the rest of the day naked, the flies crawling constantly over his skin, his feet stabbed by the rough forest floor as they performed drills. Even in summer the heat never climbed above 70 degrees and Tommy spent a lot of the day hugging his body for warmth, teeth chattering away.

"Stand up straight and hands behind your back!" she'd continually shout at him.

And, with bitterness and hatred burning in his eyes, Tommy would do so. Not because she told him, it seemed to Peter, but because he wanted to show her. Show that she couldn't break him.

TWELVE

.

ALASKA, 2021

A STRONG HAND SHAKES PETER AWAKE. HIS eyelids snap open on the visage of Magda. Silver moonlight illuminating her worried expression.

"It's Mother," she says. "She is gone."

"Ugh. Not again," Peter complains, raising himself in bed before twisting ninety degrees and plunging his bare feet down onto the cold floorboards.

As he dresses, Michael rouses in bed, the two sharing a bare attic of a room.

"You want me to go with you?" the kid croaks in a sleepy drawl.

"No. Stay here. Get some..."

Michael is already snoring.

"...sleep," Peter finishes, rolling his eyes.

Magda is already placing her shoes on at the back door

when he reaches her in the kitchen. They grab their coats and head out into the cold night.

The pine trees are soon resounding with their calls.

"Mother?!"

Her boots have made impressions in the compacted snow. When they head due west through the woods, Magda sighs. "I think I know where she is."

They find the old woman on her knees in a clearing. At first Peter thinks she is praying, but as they close in on her, he notices that she is actually digging the cold earth with her bare hands, clawing it back and sending piles shooting behind, all the time muttering breathlessly away to herself.

"Gde oni? Gde oni?"

Where are they? Where are they?

By the time Peter is right over her, she has dug a considerable hole, at least a foot square and six inches in depth. Her hands scratch away within it like a desperate cat, the skin and fingernails black with dirt, and it isn't until she stops, when he places a gentle hand on her shoulder, that he notices something in the pit.

Mother looks up sharply at him, her pale gray eyes submerged in tears.

"Look what you made us do, bastard. Look!"

She wrenches herself free of his hand and points into the hole.

He doesn't need her guidance. He is already looking into it.

Magda stays back, fiddling with her hair, looking terrified. Because there, where Mother has clawed away the topsoil, is the ulna and radius bones of a child's arm.

THIRTEEN

Eight o'clock in the morning and Peter hasn't slept since they got Mother back from the woods and cleaned her off. She is now lying in bed, wrapped tightly in blankets, holding onto Magda's hand. Soft-faced, Magda coos to her, telling her to be calm, laying the back of a hand across the old woman's hot, furrowed brow.

"They made us," Mother complains in Russian. "They made us."

Peter leaves the doorway and makes his way downstairs.

In the kitchen he takes a seat at the table and waits. Michael is out chopping wood. The sounds of the axe dropping can be heard through the thin windowpanes.

Heavy yet cushioned footsteps creak across the ceiling. They are followed by the quiet shutting of a bedroom door. Then the whine of the staircase.

The second Magda is inside the kitchen he confronts her.

"Pat Hughes mentioned something about dead children out here. It was right before I shot him in the spine."

Magda swallows and finds her way to a chair. Lumping that heavy body down on top, she fixes her gaze to the table-top. Her lips move, but no sound emerges. Peter can't be sure if it is a silent prayer or an attempt at an answer.

"How many?"

"Too many," Magda breathes, looking up with sad and frightened eyes.

"*How* many?"

"Seven."

Peter closes his eyes. *Seven* reverberates around the inside of his skull. Seven dead children—and he had brought his own son here. For what? To be number eight?

"*You* and *her* killed them?"

Not taking her eyes away from the table, Magda replies, "Not all the children took to training as well as you, Peter. There were... accidents."

"What sort of accidents?"

Her lips quiver, the tears build up, and then the levee breaks and they pour down her face. Peter doesn't have time for tears. Guilt, shame or self-pity.

"*TELL ME!*" he booms in a voice from another world, hammering his fist down and making the table jump.

Her eyes meet his, and, for the first time since he met her all those years ago in the barn, when she and Mother had taught him about pain, he sees something on her face that he thought he would live a thousand lifetimes and never see.

He sees fear. Fear of him. Of what exists deep within the wells of his own cold gray eyes. Of what *they* put there.

"There are files," Magda tells him. "In the attic. You can read *them*. But don't make me tell you."

FOURTEEN

NEW YORK, 2021

It is 10:17 Eastern Daylight Time. Semyon Mikhailovich stands on a travelator. It carries him through Kennedy Airport. At 10:26, he collects his luggage with little fuss, and as he strolls through the clusters of travelers, he is relaxed but observant.

At the gate, the customs agent takes his passport. A quick glance through it and the cheery-faced woman is shining a mouth of white teeth and saying in a syrupy voice, "Welcome home, Mr. King," before handing the US passport back.

"It's good to be back," he replies in an all-American jock accent.

Making his way out of the airport in the direction of the taxi stand, he recalls Parfyon's words of two nights before.

"You will be working entirely alone. Sourcing everything

yourself. The Russian state must not find itself exposed. If you fail, you die alone. Do you understand?"

He had nodded.

10:41. In the taxi Semyon tells the driver to take him to Brooklyn. West 8 Street. The city drifts past the windows, the spring sun lighting up the edges of the apartment blocks in outlines of fire.

11:03. The taxi drops Semyon off on a street that lies within the shadows of the overground south Brooklyn railway. He pays the driver and moves along the sidewalk. The people in this part of town are threadbare and a little crazy. A man with a head covered in knotty dreadlocks passes him going the other way. A stench of stale urine trails off him. He is very animated as he moves along, swearing to himself about *"The razzclat white devil! 'Im what take away me soul an' leave me wid nuttin but da bills ta pay! Me man Jesus gonna arize up from da eart' an' gonna wash it awl awee!"*

Train cars rumble overhead, drowning out the manic street preacher's speech.

An alleyway cuts a gap between two boarded-up shopfronts.

11:07. Semyon enters it and walks to where another alleyway bisects it. He turns right and travels down a short set of steps.

11:09. Somewhere toward the end of the alley is the type of door you usually see on a solitary confinement cell. It occupies the windowless back of a tall apartment block. The top floors are condemned and the front of the building is hidden behind scaffolding.

Semyon presses a buzzer. Hollow footsteps close in on the door and shadow covers the peephole.

"Who there?" a man's gruff voice comes through a speaker beside the buzzer.

Semyon pushes a button and speaks. "My name is Afanasy Jovic. Your boss, Josep Kirilov, is an old associate of mine."

"There is no one by that name here."

"Then I will give you his American name. Oscar Peterson."

The guy takes a few seconds. Then. "Okay. Give me a moment."

The goon makes the call. It isn't long before the bolts on the door are drawing back mechanically and it's creaking open onto the alley. The huge Slav on the other side steps out menacingly, comes right up to Semyon so that their chests practically touch.

"He asks what you want?"

"Business," Semyon replies. "He has sold to me before."

"But he says he has never met you and he wants to know why you call him Kirilov."

"Then maybe you should take me to him. So that this conversation can continue in his presence."

The goon takes a Beretta from the back of his waistband. Points it at Semyon and steps to the side. Nodding through the door, he says, "Get down there."

Semyon grins at him and does as he asks.

11:10. Everything is running on schedule.

FIFTEEN

ALASKA, 2021

WHEN MAGDA ENTERS THE KITCHEN, MOTHER IS standing by the sink, staring out of the window. Magda hadn't expected her to be here. Upon seeing her, she tucks the files she's just retrieved from the attic down the front of her coveralls.

Mother doesn't notice. Her eyes are too busy studying the open door of a shed that lies about ten meters across the dirt yard. Through the doorway she can see Peter and Michael as they finish skinning the caribou, the carcass hanging upside down from a hook.

"I don't like him being so close to the boy, Magda," Mother says without turning around.

"They are fine together," Magda assures her.

"He will take the boy away from us."

"No, he won't. I told you. This is different."

"You are wrong. He will take him away like he did the others. Take him to be a man without a face."

Magda says nothing. She simply watches Mother with a worried expression. Knowing her friend as she does, there is nothing to say. So she attempts to leave via the back door.

"Where are you going?" Mother wants to know.

"It is time for the boy's lessons. I am going to fetch him."

Mother rolls her eyes. "Huh, lessons," she mutters under her breath. "There is only one lesson he must learn: the way of the wolf."

OUT IN THE SHED, they have finished with the skinning and are now busy cutting strips from the animal in anticipation for salting.

"You're getting better with the knife," Peter tells Michael as the kid carves a piece from the shoulder.

"Thanks," Michael says, his eyes and attention fixed to his work.

"As well as not retching quite so often," Peter adds.

This makes Michael smile. He likes it when Peter attempts humor.

Nevertheless, no sooner does the joy emanate within him than his eyes go dull, his brow drops, and he asks, "What do you think Mom would say if she saw us now?"

A cloud passes over Peter's own countenance. "I don't know," he says. "She probably wouldn't be happy."

"Why?"

"Because I brought you all the way up here instead of leaving you in San Diego with your grandparents. You think your mom would be happy with that?"

Michael pauses the knife work, thinks about it, shrugs, carries on. "I guess it doesn't matter now," he says. "Her and Dad are both dead. Whatever they had planned for me is over."

Peter shudders at the kid's cool hard cynicism. It reminds him of himself. Of someone who thinks in cold logic rather than with the warmth of their emotions. Was it this place? Or was it something deeper? Something the kid had inherited from him. Something inside of Peter that he has passed on.

The shadow of Magda blocks the morning sun from the doorway, making both of them look that way.

"Mikey," she says, calling the boy by his name only when Mother isn't around. "It is time for your lessons."

"Can't I skip them today, Mags?"

"I'm afraid not."

Frowning and returning his knife to his belt, the kid leaves them alone in the shed with the hanging carcass. Magda waits until he is inside the house before reaching down the front of her coveralls and taking out the folders.

"These are the reports of all seven children. We were told to burn them, but we didn't."

Peter takes them from her.

"Is Tommy in here?"

Magda nods.

"And did you write in his report how he was killed?"

"Yes. As well as the circumstances."

Peter gazes at the folders in his hands. Then, looking up at Magda, he says, "These children deserved better than this place."

SIXTEEN

An hour later Peter sits on the end of a bed. Six already read reports lie by his side, another in his hands. As he peruses the documents, the sounds of Michael's math lesson rise up through the floorboards from the kitchen below.

He doesn't register their voices, though. Because nothing could distract him from what he is reading.

To summarize:

Asset 74 was the first to die on the farm. He ran away his first summer, obviously not believing it when they told him the summer nights could be brutal. They found him dead of exposure not even five clicks from the farm. He was fourteen.

Asset 101 had an underlying heart condition they'd not picked up in her medical. She died aged fifteen of a myocardial infarction when the abnormally narrow blood vessels leading to her heart closed up during extreme exercise. She had dropped dead right in the middle of the assault course Mother and Magda had built in the woods. When he read this, Peter recalled his own time on that same assault course. His heart was fine and it had nearly killed him.

Asset 121 drowned when he was dropped from a plane into a giant lake. Peter knew the drill. You free fell most of the way into the near freezing water and swam ten miles to Magda on the other side. When Peter had reached her, she had refused to help him out of the water into the dinghy. Even though all his muscles were exhausted and he was numb with cold. After several attempts, he had just about managed to pull himself into the boat before collapsing onto his back. Asset 121 hadn't been so lucky.

Asset 145 was killed when her chute malfunctioned during a skydiving exercise. She'd been unable to get the thing open properly or use the spare in time. She'd hit the trees at about two hundred miles an hour. They'd had to fish what was left of her out of the tangled branches.

Asset 151 died in a live ammunition training mission. He had tripped while handling a Benelli combat shotgun. As he'd fallen, the gun had gone off and the blast had removed half his face from the chin upwards. By the time the helicopter ambulance had gotten there, he was already dead from severe blood loss.

Next is Asset 160: Tommy Smith.

Peter decides to leave it for now. Let the past be for just a moment. Instead, he goes on to the last death. The only one that occurred after Peter had left.

Like Tommy, 172 was no accident. The report states that he had turned a pistol on Mother and Magda. In the ensuing standoff, he had hesitated. Mother had not. She had put a bullet hole right through the boy's forehead.

He checks the date. 11th of June. 2015. There is something familiar about it. The date resonates in his memory. But it is in a way that he can't recall clearly.

At least not at the moment.

SEVENTEEN

GLEN ROCK, 2021

Twenty-four hours after his arrival in America, Semyon Mikhailovich is taxiing a Chevy Express down a quiet suburb in Glen Rock, New Jersey. As the van creeps slowly along treelined streets, his eagle eyes scan the house numbers until he sees the place he's after and pulls into the curb.

A wood slat two-story stands alone in a yard overgrown with yellowed grass and weeds. A dirt path leads up to a screened porch. It carries a big red sign with white letters that spell out: *Beware Dog!* Barred grates cover the windows and all the curtains are drawn. A closed circuit camera sits right above the door, the lens following Semyon's approach all the way.

He presses the buzzer. Its sound is immediately drowned out by the vicious barks of some muscled dog. The barks gets louder, until the animal is bashing and scratching at the door from the other side.

A man's voice hushes it. Then an intercom speaker comes to life.

"Who are you?" the man says in heavily accented English.

Semyon steps back and looks up into the camera.

In Russian, he asks, "You do not recognize me, Luka?"

The intercom crackles. "Press button and speak into microphone."

There is a button beneath the speaker. Semyon holds it in, moves his lips inches from the intercom, and repeats the words.

There follows a brief pause. During which, Semyon comes away from the intercom and redirects his blank stare to the camera.

"I'm sorry. I don't speak Russian," the other man eventually says. "I am originally Serbian. Plus, my name isn't Luka. It is Davide."

Semyon's lips part into a sinister smile. He returns to the intercom. Holds the button in.

"You were born Luka Alexandrovich Lavrov in Omsk, Siberia, on the twelfth of July 1987. At age eighteen you were taken for national service. You excelled in basic training and were selected for the Spetsnaz program—Russian special forces. Again, you excelled. In Chechnya, Georgia and Ukraine, as well as many unofficial missions in sensitive countries, you won medals and praise from your superiors.

"Now to our personal acquaintance. In 2013, you and I completed a mission in Syria in which we eliminated the leading general for the Free Syrian Army, Mohammed

Harmoush. Just the two of us infiltrated his compound in Baba Amr and executed him along with his entire security team, before escaping. Do you remember these things, Luka?"

Nothing but crackling and the low growls of the guard dog flowed from the speaker for several seconds. Then one word. A question asked in a shaky whisper.

"Hunter?"

"*Da*."

Semyon continues. "But that isn't the end of your history. No. Three years ago you went AWOL after you and two other former Spetsnaz soldiers raided your own country's military train just north of Irkutsk. You stole over 500 million rubles worth of assault rifles and other ordnance. Sold it all for a fifth of its worth to a Chinese weapons trader working out of Hong Kong. Then, with your money, you used a false Serbian passport to emigrate to the US. Your two companions weren't so lucky. They were caught in Hungary by GRU agents. They, too, were trying to obtain papers for America." Semyon pauses and in a growl, adds, "I personally oversaw the torture of both men. It was their confessions that brought me here."

Luka takes a little while to compose himself. Then. "So what, you want me dead?"

"If I wanted you dead, you would already be dead. No, Luka. Instead of death, the Motherland offers you amnesty. All your country asks in return is that you take one last mission."

Luka Lavrov says nothing for a moment. Clearly the mechanisms of his brain are at work. Then the speaker crackles.

"I want to see your hands."

"Here they are," Semyon replies, lifting them.

Luka comes to the door, shushing the dog away. A whole host of bolts, catches and chains begin clicking and rattling, and the door opens the merest crack, so that only a face shows.

Luka Lavrov isn't as fit as he once was. He's gone to fat. Pasty white skin and black-ringed eyes. A couple of extra chins since Semyon last saw him.

"I am going to open the door very slowly," Luka says. "Keep your hands high and where I can see them. I have a gun on you."

He opens the door, staying ducked behind it. On the other side, pressed against the spy hole, is a .45 Desert Eagle, ready to blast splinters and bullets into the only man Luka has ever worked with who genuinely scared him.

"Come on in," he says cautiously when the door is wide enough to fit through.

Semyon steps into the dark realms of a musty hallway. An overweight and tired-looking Rottweiler sits beside Luka's feet, a low, guttural rumble coming between the panting.

The Desert Eagle is away from the door and on Semyon before he's even all the way in.

"Step back," Luka says as he shuts the door with a sideways kick.

"Can I lower my hands?"

"Not yet. We're going into the kitchen first." He signals the direction behind Semyon with a forwards nod of the head. "It's through there. Straight ahead."

"Are we going to have breakfast?"

"No. You are going to sit down at the table and explain yourself."

A grin opens up on the Hunter's face. "You are cautious, Luka. I like this. I liked it when we worked together, too. It is why I have chosen you."

"I haven't taken the mission yet. Now go."

Semyon turns around and walks down the hallway.

"Take the chair on the far side," Luka says as he follows Semyon into a messy kitchen, staying as far back from him as possible, outside the reach of his arms, feet—a lunge.

Semyon stops before the chair in question and surveys the room. Washing up overfills the sink. Flies circle food-smeared countertops. And there is more than a whiff of mold, damp and half-rotten cooking.

"What are you waiting for?" the former Spetsnaz asks.

Eyes back on Luka. "May I lower my hands to pull the chair from the table?"

"Okay. But slow."

Semyon scrapes the chair back along the dirty lino. The Desert Eagle trembles in Luka Lavrov's hand. His eyes sting from the sweat that drips into them, but he won't wipe it away. Won't block them long enough for this bastard to get the jump on him.

Why the fuck has he just shown up like this?

"You're still wondering what this is all about, Luka," Semyon says as he sits down. "But I assure you. The deal I offer is genuine."

Sitting at the table, his hands laid on top, the eyes of the Hunter never leave those of Luka Lavrov, and to the terrified ex-patriot, it is as if he were reading into his soul.

"The Motherland never forgives those who betray her," Luka says.

Semyon gently shakes his head. "No, no. You are wrong. She is always open to forgive those who seek redemption. Do *you* seek redemption, Luka?"

"You mean this mission?"

"I do. One mission. Tonight. All reconnaissance has been done. Weapons and ordnance sourced. All you have to do is come with me."

"What about the dog?"

It is sitting beside its master.

Semyon grins wickedly. "So do you believe me?"

"I never said that."

"But you are considering the deal?"

"I want it in writing."

"I have it."

"Show me."

"It is in my jacket pocket. Will you allow me to get it?"

Luka nods.

Semyon moves the hand ever so slowly, slipping it back from the tabletop inch by inch, the Desert Eagle shaking ever more in his direction. The hand slides into the pocket of his black bomber jacket, and, just as slow, rises out holding an envelope.

"Open it," Luka commands. "Take the letter and place it on the table. Then push it over."

Without breaking eye contact, Semyon tears open the edge of the envelope, pulls out the folded sheet of paper and unfurls it. Then he places it down on the table and slips it across, before leaning back in his chair and re-fixing his cold stare to Luka's wide, shimmering eyes.

The ex-Spetsnaz rushes forward and snatches up the document, practically jumping back to the dog, who stays in the doorway, watching the stranger as closely as its master.

One eye reads, while the other keeps on Semyon.

"It is even signed by the president," Luka mutters.

"Of course. What can we do these days without the president's say?"

Luka stuffs the page in his pocket, ponders things. Swears inwardly to himself that he might be wrong about this. Then uncocks the hammer of the .45 and joins Semyon around the table.

"Go on, then," he says. "What mission is it you need my help on?"

EIGHTEEN

ALASKA, 2021

Two hours ago Michael witnessed from the kitchen window Peter carrying makeshift wooden crosses into the woods. It made concentrating on his subsequent lessons much harder, and when he asked Magda, she went pale, telling him to mind his own business and concentrate on his algebra.

With the lessons now over and the books away, Magda sits at the kitchen table drinking tea while Michael washes Mother's soup bowl and all the other dishes that line the sink from lunch.

"Mags?"

"Yes, Michael."

"Do you think he likes me?"

Magda looks up from the table. "Who—Peter?"

"Yes."

"Of course he likes you. What makes you think he doesn't?"

"Sometimes I catch him looking at me strangely."

Magda thinks about it. Then. "It is because he sees your mother."

"No. It's another way."

"Another way?"

"Yes. Like he's angry. His jaw is tense and his eyes bulge."

Magda reflects awhile before saying, "I'm sure it is nothing. Just a thought maybe that is bothering him."

Michael dries his hands with a cloth and begins wiping the crockery stacked on the draining board.

"Was he always like this?" comes his next question.

"How?"

"So serious."

Magda once more becomes pensive. "How much do you know about him?"

"Nothing except that he met my mother when he was on some mission in Greece. They were both eighteen, fell in love, and then the people he worked for came and took him away."

"Do you know anything from before that?"

"No. He won't tell me anything about himself that doesn't involve my mother. He will only talk to me about her."

"Well, perhaps I shouldn't tell you then."

"Please."

He has turned to face her. A look of pleading in his eyes.

"What would you like to know?" Magda asks in a low voice.

"Where does he come from?"

"You mean where he was born?"

"For starters."

"He was born eleventh April thirty-two years ago in Burlington, Vermont at the University of Vermont maternity hospital."

"Who were his parents?"

"His mother's name was Jessica Black. She was a twenty-year-old waitress. His father's name wasn't on the birth certificate and he never knew him or what his name was."

"Where's his mother?"

"She's dead."

"How did she die?"

Magda goes to answer but is stopped when her attention is taken by something she spots through the window. Observing her look, Michael twists to see what it is.

Peter has emerged from the trees and is marching across the yard to the back door. The second he opens it, he tells Michael, "Grab your coat. There's something I want you to see."

NINETEEN

NEW YORK, 2021

"So do you wanna tell me why the CIA is involved in this?"

"I'm afraid, Detective, that's classified information."

Operations officers Walter Smith and Coby Jones are being escorted across a busy Brooklyn street by an NYPD detective named Blake—a squashed-looking guy with a round stomach, flat head, and short stumpy legs.

A patrol cop stands guard at the mouth of a narrow alley. He nods respectfully at the detective and holds yellow crime tape up for them to pass under. As they step into the narrow passage a train rumbles over the top of the street, making the brickwork tremble.

A short walk along the dank passage and they close in on a heavy cell door that lies open. Another patrol cop stands guard with his hands crossed in front of him.

Blake stops short of it. Turns to the two men accompanying him. "Officers attended the scene at twelve thirty p.m. yesterday after reports of shots fired. When the officers arrive, they find this big ol' door all the way open like it is now. They call inside. After they get no response, they decide to go down and take a look. That's when they find it."

The portly detective leads them down a stone staircase into the dark realms of what appears to be an underground hotel. The air stinks of mold and body odor. Yellowed wallpaper covers the walls of a door-lined corridor and trampled carpet covers the floor. The doors lie open. Inside are windowless rooms. Or cells, depending on how you see it. They look like the types of room you'd expect to find at the cheapest of motels—wavy patterned red and gold carpeting circa 1970s, wood laminated wallpaper. It is clear to both CIA men that each room is the nightmare holding pen of some poor prostitute.

"So this is the underage brothel you mentioned over the telephone," Jones says.

"Yeah. We pulled sixteen terrified girls out of here. Barely older than kids. All foreign. All trafficked over from Eastern Europe. Most of the dead belong to Russian mafia."

The bodies are all gone but the signs of violence are still there. Dried blood covers the worn tread of the carpet. Spatter rises up the walls. Bullet holes mark the plaster.

"He killed every man in the place," Blake says. "The johns abusing the dames. The guys running the joint. All of them. Can't say I'm particularly sorry about it. They got what they deserved."

"Where was Kirilov?" Smith asks.

"You mean Oscar Peterson?"

"Yes."

"This way."

Blake leads them onwards, down a short set of steps into another dimly lit corridor that is painted a dingy gray color. This one only has the one door. One which is nevertheless very impressive: a circular safe door with a spoked wheel-handle.

"Once upon a time," Blake starts up like a tour guide, "this place was a private bank. Safety deposit boxes. Stuff like that. The brothel we just walked through, that was the offices. Come on, I'll show you what these guys were using it for."

They pass another patrolman and step into a solid metal room. Impressively, the riveted walls are lined with weapons like some hunting goods store. Except these are guns you'd never find in any of the domestic marketplaces. Not even in the private sellers clubs in Florida or Texas. Only a military showroom would have these types of things on display.

Both officers stand in the middle of the safe gazing around at all the hardware.

"You see that?" Jones asks Smith, pointing at one of the walls.

"Yeah," Smith replies. "It's the new Sig Sauer XM5 rifle. It's due to replace the M4A1 carbine rifle in the US military next year."

"How the hell you think this guy got ahold of it?"

"I told you. Kirilov was one of the best smugglers I ever met. Helped me a lot during the Cold War."

On another wall hangs the M320 grenade launcher

modules that fit onto standard assault rifles. The sort of thing only special forces would get ahold of.

"He's executed your man here," Blake tells them, standing next to a solid glass counter that displays pistols and grenades. "A single bullet to the head from a 9mm parabellum. It's our understanding that he took the gun—a SIG Sauer M17—from the display here. After all, the bullets match it and it is missing from the counter."

The officers are busy looking at the walls. The weapons are back lit and spaced out in a professional manner. Like handbags on display at a Louis Vuitton boutique.

Blake goes on. If only to get this over and done with.

"He also used the M17 to murder another associate of Peterson. Hired muscle. That guy died where you both now stand."

The officers look at their feet. Their loafers are surrounded by a puddle of dried blood.

"There are gaps in the weapons," Smith says. "You have a list of what was taken?"

"Not on me, but I can get it for you."

"What about the girls?" Jones asks. "Did they describe the assailant?"

"The four that saw him only did so because he entered their rooms to drag the johns out to execute them in the corridor. They said he had a beard. Black hair. Crazy eyes. We got them to sit with an artist. I'll get you the picture."

"That'll be good. Make sure you do."

"Who *was* this guy Kirilov exactly?" the detective then asks. "When I looked up Peterson, I found the files were all sealed and the next thing the CIA is calling me up and arranging to come down."

"I'm afraid," Jones reiterates in a deadpan tone, "anything I tell you would be classified."

This makes Blake roll his eyes. Before someone calls the detective from outside.

"I better get this," he says, making his way out of the refurbished safe.

Jones cozies up to Smith.

"You were close to Kirilov back in the day," he says. "After all, he was *your* contact. Who do you think would do something like this?"

"He *was* my contact," Walter Smith replies. "I haven't spoken to him in over thirty years. Not since I got him American citizenship. I was hoping that he'd become a productive citizen."

Gazing about the room of blood-spattered weapons, Jones says, "I think it's safe to say that assumption was a little *off.*"

"Yeah. I guess it was."

"So tell me what you know, old-timer."

Old-timer. It makes the skin on Smith's back ride up his shoulders. It is six years since Venice and Deputy Director Walter Smith is no longer deputy director. He's simply Operations Officer Smith. And even that he'd had to beg for.

What should have been the glory days of his career became the beginning of its dreaded fall. After losing the Fallen Angel program, he had ended up losing a lot more than just a bunch of assassins.

A *whole* lot more.

The aftermath had almost cost him his sanity. His career up until that point had been one endless elevator ride: top of his class at Camp Peary; constant praise in the field; promotion after promotion; and then, at only forty-nine, becoming the youngest deputy director of the CIA ever. The top seat was next and it was all *his*. The only thing he had to do was wait.

Except, often when waiting for one thing, another thing altogether comes crashing around the corner. And when that thing costs you everything you hold dear, your career is bound to suffer. It made the fall all the harder because of how high he had to drop. Men and women he had led and reprimanded were now leading him. Reprimanding him. He had fallen down so many rungs of the ladder that he found himself almost footing the bottom.

"Didn't you hear me, Smith?"

"I heard you," he answers gruffly.

"So?"

"Josep Kirilov used to smuggle people out of the old USSR."

"Okay. So is that how you know him?"

"Yes. He was a contact of mine. Used to help get operatives in and out of Russia."

"So he's someone Russia might still want to kill. Like Skripol in England."

"Yes."

"And do you think it's them?"

"It's not the usual style. Like Skriple, dissidents are usually poisoned. This is mass murder."

"So you think it's more to do with Kirilov's recent activities?"

"I didn't say that. I mean, this type of hit. One man. It would have to be someone far more organized that just some local mafia."

"Is that a yes or no?"

Smith thinks about it. "If it is," he muses loudly, "then I can think of only one Russian asset that would do it this loudly."

"Who?"

"The Hunter."

TWENTY

ALASKA, 2021

"I DON'T WANT TO LIE TO YOU, MIKEY," PETER SAYS as they stare at the six crosses sticking up out of the frozen dirt like wooden flowers.

The kid stands beside him, reading the six names. Ostensibly looking for Tommy.

He's not here.

"Who were they?" Michael asks.

"Kids who came to this place. Like me and Tommy."

"Why's *he* not here?"

Peter swallows. Then. "He's somewhere else."

Michael glances sideways at Peter. His face is as pale as the gray sky.

"How'd they die?" the kid asks, turning back to the mini cemetery.

"That's what I want to tell you. They died, Mikey, because of *her*." He's pointing in the direction of the farmhouse. "Because of the things *she* had us do. You cannot trust that woman, Mikey, do you understand?"

"She didn't kill them, did she?"

"She may as well have. They all died because of this place." Turning to face Michael, he adds, "So you need to get ready to leave."

"Leave?"

"Yes. Say nothing to Mother or Magda, but by the end of the month we will be leaving. I was a fool to bring you here. It's not safe."

"But what about my training?"

Peter groans. "Look. If you want to be trained, then *I'll* train you."

The kid's face lights up. He smiles. "You mean it?"

"Yes. I'll train you."

Anything to get the kid to agree on leaving here. Even if it is a lie.

TWENTY-ONE

WASHINGTON DC, 2021

WALTER SMITH IS DRIVING COBY JONES HOME from Dulles Airport. It's almost nighttime as they slide along the freeway. The last of the sunlight turns the horizon a deep yellow. In the distance is the shadowy silhouette of the capital. The fiery skyline brings to mind that late summer evening of 1814 when the British invaded and burned it down.

"Penny for your thoughts?" Jones asks.

Smith clears his throat. "I was trying to think who else the Russians would be coming for."

"And what have you come up with?"

"Me, for one."

"You?"

"Yes. I was pretty involved with Kirilov back in the eighties. I got a hell of a lot of people out of the USSR. I was the one who debriefed them. Kirilov was *my* man."

"Who else?"

"There's a few KGB assassins we got out. People who helped with our training programs."

"You mean the Fallen Angel program?"

"Yeah."

"Well, let me know if anyone significant comes to mind."

They leave the freeway via a turnpike and enter the upmarket suburb of North Potomac. The streets are lined with elm trees and carriageways spread out from the front of six bedroom houses in the Greek revival style. It is the type of wholesome suburb you'd expect to see in a John Hughes movie.

They pull up in Jones's carriageway.

"What's the plan of action?" Smith asks when his colleague cracks the door open.

Turning back into the car, Jones replies, "Call your contacts in Russia. See what they know. Until then, we should hold back."

"What about PD?"

"Let's keep the FBI out of it for the time being."

"I agree."

There follows a few seconds silence. Then Jones comes to some internal agreement. "Okay," he says. "Get some rest, old-timer. It's been a long day and tomorrow could be even longer."

The two men finish their goodbyes before Jones gets out the car, retrieves his luggage from the trunk and wheels it to the front door of his house. By the time the key is in the latch, Smith is already pulling out of the driveway.

"Daddy's home!" Jones calls out as he steps into the hallway.

There is no immediate response from his family. The only sound comes from the television in the living room. So he leaves the luggage at the door and makes his way there.

"Hey, Chantel, sweetie, where is every... one?"

He stands frozen in the living room doorway, his heart aching in his chest. About three yards across the polished parquet floor are his family. They sit in a line on the couch. His wife and two young daughters. All three have their arms behind their backs, duct-tape over their mouths, tears in their eyes.

A man in a ski mask steps into view. He is holding an XM5 battle rifle. It is aimed at his wife and daughters. Enough firepower to decimate them in a few pulls of the trigger.

Jones goes to pull his service pistol, but before his hand even touches the grip he is thrown forward by a blow from behind that hits him between the shoulder blades. It comes from the butt of a pistol and sends him down onto his knees. Before he knows what is happening, a hand is on his gun, snatching it from the holster.

His attacker, a second man, strolls around the front of him, holding both Jones's pistol and a SIG Sauer M17. Unlike his partner, he isn't wearing a mask. Even if his face does retain a mask-like presence. Flat and lacking in angles or definition, it is the face of an *everyman*.

"Welcome home, Agent Jones," he says.

"You hurt my family," Jones seethes through the pain in his back, "I'll kill you."

Semyon grins. "What an odd thing to say from down there."

Jones glances past him. At his family.

They are all looking to their patriarch with tearful fear.

The CIA man closes his eyes tight. "What do you want?"

"Good," Semyon says. "You realize how this works."

TWENTY-TWO

ALASKA, 2021

Peter, come back! Don't leave me!

The cry echoes in his head as he sits bolt upright in bed. Heaving in breaths, sweating, humming Irving Berlin from between clenched teeth.

What'll I do?

Peter takes himself to the bathroom with his mumbling. There, he positions himself over the sink. Gripping the cold porcelain in his hands, he stares into the faded mirror at the strange, featureless face that stares back. He lifts a hand up and runs his fingers over the planed-down features. The result of countless operations to alter his appearance.

It doesn't even feel like me anymore. Nothing but the killer left.

"You couldn't sleep?"

Michael stands behind him in the bathroom doorway.

"No," Peter says, running the faucet and splashing water over his face.

"Me neither. Especially after you woke me up with your humming."

"Sorry about that."

"It's okay. Were you having a nightmare?"

"I think so."

"You don't remember?"

"Only residually. But it could be anything. There's so much I've seen in my life, it could be any number of dark memories."

The two hold each other's looks in the reflection of the mirror for a moment before Peter says, "Mikey?"

"Yeah."

"Do you, maybe, want to go home?"

Having said this, Peter turns to him from the mirror.

"There is no home," the kid says with certainty.

"But you have your grandparents in San Diego."

"Why are always trying to get rid of me?"

"I'm not. I just... I mean... Come on. Look at this place. These people. *Me*. Do you wanna end up like us?"

"You think I can just go back to being a normal teenager after the things I've experienced?"

"No, but—"

"My world is your world now, Peter."

"But what world, Mikey? What world is it *I* live in? Because you really don't know what you're talking about if you want to end up like me."

"You mean someone who can survive? Who isn't bound by laws. Who can go anywhere and do anything."

"I *am* bound by laws. And I *can't* go anywhere and do

anything. All I ever wanted was to be with your mom. That's all. And look how that turned out."

"You survive, though, Peter. Don't you? All those people trying to kill you and *you* survived while they're all dead."

"And so too is your mom."

The two stand staring at each other when the landing light snaps on and they look to see who it is.

Mother stands in her doorway, leaning on her cane with both hands.

"Peter?" she calls groggily to Michael. "Peter, come away from him."

She shuffles rapidly across the landing, the cane tapping a rapid beat on the floorboards. Reaching them, she shoves Michael aside and swings the cane at Peter. He manages to catch it before it strikes his face. Clasping it tight, he pulls her easily toward him, until their faces are inches apart.

"*I* am Peter," he growls at her, their eyes locked. "It is *ME* who you took from that orphanage and brought here to the edge of the world. *ME* who you trained almost to death. *ME* who you had Magda shoot, trainers bully, fighting masters break the bones of. *ME* who you beat the shit out of. *ME* who you showed nothing but coldness to. It is *ME* who you owe your apologies to for eroding away the boy you now see in *him* while you see nothing but a ghost in me. *Me! Me! ME!*"

TWENTY-THREE

WASHINGTON DC, 2021

A full seven blocks from the George Bush Center for Intelligence in McLean is a set of much smaller and less important offices. It is where they place low-level agents. Mostly those who deal with records.

Surrounded by windows, the security gatehouse at the edge of the site shines like a beacon in the black night. It is the only entrance into a two-acre lot surrounded by a fifteen-feet-tall chain-link fence crowned by roiling razor wire. In the middle of the lot is a two-story office building, rectangular and flat-roofed.

Jones pulls up in front of the electronic gate. The window on the gatehouse slides down and a security guard with black curly hair leans out. Another sits behind him in a corner of the gatehouse reading a copy of *USA Today*.

Jones unwinds his window. Flashes his pass at the guard.

"Who's your friend, Mr. Jones?" the guy asks, nodding in the direction of the man in the passenger seat.

"He's an IT contractor," Jones replies. "I was hoping your colleague at the lobby could get him a contractor's pass."

"Is he on the list?"

"Afraid not. But—and I know this is short notice—it's real important I get him in to my office so he can take a look at my computer."

"I'm not sure, sir. See, he needs to be on the list of approved contractors. Otherwise our asses could get canned. It's protocol."

"But this is really important. An emergency."

"How so, sir?"

"Son," Jones says harshly, his endangered family constantly at the forefront of his mind. "This is a national emergency. There are files on my computer that may have been compromised by a foreign power. I need this man inside my office so that he can help me monitor this activity."

"Then I'm afraid you'll have to inform the area captain. You can call him on…"

The security guard stops speaking and pulls a frown.

Jones's passenger has just gotten out and is walking around the front grille.

"Sir, if you can just get back inside the car," the guard says from his window.

Semyon says nothing as he walks right up and raises a silenced pistol.

"Sir, you can't—"

The bullet goes straight through his head, brains and

blood decorating the walls and ceiling of the gatehouse like a Jackson Pollock. The other man throws down the paper but is shot in the throat before he's even got to his gun. Semyon then leans in through the window and sends another two bullets into his twitching body.

After that, he presses the button and opens the gate.

"You didn't have to kill those men," Jones says when he's back in the car.

"Yes I did. Now drive."

TWENTY-FOUR

ALASKA, 2021

PETER STANDS AT THE FOOT OF MOTHER'S BED watching her sleep. She begins tossing and turning under the sheets. Her lips murmur sounds. He thinks she is saying *Misha*.

Peter has never heard her say this word before.

Suddenly she's up, rising. Her old eyes snap open and stare at Peter. At first she looks confused. Then the expression softens. She reaches out a hand. Says in a soft voice that doesn't seem hers, "*Misha? Eto ty?*"

Misha? Is that you?

She squints her eyes. Then grimaces when they focus, the hand recoiling sharply back.

"Oh, it's you," she says gruffly in English.

"Who is Misha?" Peter asks.

Her wrinkled face knots up into a scowl. "Get out!" she shouts.

Downstairs in the kitchen, Peter finds Magda drinking tea at the table. Taking a seat opposite, he asks her who Misha is, and her face immediately darkens.

"How did you get that name?" she wants to know.

He tells her.

Sadness envelops Magda as she tells him. "Misha was Mother's husband."

"She was *married*?"

"Yes. And in love, can you believe it?"

"No. I can't."

"Well, it was," Magda says sharply, a little annoyed at his tone.

"And where is he now?"

The sadness returns to sweep away the irritation. "He's dead," she says in a hushed voice. "Murdered when we betrayed the Motherland. You could say it broke her," Magda adds pensively.

"So she did have a heart once, then."

The irritation is back on her face. "You think she is nothing but coldness, Peter, but it isn't true. There is warmth inside her. Even now when she is no longer in her right mind."

"She never showed any warmth to me."

Magda shakes her head. "You are wrong. She loves you, Peter. Even if she only shows it to the boy."

TWENTY-FIVE

WASHINGTON DC, 2021

AT THE CIA OFFICES IN MCLEAN, THE SECURITY guard on the front desk sits right back in his chair. A hole through his head. Blood spatter up the polished wall.

Jones had hoped that the one in the control room would be watching the monitors, but he was only watching television. The murder of his three workmates going on behind him while he watched *Squid Game* on Netflix.

He didn't get to see the end. Like most of the contestants in the Korean series, he got his brains blown out. Semyon putting two bullets into him when he snuck up from behind.

In a glass-faced office overlooking rows of desks, Semyon stands over Coby Jones as the CIA operations officer sits at his desk, his face illuminated in the garish light of a computer monitor.

"Okay," he says. "Is this what you're after?"

He twists the monitor around to face the Hunter.

"This is satellite imagery of the place?" Semyon asks.

"Yeah. As you can see it's still there."

"And she—she is still there?"

"As far as we know she and the other one are living on the farm to this day."

"And these are the coordinates?"

"Yeah. You reach it via Fairbanks. There's an airfield there. Now will you free my family?"

Semyon remains stone-faced for a moment. He appears to be considering something. His mouth curls into a grin and he nods.

"Of course," he tells Jones.

Semyon takes his cell phone out and calls Luka. The words he says to his partner, however, send terror racing through Jones.

"Kill the family," he tells his compatriot in a dead voice.

"No!" Jones cries out.

Three things happen.

First, gunshots are heard coming from Semyon's phone.

Second, Jones lurches out of the chair at him.

Third, Semyon pulls the trigger of the SIG Sauer M17. The bullet racing through Colby Jones's head before he's even halved the distance between them.

TWENTY-SIX

ALASKA, 2021

MAGDA IS TAKING MOTHER FOR THEIR DAILY walk. In the meantime Peter and Michael begin their preparations for departure. In the attic the two of them search through a box. The words *Peter's Things* are written in black marker pen across its front.

Peter is attempting to gather what he can of his life. Because he never plans to come back to this farm ever again.

"Is this you?"

Michael is holding up a small photograph. The type clipped to the top corner of a personnel file. A serious faced boy with bleach white skin stares back. Peter takes it from the kid. Stares at the boy.

Features, whispers in his head. *Actual facial features. Not this mask I wear now where once was a face.*

"Yes," he says, handing it back.

"You look different," the kid remarks, glancing back and forth between the photo and Peter's face.

"It was before they changed me."

The kid looks at him sadly.

Searching further, Peter finds what he is looking for. An old, frayed leather dog collar with a bear's tooth dangling from it and a little brass tag. He twists the tag around in his fingers. *Charlie* is written across it in flowing cursive.

"You had a dog?" Michael asks, amazed.

"Yes. It was the only thing she ever gave us."

TWENTY-SEVEN

ALASKA, 2004

ONE EVENING AFTER TRAINING, TOMMY AND PETER were eating in silence when Magda came into the kitchen holding in her thick arms the only thing that could take those hungry boys' attention away from the food. She brought with her a puppy. A red-furred mongrel that made both boys leap up from their chairs and rush over to her the instant they saw it, their hands reaching out to stroke the dog as if they suspected it was no more than a mirage brought on by exhaustion from the day's heavy training.

But they didn't. Instead, they spent the rest of the evening playing with the skinny little mutt they quickly agreed to name Charlie.

Mother lectured them briefly on the rules. They would both be responsible for the upkeep and feeding of Charlie. He was their responsibility and theirs alone.

"Can he sleep in our room?" Tommy asked brightly.

To Peter's astonishment, she said yes. They would make a bed up for him on the floor in their room.

"Just remember," Mother warned as they prepared for sleep. "Make sure you look after him."

THEY HAD no idea exactly what Charlie was. Other than male and a dog. For the first weeks the boys tried to guess what breed he was from an old copy of the American Kennel Club's book on dog breeds that they found on a dusty bookcase. Red haired, bony and medium sized, he had a pointed face like a Collie, a fluffy curled-up tail like a Chow Chow, and sticking up ears like a Corgi. It was impossible to nail him to any single breed. Or even whittle it down to two or three. In the end they had given up. "He's a mongrel," Mother had told them. "Pure and simple. A mongrel like the pair of you."

As for how Charlie had ended up on that lonely farm, the boys were pretty certain it wasn't via an orphanage. The explanation had turned out to be quite simple. During a visit to a wholesalers on the outskirts of Fairbanks to buy the few provisions they brought in, such as soap, Magda had come across several flea-bitten puppies hanging around the back door of a warehouse. Having spotted them while lifting sacks of lye onto her shoulder, she had asked if she could take the last male. The next thing, the dog was standing on the passenger seat of Kitten the Sno-Cat with his head hanging out the window and his tongue out his mouth.

By two months Charlie was a beloved part of the household. To those boys, it seemed like he was some essential part of the farm now. That without his presence it would fall apart.

He had breathed life into that dead place with his antics, with his continuously wagging tail, his simple lust for life. Light now existed where only shadow had previously dwelled. To take him away would have been to kill that place for both boys.

He was their number one.

Their responsibility.

Their bond.

At the crack of every dawn, Charlie woke with the boys, standing to attention at the foot of Peter's bed by the time Mother and Magda were stepping into the room for inspection. When they left he would follow them all the way to the front door, before retreating to the upstairs. There, he would watch them from a window as they left to perform whatever training, chores, or punishment they had been set. Most of the dog's day was spent curled up by that same window waiting for their return.

Then, one day, something happened that fused their bond forever.

They were silently stalking through the woods hunting deer, their rifles strapped to their backs, the dog following closely behind.

Peter held a hand up.

Stop.

Charlie stopped with them, getting down low in the bracken. Peter knelt beside a set of tracks pressed into the mud. A mound of droppings lay amongst them, steam rising off it.

Peter made a series of hand signals at Tommy that essentially translated as: *It's fresh. He's close.*

They continued through the scrub, moving down an embankment that led to a river. A short ridge blocked their view of the rushing water. If the deer was drinking, as they supposed, the uprising of rock would give them cover.

They got down on their bellies and crawled the last few meters to it. Their suspicions were proved correct when they peeked out from behind the rock and spotted a giant buck dipping his head in the passing water. Raising it up every now and then to check his surroundings.

The sun strobed through the trees on the other side. The light making his huge crown of antlers glow golden.

It made for a beautiful sight.

The boys slipped their bodies back behind the ridge. Tommy caught Peter's attention and with his hands reminded him: *This one's yours.*

Peter nodded and began making his way back around the rocks. As for Charlie, he wasn't even looking their way. The dog appeared mesmerized by something he'd smelled deep in the thick scrub they'd come from. His nose sniffing the air.

Peter lay on his belly, hidden in deep bracken, an eye lined up with the scope of the rifle, keeping his breathing down to a calm minimum.

He slipped the bolt back.

Held his breath.

Didn't get to make the shot.

Charlie had let off a loud bark that sent the deer scattering.

"Charlie?!" Peter complained, glancing a sore look over his shoulder at the mutt.

The dog wasn't listening. It continued to bark into the woods.

Tommy stood searching the distance where the dog's fierce attention appeared drawn. "What is it, boy?"

He soon found out.

The forest came alive. The green scrub moving and shaking. It confused both boys. They just stood there stunned. The sound of a roar made it over the hiss of the river and there it was—a giant grizzly rushing at them on all fours, the fur along its spine shaking with every beat of the dirt from its huge paws. It was coming in so fast both boys forgot all about their rifles. Peter had left his on the ground. Tommy wheeled around and went to run, but the beast was on him. It lurched forwards, grabbed him at the back and lifted him up, began swinging him from side to side, Tommy screaming into the woods.

Peter did everything he could to push back the fear. Charlie bought him the time he needed to get his focus. The little red dog leapt at the bear and caught ahold of its flank, clamping on with his teeth and mauling it.

The bear roared and in doing so released Tommy. Dropping him face first onto the mud. Peter expected to see blood, an exposed spine, but there was nothing of the sort. The bear had only gotten ahold of the rifle on Tommy's back.

Grabbing Tommy by the hands, Peter dragged him down the hill, picking his rifle up on the way.

"Did he get me? Did he get me?" Tommy called out frantically.

"No. He got your gun."

All the time the dog was barking and snarling, blocking the grizzly off from the boys. The bear growling as it pushed them back. Not quite sure what to make of the dog. For now at least.

It gave them time to get themselves together after the rush attack. Their Bergara B-14 HMR rifles now at the ready, Peter and Tommy pulled the triggers and blasted that bear into oblivion before it figured it could crush the dog into the dirt if it wanted.

After the first few hits from the .308 Creedmoor rounds, it tried to run, but they followed it down the bank, continuing to fire until it let out a howling gasp and collapsed onto its front at the edge of the river.

Panting and breathless, both boys turned to the dog. Their hero.

TWENTY-EIGHT

VIRGINIA, 2021

"How much further?" Luka asks.

"Another mile or two," Semyon replies.

Luka drives them north along the freeway, headlights eating up the road. Across a wheat field, the moon's reflection stretches across the quivering waters of the Potomac. A half hour ago, they passed through the sleepy town of Leesburg and are now back on open road. Nothing but Virginia country either side.

Their lights illuminate a sign for the small town of Lucketts.

"Take the next left," Semyon tells Luka.

The next left takes them off the freeway onto a farm track. The car bumbles along for a couple of miles through tall cornfields, until they're reaching a dirt clearing where a silver Buick Verano waits.

Without a word, both men get out and retrieve the guns

and other luggage from the backseat, transferring it to the trunk of the Buick.

Luka slams the lid shut and turns.

He freezes.

Semyon is aiming a pistol at him.

"Hey. You don't ha—"

The shot hits him between the eyes and he drops like spilled clothing.

"*Predatel'*," Semyon grumbles as he steps over the body and fetches a jerrican of gasoline from the passenger footwell of the Buick.

Traitor.

TWENTY-NINE

ALASKA, 2004

"CHARLIE?!" THE BOYS CALLED OUT IN UNISON AS they wandered the farm.

It was strange. Normally when they returned from training the dog would run from the house and meet them before they were halfway across the yard. But today nada.

With night falling, the surrounding woods and mountains had a colorless hue to them.

"You think he's in the barn?" Peter suggested. "Got hisself trapped in the corn cellar again chasing rats."

"Maybe. Let's take a look."

It turned out he wasn't in the corn cellar.

He was in the barn.

Just not the cellar.

Both boys walked in side by side. The second they saw Mother standing in the center, the well-beaten punch bag dangling behind her, they knew something bad was about to happen.

Because sitting beside her feet and shivering on the end of a leash was Charlie, the bear's canine, a memento from the day he saved their lives, dangling from his collar.

"Look at the two of you," Mother said. "You have gotten so big and strong. Plenty of nutritious food. Nevertheless." Her voice darkened. "Since Charlie joined our ranks, the rations have suffered." She paused. Then. "Peter, can you come here, please?"

It was not a question, it was an order. And like any good soldier he was in front of her seconds after she finished giving it.

Mother removed the pistol from her hip holster and held it out to him.

"Take it," she said.

Like always, he did as he was asked. No question.

"Peter," Mother said in an emotionless voice, "I need you to shoot the dog."

Tommy shuddered. "No!"

"You stay there," Mother barked, pointing at him.

He stayed put. He, too, knew the rules by now. You always did exactly what she told you. Otherwise she would make life hell.

Eyes back on Peter, Mother said, "If you do not get rid of this dog, you will both be on half rations until it dies naturally in around twelve years."

Peter was shaking as much as the dog. He looked from the animal, to the gun, to her. "You can't do that," he half whispered.

"I will," she assured him.

"Please."

He stared at the dog. Its almond eyes gazing up at him.

Tommy shouted, "Why can't you just let us keep him?"

"Peter, shoot the dog."

Charlie began whining. Like he knew what was about to happen.

"I can't," Peter said, looking into the dog's eyes.

"You must, or I will starve the pair of you into oblivion. Now shoot the dog?!"

"No," Peter sobbed, closing his eyes tight and wishing himself somewhere else. Anywhere, so long as it wasn't here.

"Shoot!" she screamed.

"I can't."

"Shoot the fucking dog!"

She yanked the leash, making Charlie yelp. Then lurched forwards, attempting to snatch the pistol back.

Peter avoided the swipe and stepped away.

She froze, her cold eyes widening into a terrible scowl. In some ways, she looked hurt. Hurt that he had disobeyed her like this.

In a voice trembling with fury, she said, "You have no idea what will happen if you do not..."

Her speech was killed when Tommy stepped forward and ripped the gun from Peter's limp hand.

A shot rang out. Sending the birds nesting in the rafters into a frenzy.

Peter opened his eyes.

Tommy was standing beside him. The gun smoking in his hand. Eyes trapped on the image of the little red mongrel lying on its side with its brains blown out.

Years later Peter would discover that this was part of the

training. That none of it was, as both boys thought at the time, another of Mother's cruelties. It was, in fact, the fevered brainchild of some CIA shrink tasked with coming up with ways to break children and make them into assets. You get them to love something, care for something. Then you get them to kill it.

THIRTY

CRIMES AGAINST GOVERNMENT EMPLOYEES ON US soil are a federal matter. Therefore, the FBI had been called immediately and are now all over the small two-story office block in McLean like ants on a spilled donut.

That's not where Smith is heading, though.

Since he took the call his head has been writhing. A hundred thoughts surge through him at once as he drives furiously towards Coby Jones's family home.

Police tape cuts off the driveway to the street. Neighbors crowd the opposite sidewalks. Police officers hold them back. The press line up next to them, recording the whole thing.

A line of police officers blocks the street. Smith parks, gets out, breaks through them.

"Hey!" one of the cops shouts, coming after him. Catching up, the guy takes hold of his shoulder. Smith shrugs him off, flashes his ID.

"I'm CIA," the old man growls from a corner of his mouth.

"Yeah, but this is FBI jurisdiction. You can't go back there."

"He was my colleague. I may be able to help."

But he hasn't come here to help. He's come here to see it. To see if it's *him*.

The cop walks with Smith, nodding to the officer manning the driveway so that he lifts the tape for them to pass underneath.

Two FBI special agents chat to each other in the hallway. The cop leaves Smith standing at the door and goes to them to explain who the old man is.

Smith hears nothing of their muttering conversation. All the blood has gone to his ears and the only thing he can hear is his thudding heartbeat.

He walks hypnotically toward the living room. Through the open door he can see two crime scene investigators. One is taking pictures while the other collects fibers from a rug.

Walter Smith steps into the room. Whatever the photographer is shooting, Smith's view of it is blocked by the couch. He moves around it. The men in the hallway don't notice his absence until he's all the way around and staring down at the three dead bodies.

They are huddled together, mother in the middle, her children pulled into her. They lie on their sides, legs bent from where the gunman has had them kneel in front of him while he stood behind. Each has died from a single gunshot wound to the back of the head. High caliber. The exit wounds have destroyed the faces. He's not even afforded the family the luxury of an open casket.

In a way, Smith isn't even looking at them. He is seeing another scene, three different dead bodies, superimposed over these ones.

Once more he is in Venice.

"Hey!"

The FBI agent grabs his shoulder, twists him around.

"You can't be here," he says when Smith is facing him.

The agent frowns at the blank expression on the other man's pale face. It is like Smith has seen a ghost. Or three of them.

He walks with the agent back to the hallway, not hearing a thing he says. Not even when the guy calls after him after he continues walking out the front door and back to his car.

They let him go. Staring after him from the driveway with bewildered expressions.

Back in his car, Smith makes a call.

A female answers. "Hello?"

"Ibliss?"

There is a pause that lasts a few seconds. Her slow steady breathing purring down the line into his ear.

"I don't know who that is," she eventually says. "You have the wrong number."

"No, I don't. I know exactly who you are and where you are."

"I have no idea what you are referring—"

"Okay. Play it like that, if you want. I'll just hand what I know about you over to the CIA then. Tell them I've found one of their missing assets. The ones they want dead."

"You know nothing about me."

"I know you live in Toronto, Canada, with your husband and daughter. I know you work for Amtrak

Communication Systems as a sales consultant. Corporate sales. Neat swap from being an international assassin. I also know you call yourself Sara these days."

On the other end, the woman is speechless. Smith feels the need to ask if she's still there.

"I should put the phone down and run," she says.

"And leave your family behind?"

More silence. Then. "What do you want?"

"Good. I'm glad you're onside. Because I'm in need of your unique skillset."

THIRTY-ONE

ALASKA, 2021

Dawn and the air is deep blue when Peter and Michael emerge silently from the barn, wheeling a pair of dirt bikes into the yard. Peter kicks his over first try, the Yamaha bursting alive and filling the trees with rattling noise.

When Michael tries his, it falls flat on the first kick. So he tries again. A hollow rumble, still no life.

He goes to kick it again when Peter stops him.

"Look," the latter says, pointing down at the carburetor. "The seal's opened up. There's no air getting into the chamber."

"Ugh," Michael groans.

"I don't have time to fix it."

Michael becomes sullen. "So what? You'll be hunting alone today?"

"I guess."

"Great," the kid complains. "That means I get to stay here and help Magda with the laundry."

"It does."

Minutes later Peter—a lone wolf on the hunt—zigs and zags through the trees, the bike climbing up the steep banks of the forest. Today's hunting ground is far. At least twenty miles away through knotted, hilly climbs, the ride estimated to take around two hours.

An hour and a half into it, Peter finds himself gliding past a familiar spot. He can't help stopping the bike and dismounting.

Leaving the Yamaha on a ridge, he pushes through thick scrub, climbing an embankment all the way to a line of rocks. Reaching them, he stands staring down at a small clearing where bushes grow over a thin gorge.

As he stares at it, he hears a voice call his name.

Peter?!

THE LAUNDRY DONE, Michael suggests a game of hide-and-seek to eat up the time until Peter returns.

Mother counts down in the house while Michael and Magda run outside to hide. They head straight for the barn. In the center of the well-worn floor is a trapdoor that leads to an old corn cellar.

"I got dibs on the cellar," Michael says.

"No problem," Magda replies, her eyes honed on Kitten the Sno-Cat, the all-terrain vehicle under tarp at the back of the barn. "I'm too big for down there, anyway."

"But I'm gonna need your help."

She stops and rolls her eyes. He is struggling with the weight of the door. She comes over, practically swats him out the way, grabs the iron ring, and lifts it open with a whining creak.

"You're the best, Mags," Michael says with a wink as he heads down into darkness.

The door closed back up, Michael calls to her.

"Pull that table over the top," he tells her from a gap between the floorboards. "That way she won't think anyone's down here."

"How much time do we have?" Magda asks.

"Thirty-six seconds. Enough time."

The boy retreats into the shadows while Magda drags a scratched and battered table over the trapdoor.

Right at that moment Mother emerges from the house.

"Ready or not," she announces, "here I come."

Magda makes a dash for it, reaching Kitten before Mother is far enough across the yard to see all the way into the barn.

Taking a position equidistant from the house and the barn, Mother stops and scans her surroundings. Her spotlight-gaze moves across the trees, scrutinizes the cooler shed, the stores, the work shed. Reaching the arched entrance to the barn, they narrow, hone in, sharpen.

However, when she goes to step toward it, the low guttural sound of an approaching engine stops her in her tracks. She gazes in its direction, and soon the ominous sound is filling the woods.

Having heard it herself, Magda steps out from behind Kitten and makes her way out of the barn.

"Stay hidden, Mikey," she says when she is standing over the top of the cellar.

"What is it?" he calls up through the gap.

"Company. I don't know who. I'll let you know when it's safe."

By the time Magda reaches the yard, the colossal front of a Viking all-terrain vehicle is coming into view through the trees, its six deeply rutted tires churning up the mud as it pulls in front of the house. The ugly thing resembling a mechanical toad on wheels.

Magda joins Mother and the two watch as the hatch-like door of the Viking opens.

"Probably another child to train," Mother puts to Magda.

"We don't train children anymore," comes her friend's curt reply.

A single occupant climbs out. He is dressed in hard-wearing civilian clothing; the type you'd expect out here. His hair is black and his skin is bone white. He greets both women with a smile.

It is then that past and present wash into each other. Mother tilts her head. Her eyes begin to pierce and a frown slowly forms on the wrinkles of her face.

"Misha?" she says as if gradually recognizing him.

The man narrows his eyebrows at her.

"Misha?" he says.

Mother's only reply is to leap forward, throw her stringy old arms around him and bury her face in his chest.

"*Ty prishel. Ty prishel*," she murmurs gladly into him.

You came. You came.

"Is she okay?" he asks Magda as the old woman sobs into him.

"No," Magda replies bluntly. "She is *not* okay. Now explain yourself. Who are you and what do you want?"

"My name is Jason Hammond. CIA. I happened to be the closest agent to you guys, so I got the call. I must admit, you're way out here. It was a real doozy to—"

"What call did you get, Agent Hammond?" Magda interrupts.

Hammond glances down at Mother, her arms wrapped around his shoulders. "Maybe we should do this indoors?"

"*Da!*" Mother announces, removing her face from his chest. "Let's have tea."

She grabs his hand and leads him toward the house. Magda following with a sullen look on her face.

HAVING ABANDONED the Yamaha to continue on foot, it isn't long before Peter comes across fresh deer tracks and begins following them up and around the crags and ridges of the gloomy forest.

Led on by the tufts of loose malting fur he finds on the ends of tree branches, he moves through the forest, making as much sound as the breeze, shaping his body so that he fits perfectly between the overhanging scrub, stalking his prey like its own shadow.

The higher he gets up an almost vertical slope, the more the thunderous rumble of a tumbling river beats at his ears. Grabbing the exposed roots of trees to climb, he reaches the top. Crawling over like a soldier breaching a trench, the river's rumble bursts into a roar.

He keeps his chest tight to the ground, stays hidden

within the confines of thick bracken, and from there spots his quarry.

A huge buck stands at the river's edge taking a drink. Peter's hand reaches over his shoulder and takes hold of a Super Kodiak archer's bow that lies on his back. He removes an arrow from his quiver and loads the bow. Drawing it, he pauses a moment to watch the majestic beast before its death.

IN THE KITCHEN Magda makes the teas while Jason Hammond sits next to Mother at the table. The old woman still has hold of his hand.

"It's wonderfully isolated out here," Hammond remarks.

Magda grunts back at him over her shoulder.

"*Misha,*" Mother cuts in in Russian, "*why do you speak in English with us? Are we all not Russians?*"

Hammond, a little red in the cheeks, picks her hand from his lap and tells her, "I'm afraid I don't understand you."

She smiles. "*You lie.*"

She points a bony finger. "*You always were good at acting, Misha. Always. Even in times of...*"

She catches a look at the finger pointing in his direction and goes silent. Bringing the back of her hand to her eyes, they widen, then shimmer. She notes the amount of liver spots speckling the hand, the deep color of the skin, the protrusive veins wrapping the bony fist like wires.

"This is not my hand," she mutters. "Magda," she looks up at her friend, "when did I get so old?" She turns sideways to Jason Hammond, gives him a curious look. "Why is Misha still young?"

"Because he's not Misha," Magda says, placing the tea things on the table. "Now," she adds, lumping herself down opposite them and addressing Hammond, "what is it you want?"

Hammond smiles. "You trained children here, right?"

"You know we did."

"Children?" Mother says, breaking into English. "Training children?"

"Yes," Hammond says. "Part of the Fallen Angel program for the US Government. You and your friend here used to house children at the farm with you and teach them certain... skillsets."

Mother begins shaking her head at him. "No, no. You are wrong. We are KGB. We would never train children for the Americans. Only for USSR. Is this a test, Misha? You've come here to test us before taking us back?"

The deep wrinkles of her face bend and twist.

"This isn't a test," Hammond says. "I'm here to warn you."

"About what?" Magda wants to know.

"Is this about *him*?" Mother cuts in.

"Him?"

"The man with no face?"

Hammond narrows his eyes, stares at her for a moment, then turns to Magda and asks, "Dementia?"

"Partly."

"Partly?"

"Yes. Some of it was always there, one way or another. You see, Agent Hammond, she's led a hard life. We both have. Especially since you sent us all the way out here to this place to train your killers."

Hammond's face darkens. In a cool voice, he says, "You didn't have to come."

Magda doesn't like the tone. Her eyes cut at him. "What do you mean by that?"

"You could have stayed in Russia in 1980 instead of defecting."

Magda's eyes are two slits in her face.

PETER LINES the Super Kodiak up with the deer as it drinks, the tight bowstring pulled all the way back. The arrow primed between his fingers. His eyes focused.

He can see the individual hairs of the deer move as the breeze plays with them. He can see the jugular throb with each mouthful of water. He can see a tuft of white hair that sticks out behind its right ear.

Peter pulls in a steady breath, holds it, lets go.

The arrow whistles through the forest. The deer looks up. It's too late. The animal half leaps, half runs, before dropping onto its side within a few feet of the river, the arrow sticking out of its neck.

Peter returns the bow to his back, makes his way down to the riverbank, kneels by the dead deer. He plucks the arrow out, places it back in his quiver, then loads the buck across his shoulders, needing all the strength in his legs to rise and carry it away.

. . .

"I DON'T UNDERSTAND," Mother says, glancing from Jason Hammond to Magda and then back again. "You're *not* here to take us back?"

"Would you like to go back to Russia?" Hammond puts to her.

"Yes."

He turns to Magda. "What about you?"

"Only death awaits us in Russia," she tells him frankly. "Now, please, tell us what you've come here to warn us about."

"You are both in danger," Hammond finally comes out with. "Like I said, I was the closest in your area, and being that you have no lines of communication, I was enrolled to come and speak with you both."

"About what?" Magda snaps impatiently.

"Are you aware of a Russian agent nicknamed the Hunter?"

"No," is the straight answer to that.

"To put it bluntly, he is Russia's most accomplished assassin. And we are under the impression that he has been sent for *you*."

"Us? Why?"

"The two of you defected from the Soviet Union in 1980, right?"

"The Soviet Union no longer exists," Magda points out.

Jason grins. "Be that as it may. But back then it did. And you were both assassins in the KGB. Very good ones, if I'm right. You, Magda, dispatched Giorgi Markov in 1978 on Waterloo Bridge, London. You did so using a poison dart fired from an umbrella. The dart was dipped in ricin and—"

"So what?"

He grins. Turns to Mother. "You, she-wolf, have a very long and extensive history. Being that before the Hunter, it was *you* who was Russia's darling killer. In 1954 you were used in the assassination of Abdurrahman Fatalibeyli in Munich. Fatalibeyli was a Red Army general who defected to the Nazis in World War Two, then later to the CIA. Stalin had wanted him dead for a long long time—"

Magda hammers her fist down on the table.

"So what?!"

Still staring into Mother's eyes, Hammond, unperturbed by the show of aggression, goes on, "You were only twelve years old when you garroted Fatalibeyli. See, the old traitor liked young girls, and the KGB had just the young girl for the job. One who was already a killer. One who had already killed by age nine and by twelve, the age she was when she ran that garrote around Fatalibeyli's pedophile neck, had already taken the lives of seven men and two woman." His expression is one of admiration. "My word, no wonder the CIA thought you perfect to train the little devils they sent up here."

Magda stands up sharp. Her chair clattering against the stone floor.

Hammond still ignores her as he tells Mother, "I have learned so much about you, Mother."

The old woman tips her head to the side. "Why do you call me Mother, Misha?"

"Because that is who you are, she-wolf."

"*You* are not CIA," Magda puts to him, her eyes two slashes across her face.

Jason Hammond holds his hand up. "*Hush now,*

Magda," he says in Russian. "*Look at her. She is seeing the past with those old eyes of hers.*"

Indeed, Mother does look to be weighing things up, a pensive expression bending the contours of her wrinkles, a blank stare, finger to her lips.

Still in Russian, Hammond says, "*She is seeing all the terrible, terrible things she has done. The evil that has come from her wicked hands. No wonder the Americans kept you locked away out here. Didn't dare to let a wolf so close to the flock.*"

Magda makes a dash for the sideboard. Grabs a knife from the block. Wheels around. He's right there.

THE BUCK, heavy and cumbersome, flops unevenly about on Peter's shoulders as he carries it through the woods. As is often the case for a hunter, he hadn't realized how far he'd gone whilst silently tracking the animal. Eyes peeled on the marks in the icy mud, ears to the wind, thoughts, feelings and instincts honed to the point of hypnotic tunnel vision. He'd traveled at least two miles from the Yamaha.

When he finally reaches the bike, Peter loads the buck onto the back of it, tying it to the rear mudguard, its hooves already bound. Then he jumps on the front, kicks the Yamaha over, and begins his journey back to the farm.

SEMYON AND MAGDA burst out of the house, the brawl spilling into the yard.

Now that they're outside, they can get some space, draw breath. It had been a scramble of blows and counterblows in the tight spaces of the house, Magda having been dispossessed of the knife early on.

In the background, Mother staggers to the open door of the farmhouse. She leans heavily on the frame.

"I feel weak," she says before crumbling to the floor in a heap, having succumbed to the large dose of benzodiazepine Semyon had slipped into her tea when Magda's eyes had been too busy watching his own.

"What have you done to her?" Magda demands.

Her nose is already bleeding. A testament to the headbutt he'd landed when their limbs had become locked in the hallway, when she'd almost gotten him in a hold which would have seen her try and break his back.

"Just something to make her sleep," Semyon says without taking his eyes off his opponent.

He attacks, full speed. Kick meets stop kick, punches are diverted, jabs dodged, blows absorbed against arms, legs, hips. There are no tricks, nothing showy. Just speed.

In the midst of the flashing limbs, Magda does her best to parry and block, looking for an opportunity to grab ahold of him. Younger than Mother, she is still well in her sixties, and though immensely fit for her age, her creaking joints don't move anywhere near as fast as they once did. This is why she doesn't attempt many kicks or punches herself: she is just too slow for the type of speed coming at her. Therefore, she must wait for her chance of a counteroffensive using the technique of Sambo. The martial art taught to Soviet special forces and developed by the Red Army with the primary goal of being able to end a fight as quickly as possible through chokeholds or limb grapples that break bones and ligaments.

But Semyon is too good to give her a chance.

With reluctance, Magda realizes that her opponent is stronger, quicker and better. She spots several fighting techniques being merged into one constant flow. The Brazilian style of Capoeira, that combines elements of dance and acrobatics. Israeli self-defense Krav Maga, utilizing a combination of techniques used in aikido, boxing, judo, karate, and wrestling. The African martial art of Dambe, which focuses primarily on boxing but also uses kicking techniques. And the Indonesian martial art of Pencak silat with its emphasis on speed and accuracy.

She would be impressed if she wasn't so busy deflecting his blows, their dance moving toward the barn, Magda being backed along the dirt, her forearms and shins aching from the pounding they are taking.

All the hope she has is that she can keep him from killing her before Peter gets there.

FOUR MILES FROM THE FARM, Peter is riding steadily down a rough hillside when he hits a patch of loose dirt that causes the back wheel to slide out from under him.

He's too quick to fall. Jumping off the bike in time and landing on his feet. The Yamaha slips sideways down a bank, the weight of the deer pulling it. The engine revs hard, filling the forest with its furious noise, and the stench of gasoline and oil hang in the air.

Peter is forced to follow it down, his boots surfing through the loose dirt of the hillside. Reaching the bike, he stops its descent by holding on to the handlebars with one hand while using the other to grip exposed tree roots for leverage.

There is further dismay when he finally gets the bike upright. The deer has come loose and hangs at an angle. If he doesn't retie it, he'll have to drag half of it through the bracken.

"Great," he grumbles under his breath.

SEMYON LOSES focus and Magda sees an opportunity. A window through his lightning kicks and punches.

She unleashes a jackhammer of a low spear jab. It breaks through. Just. Semyon steps back so that the worst of the blow doesn't quite reach. But it still hits.

He recoils involuntarily from the strike. The window widens. She sends a left jab at his chin—stops it halfway. His block is already up, but the blow doesn't come from where he thinks it will. He feels the air move next to his left ear before it is followed by a right hook lashing into the side of his head. It is like being hit with a brick. The blow sends him reeling sideways. She swoops in for the grab. Semyon evades it. He leaps backwards into a reverse flip, his rising feet clipping her on the chin and sending her away.

By now the fight is inside the barn. She backs him into the center and the two stop a few yards from the table to take a breather.

Semyon shakes his head. His arms. His legs.

"Whoa!" he exclaims. "That was some punch. I'm seeing double."

Magda is moving slowly toward him, trying to shake off her throbbing chin.

Semyon smiles.

Exploding forward, he feints by dropping his right shoulder and snaps off a quick left at her face. She falls for the dipped shoulder and the punch sneaks through her misplaced block.

His fist crushes her eye and her vision immediately blurs. If he is seeing double, then she can now hardly see at all.

Semyon presses his advantage, unleashing a flurry of punches. Caging her head with her forearms, Magda backpedals blindly into a corner of the barn, his fists blasting at her.

A strike to her stomach makes her almost vomit and the dull, sickly pain washes through her. Fury erupts, pushing the throb out of her muscles as she manages to shove him off. Then she goes for him, forcing him to skip backwards, to constantly send out blocking moves and parrying punches. Betting it all on one horse, Magda opens herself up and lurches for him. As she comes in, a palm strike crushes her nose further into her face. The crunch it makes reaches the rafters. But she does get her man. Throwing those thick tentacles around him, she traps Semyon's arms at his sides and holds on. She takes a few seconds to store up her strength. Then she begins to do what all good anacondas do: she begins to crush her prey.

"No," he begins to mutter as he struggles.

His exposed legs kick at her. With a well-aimed toe poke, he cracks her knee and she goes down on it, crying out into the barn. Caught out by the pain, her grip loosens for a split second.

It is enough.

Semyon manages to get one arm free as he feels her constricting grip begin to force his ribs inwards. As the pain builds and it becomes impossible to breathe, he digs his thumb right into her eye socket, gripping the back of her skull with his fingers and forcing the thumb into the eye.

She screams in agony. Her grip loosens a second time and his other arm is out and both hands grip that poor woman's head.

Her screams are bloodcurdling.

All the way until the end.

She releases him, and when Semyon retracts his bloody thumbs, she falls sideways onto the floor, kicking up dust as she lands.

The Hunter takes a while to cough and pant. He checks his ribs. Is thankful that he hadn't been within that vise of arms another second. Otherwise, he would be drowning on his own blood by now.

Having gathered himself, Semyon staggers out of the barn. Reaching his vehicle, he opens the door and retrieves his handgun. Returning to the outbuilding, he marches up to the huge woman and unceremoniously puts three bullets into her to make sure.

Then he spits on the ground and walks back to the yard. There, he scoops up the almost weightless body of Mother and carries her into his giant vehicle. Placing her across the backseat, he places plastic zip-ties tightly around her wrists and ankles.

Moments later, he is leaving, the low guttural sounds of his vehicle's engine gradually fading.

· · ·

When it has faded completely, Michael climbs out of the cellar and runs straight to Magda. Grabbing a shoulder, he rolls her onto her back. Something that takes almost all his strength.

He bursts into tears the second he sees her mangled, eyeless face. Dropping to his knees beside her, he begins to sob.

"*Magda?*"

He almost jumps out of his skin when she coughs, a rivulet of blood slipping down from her mouth.

"Oh, my boy," she wheezes, reaching a hand up to him and touching his face. "You must stay hidden... until Peter is back. The man who did this might come back."

"Magda, are you going to die?" the kid whines.

"I think so."

His face creases up.

"Don't cry, boy," she says tenderly. "Don't cry. It's okay."

She pats his chin and runs the back of her hand down his cheek, wiping away the tears.

"We have to stop the bleeding," Michael says, shaking himself. "I'll get the first-aid kit from the house."

He goes to leave her, but she grabs his arm and stops him.

"No," she says when he turns back to her. "It is too late for me, boy. You must... huh... wait... for Peter..."

It is eerily quiet when Peter returns to the farm.

Usually this wouldn't bother him. This place has always

borne a somber mood. But Michael, like Tommy and Charlie before him, has brought an especial life to it, and he expects to find that life in the yard when he pulls up.

"Hello?!" he calls out, getting off the bike and tending to the deer flopped over the back.

Feet crunch rapidly across gravel. They make him turn in the direction of the barn. Michael is running toward him. Upon spotting the look on the kid's face, Peter's stomach kinks and he leaves the deer.

Michael throws his arms around Peter, gripping him hard and crying.

"What happened?" Peter says, scanning the farm, every cell in his body hardening.

Michael lifts his face. Anger floods it.

"A man came," he says through his teeth. "He..." Michael glances over his shoulder at the barn. "He killed her."

"Who?"

"Magda."

Peter follows Michael to the body. She is on her back. The kid has crossed her hands over her chest. He'd thought about closing the eyelids, but hadn't been able to bring himself to do it. Not with the eyes like that.

Peter does the job. Then he kisses his former mentor on the forehead. His fists gripped tight at his sides, he tries his hardest to nullify the rage swelling inside him.

"Where's Mother?"

"He took her."

"The man?"

"Yes."

"Did you see him?"

"No. I was hiding in the corn cellar."

Peter turns to the kid. "I need you to tell me everything."

THIRTY-TWO

ALASKA, 2004

PETER WAS SITTING AS CLOSE TO THE OPEN DOOR of the stall as the chain around his ankle would allow. His red eyes stuck on the dead dog.

A day later, Charlie was still there. Lying on his side, the top of his head missing, blood spread across the wooden floor. Going black as the flies writhed about in it.

Magda walked in from the dark holding a blanket and made her way to him.

"Here," she said, holding out the thick gray cover as she stood before him.

"Thank you."

The second he took it, Peter unfurled the harsh woolen blanket and draped it over his shoulders.

Magda sighed. "These things are done for a reason, Peter."

He looked up at her. "What reason, Magda?"

"To prepare you for out there. It will be harsh, Peter."

"As harsh as this place?"

"Harsher. There will be no one to trust. No one to help you. Your government will deny you. May even hunt you if it has to. You must learn to trust nothing and nobody."

Peter's lip quivered. "And where does that leave a person, Magda? If they can't trust anybody."

"This is our fate, Peter. That is all there is. Fate."

And with that she turned on her heels, made her way to the dog, and lifted its lifeless body from the floor. Peter watching her carry him out, all the way until she was swallowed up by the darkness.

IT RAINED the night it happened. Rained hard.

Peter finished the food that Magda had brought him, then crawled into the blanket to escape the cold air of the barn. Eating tired him and he fell into a deep slumber on the damp, hay covered ground as the rain rattled the tin roof.

Soon after, however, he awoke in a fever. His stomach writhed and cramped and he jolted forwards to spray vomit across the barn.

The burning pain deepened in his stomach. Cramps spread through his arms and legs. He pulled himself into a ball, felt his bowels lurch. Diarrhea oozing involuntarily down his leg.

Lying where he was, he could see right out into the yard.

A great bolt of lightning lit up the farmhouse right at the moment Magda stumbled out the front door, vomit spread down the front of her coveralls, and collapsed in the mud.

A second person followed her out, stepping into the rain. They were holding something, and when they reached Magda, Peter saw that it was a rope. They went about hogtying her. At one point she weakly tried to push them off, her hands clawing at their face. But they easily beat the attempts away and got the wrists tied up with the rest of her.

After that the person moved to Peter, strolling into the barn with a calm authority. Coming right up, they crouched in front of the helpless teenager, leaned forwards and pressed a flask of water to his lips. Peter used the first sips to wash out the bitter bile which filled his mouth. The second sips he drank down. Though his aching stomach didn't thank him for it.

"Don't worry," Tommy said afterwards. "You haven't had anywhere near as much as they have. I wish I could have avoided giving it you at all, but I had to put it in all the food to make sure."

"How... come... you're not... ill?"

"I've been taking small amounts since I got here. Building up my resistance and waiting for the right moment."

"What... is it?"

"Zigadenus venenosus," Tommy announced like a botany professor. "Commonly known as Death Camas. A toxic, weedy perennial that grows mostly in the western US, across the Plains states, as well as here in Alaska. My first Father was into botany. He would spend hours telling me all about the forest flora."

"What does it... do?"

Reeling off the information, Tommy tells him:

"The effects of the toxic alkaloids may appear from one

to eight hours after ingestion. Symptoms include excessive salivation, burning and numbness of the lips and mouth, thirst, headache, dizziness, nausea, stomach pain, persistent vomiting, diarrhea, muscular weakness, confusion, slow and irregular heartbeat, low blood pressure, subnormal body temperature. However." He held a finger up. "Recovery usually occurs within twenty-four hours. Not a nice experience, but one that doesn't kill."

Peter's eyes moved past him to Magda.

Tommy followed the gaze, then looked back at him.

"Don't worry about her," he said. "We'll figure out what to do with them later. Now let's get that chain off you."

He came around Peter and unlocked the clasp around his bruised ankle.

Peter was filthy, having been out there almost a week. Exhausted from the sickness, he needed Tommy's help to walk. Staggering out of the barn, he immediately began shivering under the beating rain.

As they moved past Magda, she gasped, "Peter! Peter!"

He glanced at her for a few seconds, before continuing inside with Tommy.

Mother lay tied up in the hallway, sickly white, vomit shining down her front like gloss paint. She lifted her head when they came in and her face screwed into a look of absolute hatred.

"Peter... untie me... now!" she shrieked. "Untie—ooff!"

Tommy kicked her in the ribs.

"Shut up!" he shouted.

The fierceness faded from his face when he turned it to Peter. In a soft voice he told him, "Come on, Pete. I ran you a bath."

Peter couldn't help glancing back at Mother as Tommy helped him climb the stairs.

"Leave her," Tommy said. "*We* are all we have now, Pete. Just you and me."

THIRTY-THREE

ALASKA, 2021

EVEN IN THE VIKING ALL-TERRAIN VEHICLE HE'S driving it will take four hours to get to the airfield in Fairbanks. Semyon is glad that the sun is still out and he has visibility. Because the mountainous terrain is treacherous.

"Misha?"

He glances up at the rearview mirror. Mother has roused and is looking up at him from the backseat.

"Why am I bound?" she asks in Russian, holding her zip-tied hands up to him.

"You still think I'm Misha?"

She smiles. Cocks an eye. "A joke, love?"

He cocks one back. "If I untie you, will you be good?"

"Of course, Misha. I don't understand why you tied me up in the first place. Maybe some kinky fun?" she adds with a salacious wink.

She thinks I am this Misha, Semyon thinks as the skin of

his back gradually retracts to its original position. *Then I shall be her Misha. At least that way, she'll be easier to control until we reach our destination.*

Semyon stops the Viking. Leaning into the back, he flicks out his Finka folding knife and holds it before her. "You promise to be good?"

She smiles, screwing her wrinkles up.

"Oh, Misha, I have missed your games so much."

Shaking his head gently, Semyon cuts the ties and helps her into the front with him. In the passenger seat, she sits like a cat, gazing at him through simpering eyes while he pushes the all-terrain vehicle onwards.

After a while her staring becomes uncomfortable.

"Why are you looking at me like that?"

"You always were so handsome, Misha. I'm so glad you found me. I thought after Shoyna, I'd never see you again."

"What is Shoyna?"

"Don't you remember?"

"No."

"Shoyna is a place. A godforsaken place."

"What happened there?"

The soft expression creases into confusion.

"You know what happened."

"I have forgotten."

The look of uncertainty brightens into a smile.

"You're playing again."

Then, without warning, she leans across the vehicle, grabs his thigh, just below his manhood, and kisses his cheek.

"Hey!" Semyon exclaims, jumping half out of his skin and quickly retrieving the hand as it moves further up his leg. "No playing around. I need to concentrate on driving this thing."

"I thought after all this time," she remarks disappointedly, seeping back into her own seat, "you'd want to snuggle."

Semyon aims a sullen eye at her. "Not during missions."

"This is a mission?"

"Yes. We have to reach the extraction."

THIRTY-FOUR

I T T A K E S T H E M H A L F A N H O U R T O D I G U P T H E
million Peter took from Fred Wilson. They load it onto the
flatbed of Kitten and get into the cab at the front. The Sno-
Cat coughs and hacks her guts up as the engine shudders
into grumbling existence and the caterpillar tracks begin
creaking forwards.

Not long after setting off, Michael has a question.

"How are we gonna get Mother back?"

Peter has a simple answer.

"We're not."

The kid's gaze jerks to him. Big eyes. Lip out.

"Please say I heard you wrong."

Peter's eyes don't leave the rugged terrain. "I'm sorry," he
says, "but I'm not risking both our lives taking on whoever it
is that's got her. We don't even know where they're
heading."

"But we have to save her. She's family, Peter."

"She is *not* family, Mike."

"Yes, she is. You said yourself she's the only mother you've ever known."

"I had a real mother once. *That* was my mother."

"Where is she now?"

Peter has a vision of a corpse lying in a bed. Of reaching out and touching the fly-covered face.

"Dead," he mutters.

"Then Mother is all you have."

"No, she's not," Peter says, turning to meet the kid's look. "*You* are all I have."

THIRTY-FIVE

FAIRBANKS, 2021

PEGGED IN BY MOUNTAINS AND SURROUNDED BY
roaming forests, the city of Fairbanks is an isolated place. A
carpet of one and two-story buildings with the usual
suburbs and commercial districts, it snows seven months of
the year and is the coldest and largest city in the Interior
region of Alaska.

There really is not much else to tell.

On the outskirts of Fairbanks a private airfield takes up
an area of land bordered by a looping stretch of the Chena
River. It consists of three runways, a few shacks at the edges
where commercial fliers advertise, and a hangar the size of a
football field that stands at the end.

It is now nightfall and a frozen fog has been slipping
down from the mountains and washing over the city. As
Semyon drives the Viking across the flat asphalt, only the
blinking runway lights and the semicircle outline of the

hangar can be seen with any clarity. Most of the planes are inside or covered over in tarp. Only a single plane stands ready to fly. A Cessna Seahawk four berth that slowly emerges from the mist the closer they get.

"Where will we live in Russia?" Mother asks.

"At my place," Semyon replies blankly, hawk eyes searching the open space they travel across.

"Where do you live now?"

"Moscow."

"Ugh! Moscow? You always hated Moscow. I thought you would have been given a dacha in Crimea by now. That was what was promised, wasn't it?"

"We're not retired yet," Semyon says, continuing with the *game*.

"We should be."

Semyon ignores her while he parks as close to the plane as he can. Following that, he helps her out. The pilot leaves the Cessna and comes to them. He's a short, round man, and the jowls of his face are creased into an expression of worried angst.

"Mr. Hammond," he says in a shaky voice. "Look, I think you should reconsider flying. The wind is pretty strong to the southwest and visibility is real low."

"I told you. Whatever the weather, I don't care. Just get me to the coordinates and you will receive the sum promised."

"But this fog wasn't expected. The darn wind changed."

"You have state-of-the-art GPS navigation?"

"Yes."

"Then stop being a pussy and get in the plane."

The dark look Semyon gives the pilot leaves the man in little doubt that the conversation is over.

"Yes, sir," he says.

Semyon's biggest concern isn't the weather. It is the danger of the open ground all around them. From the north and south, they are completely exposed. Nothing but the plane to the east and the Viking to the west for cover. It is only the fog hanging in the air that gives him any type of reassurance that they're not simply sitting ducks.

"Now," Semyon orders the pilot, "help her into the plane while I retrieve our luggage."

The pilot goes to take Mother's frail hand. She instantly snatches it away.

"I can walk myself, *pervert*," she says with a curled lip.

Semyon, meanwhile, slides a long, heavy gym bag from the trunk space of the Viking. Then, as he follows the others to the Cessna, he strains his eyes to see into the swirling gray, settling his vision on the hangar roof.

That's where I would—

Something up there flashes.

"Get down!"

Semyon drops onto his front. He feels the air move above his back as the bullet passes over him. It hits the pilot. Enters his abdomen, carries on through his stomach, pancreas, liver, exits through his spine.

The blow from the 6.5mm Creedmoor almost cuts him in two. For a moment he sits on the frozen ground blinking.

"What the...?"

The sentence finishes in a wheezing death rattle.

Semyon takes cover underneath the wing of the Cessna.

Mother has molded her body tight to the nose of the plane, blocking off the hangar. She too had seen it.

"Give me a gun, Misha," she shouts.

He is watching the hazy contours of the hangar roof.

Muzzle flashes light up the arched doorway below.

The shooter has moved.

He must too.

The asphalt chips up around Semyon as he dives for the cover of the fuselage, the gym bag swinging from his tight fist.

Reaching the rear of the plane, out of view of the hangar, he drops the bag to the floor and unzips it as more shots ricochet, ping and spark off the Cessna.

"*b'lyad*!" he says aloud, grabbing an AK-74M from the bag.

Hefting it into his arms, he bursts into the open and sends covering fire at the hangar doors, spreading it across the wide space. His intention is to force the target into cover rather than get a definite hit. Therefore, buying them time.

He unloads the clip and turns to Mother.

"Get in the plane! Get in the—"

The sniper gets a shot on him. The Creedmoor round smacks him right over the heart. It is like being gored by a bull and he is sent straight down onto his ass.

"Misha!" Mother screams, running to him and picking up the spilled AK.

She goes down stiffly on one knee, wedges the buttstock into her shoulder and fires off a neat stitch of bullets. She gets a hit; a woman's shriek emerges over the howling wind.

Mother shoulders the gun and rejoins Semyon. He is

sitting up, desperately pulling in gasping breaths. He lifts his shirt and Mother is instantly relieved.

"Body armor," she says, looking at the huge, smoking dent over the left breast, the crushed slug smoldering in it.

"Help me, huh, get it, huh, off."

The dent is pressing on his chest. They scramble to get the armor unstrapped and off, and when they do, Semyon checks his torso, the flesh already turning yellow over his heart.

A motor starting brings their attention back in the direction of the hangar. It revs and begins bearing down on their position. A shape moves through the fog at ramming speed.

Mother unshoulders the AK and trains her fire on it. Semyon launches himself at the gun case and rips out an OTs-27 Berdysh—essentially an updated version of the Makarov semi-automatic pistol—and begins unloading on the target.

The fog explodes in a ball of fire and soon the flaming remains of a snowmobile are sliding past them.

It is lacking a rider.

Semyon whirls around just in time to see the muzzle flashes of an assault rifle light up the fog from the south. He dives for the cover of the plane. As he stoops under it, several bullets puncture the fuselage.

With fuel leaking onto the asphalt, he zips the gym bag up and carries it to the plane.

"Get in!" he shouts at Mother.

Semyon rips the door of the Cessna open, tosses the bag into the back, and lumps himself down in the pilot's seat. Mother follows, getting into the other side. As the fuselage crackles and pings with bullets, Semyon hurriedly starts the engine, flipping switches and sending the craft into motion.

The sniper has repositioned themselves at the end of the runway. It means they'll have to face them during takeoff.

"Get down," Semyon tells Mother as he does so himself, operating the plane from a crouched position.

The plane begins moving forwards, accelerating toward the figure in the fog. They open fire. The windshield shatters but doesn't break. Semyon pushes the throttle forwards as far as it goes and pulls down on the controls. The Cessna lurches upwards and he feels the air carry it away.

Once clear of the airfield, Semyon and Mother sit up.

"Are you okay?" he asks as they head into the gray sky, only the plane's navigation equipment to guide them.

"Yes," she replies. "A little sore. But I'll live."

There's no time to rejoice in their escape. An alarm sounds and Semyon's eyes fix to the gauges.

They're losing fuel, and fast.

"*b'lyad*'," he mutters.

A SINGLE SLENDER female dressed in a charcoal colored catsuit emerges from the murk. She lifts a pair of field glasses to her eyes and watches the Cessna bob and weave across the top of a vast forest that spreads out from the south of the city. She watches all the way until the fog eats the craft up completely.

Clipping the glasses to her utility belt, she checks the gash on her upper right arm—where the bullet had struck. The fabric is torn, the flesh covered in blood, and the arm is a little numb. But apart from that, nothing to warrant engaging her pain training. Nevertheless, it will need stitches.

Thankfully, she has a full first-aid kit on the back of the belt. After all, Ibliss tends to come well prepared for such eventualities as being shot. Or at least she used to before the end of the Fallen Angel program.

Other items of preparedness are the Heckler & Koch G36 assault rifle and Bergara B14 HMR sniper rifle that she carries on her back. As well as the Ruger LCP pistol she has swaying from side to side on her right hip. Not to mention the Kershaw boot knife that sits tucked in her right Hunter Commando.

Best to come prepared.

As for her appearance, her cropped raven-black hair shows not a single strand out of place. No sign of all the effort it took to get as close as anyone has ever got to killing the Hunter.

Plucking a phone from a tight pocket of the catsuit, Ibliss checks the screen. A red dot blinks as it moves away from her position.

She places the phone back and makes her way to the hangar. As she moves, her muscular hourglass figure flexes underneath the hardwearing fabric of the catsuit. She spots a man in a Chicago Bulls baseball cap emerging cautiously from behind a yellow helicopter that sits in the middle.

"What in the hell just happened?" he asks.

He is middle-aged and dressed in denim dungarees. A bushy gray moustache drops over his mouth and moves when he talks.

"That helicopter," she says, pointing at the Ultramarine. "Can you operate it?"

"I ain't operating shit, lady. I'm calling the cops."

She takes the Ruger LCP from her hip holster and points it at him. "No you're not. You are going to fly me in the direction of that plane."

THIRTY-SIX

ALASKA, 2004

THE MUTINEERS WERE IN THE YARD PLAYING WITH their very own shooting gallery. Not long after their rebellion, they had seized the keys for the armory and emptied the shed of ordnance. That done, they had turned the yard into a firing range, lining up all the furniture from the house and sheds. The cupboards. Their beds. Mattresses. The chest of drawers Peter had helped Magda make the summer before. Mother's wardrobe. Magda's too. Even Kitten hadn't escaped and the ugly Sno-Cat was lined up with the rest of it. Books, crockery, pictures, framed photographs—all the two women had left from their former lives in Russia—all of it was sitting like ducks in a row on top of the furniture.

"Try this one, Pete," Tommy said, lifting an M4 carbine from off the kitchen table, which now sat in the yard. "You want the sight?"

"Sure."

After the gun, Tommy handed him a Trijicon TR24 AccuPoint. Peter slapped the optics on top. Instinctively, he checked the weapon over, and once he was sure it was in operational order, he lifted the carbine to the small of his shoulder and lined his eye up.

The oil painting of a bear lifting a salmon out of a river with its paw jumped at him through the scope. Magda had signed her name in the bottom corner.

Tommy took a seat behind him on the table, his legs dangling off the edge. "Tell me, soldier," he said in the tone of a drill sergeant, "the specifications of that there weapon you're holding."

"This here," Peter replied in a monotone, "is an M4 carbine. It is a NATO, gas-operated, magazine-fed carbine that was developed in the United States during the 1980s. It is a shortened version of the M16-A2 assault rifle."

He squeezed the trigger and put a single bullet through the head of the bear and the picture exploded with the impact.

Peter breathed out through his nose. Sought the next target. Scanned across framed photographs of Mother and Magda. Both of them when they were much younger.

"The M4," he continued, settling the crosshairs on a picture of Mother receiving the Order of Lenin from Leonid Brezhnev, "is extensively used by the United States Armed Forces and is the primary infantry weapon and service rifle of the United States Army and the United States Marine Corp."

He sent a bullet headed straight for the thick monobrow of the General Secretary of the Communist Party. When it hit, the picture flipped backwards into the woods.

"The M4," Peter droned on, "has been adopted by over sixty countries worldwide and has been described as one of the defining firearms of the 21st century."

He placed the gun on fully auto and punched a line of bullet holes across the tops of the furniture, the pictures and photographs popping and flipping, Tommy plugging his ears with his fingers, yipping and cheering the whole time until the M4 was clicking. The magazine empty.

Tommy rushed past him. Peter spotted the grenade the second it left his hand and arc into the trees.

"Fire in the hole!" Tommy shrieked.

They dropped for cover as it exploded between two pines, blowing both into splinters that scattered across the yard.

Tommy got up and began dancing in the raining wood.

The lunatics really had taken over the asylum.

As Peter released the clip from the M4, he couldn't help glancing off into the barn. Shadow filled the end of it and he couldn't see them.

"What are we gonna do, Tommy?" he asked as he slapped in another magazine.

Tommy stopped dancing. He joined Peter in staring into the barn.

"We gotta kill them," Tommy said coldly.

"That's gonna cause a lot of trouble."

"Don't matter. We'll be long gone. There's hunting lodges about a hundred miles to the west. I seen them when she took us up in the plane that time over Beaver Creek."

"I seen them too."

"We could take the bikes. Get to one of the cabins and work our way back to America from there. I mean, come on,

Pete. The shit they've taught us. We could survive out in those woods till next summer if we wanted."

"Then why do we need to kill them?"

Tommy turned a disappointed expression on Peter.

"Sometimes, Pete," he said bluntly, "you scare me."

"I don't mean to. It's just, if escape is what we're doing, there's no need to kill them."

"We let them live, they'll alert people to come after us before we're hidden. It's what happened before when I got loose. No. This time they have to die. We need a head start."

"Then keep them tied up."

"It'll be the same as killing them. Some bear will come onto the farm and get them. Or they'll die from dehydration. How you expect them to drink water or feed themselves?"

"I don't know, Tommy. It just doesn't feel right killing them."

"Really, Pete?! They treat us like shit. Get us to shoot our own goddamn dog! They deserve much more than just death. Now come on. Don't let me down. Please. I'll let you do it. Real easy. Bullet to the head."

And with that he held out a Heckler & Koch HK45 semi-automatic pistol.

A MINUTE later Peter was stood over Mother and Magda, the HK45 dangling at his side. His senses on high alert, the stink of the barn filled him.

The sweat, the sawdust, the blood.

The gun felt heavier than usual as he brought his aim up and focused it on Magda. Looking straight into her swollen eyes, he dared to stroke a trembling finger over the cold trigger.

She looked accepting. Like now was as good a time as any to be sent wherever it was she was due to go: heaven, hell, oblivion.

Peter lowered the gun. He couldn't start with Magda.

His aim moved to Mother. Her look was less beseeching. It was cold as ice. Hard as stone.

"They don't deserve to live, Pete."

Tommy's voice pounded in his head.

"The things they've done to you."

"They were training me," Peter replied in a hollow voice.

"They were abusing you, Pete. They are your abusers. Not family. Not friends. Abusers. Just like that priest. Now shoot them. Before *I* do. Just like I had to with Charlie."

The breeze prickled Peter's hot skin. Time slowed. The smell of sweat and fear and blood filled him until he could taste it all in his mouth.

"Just pull the trigger," Tommy hissed.

Peter closed his eyes.

He weighed it all up.

Came to a decision.

Turned around to face Tommy.

"I can't kill them," he said, opening his eyes.

Tommy's top lip curled into a snarl and his fists clenched.

Peter told him, "This is no better than Charlie."

Tommy glowered at him. "Charlie didn't deserve it. They do. Now if you won't put a bullet in their skulls, I will."

He went to snatch the M4 carbine from his shoulder

when Peter lifted the aim of the HK45 and trained it on him. Tommy's hand froze over the carbine's buttstock and he narrowed his eyes into a pair of evil slits.

"Peter," he said slowly, "you need to think real hard before you take the next step. Real hard. Because if you..."

The pistol exploded in Peter's hand.

But nothing happened.

And when he spotted the cruel grin on the face of the still-standing Tommy, he realized that the HK was loaded with blanks.

"Sorry, Pete," Tommy said, lifting the rifle slowly from his shoulder and training it on him, "but I've never trusted anyone in my life. That includes you. I thought I could. Wanted to. Call this a test. One which you've failed."

Before he could fire, Peter hurled the pistol at his head. It gave Tommy no time to get the shot away. He had to throw himself backwards like an expert limbo dancer to avoid it.

As the pistol hit the wall of the barn with a thud, he whirled around with the carbine.

Peter was right there.

He got both hands on the barrel. Forced it upwards at the moment Tommy pulled the trigger.

Bullets sprayed across the rafters, sending every bird in the barn scattering. The air filling with feathers.

With the barrel burning his hands, Peter managed to tug the carbine out of his opponent's grasp. But Tommy was quick to release the cartridge so that by the time Peter had spun the M4 around in his hands, it did nothing but click.

Tommy charged him, his lead foot stepping rapidly forward. Thrust punches came in—left, right—followed by an upward-canon punch. Tommy sending them out from his core exactly like their Wing Chun master had taught them.

Peter deflected the blows using the rifle. Found a gap. Pivoted around the back of him. Spun the rifle in his hands and went to jab the buttstock between Tommy's shoulder blades.

But Tommy sensed it.

His upper body lurched to the side as the M4 thrust forwards. It missed its intended target, the weight of the gun dragging Peter into a half stumble. By the time he had rearranged his feet, Tommy was on him.

He launched himself into a 540 back kick. Spinning through the air at Peter and landing with a feinted front kick. Then, using his momentum to pivot 360 degrees on his supporting foot, he knocked the rifle out of Peter's hands with a reverse roundhouse.

Now it was just them. Mano a mano. Two trains meeting at full speed. Who was going to flinch? Who would see a brother and who would see an enemy? Who would go for the jugular while the other lost his stomach?

Tommy was initially the fiercest, and Peter did well to deflect the subsequent barrage of punches and kicks that came furiously at him.

They parted. Neither out of breath yet. Circled. Fists clenched. Only a few feet of stale air between them. The entrance of the barn faced westward. It was now early evening and the orange sun was shining into it, casting the fighters in golden light.

"I thought I could trust you, Pete."

"You can't just kill people because they become a problem for you, Tommy. That's what crazy people do."

"You dumbass. Look around you. Think back to the past years of your life on this farm. This is how you make crazy people, Pete. In places like this. Well, if they want it: I'll show them crazy."

He came at Peter. The two becoming a flurry of kicks and counter kicks. Punches and counter punches. Peter found himself going backwards. The wall of the barn close behind him. He continued to retreat. Tommy continued advancing. Then, right at the moment his back was to hit the wall, Peter thought he'd found a gap. He countered with a forearm strike.

Tommy blocked it.

Their training had been almost identical. Peter had a total of six months on Tommy, but their level was pretty much the same. When one moved, the other appeared to know exactly where they were going. What they were going to do. It was like two ancient chess masters going at it for the thousandth time. Breaking each other down piece by piece, until only two remain.

Mother and Magda watched on with rabid eyes.

Having escaped being cornered, Peter brought the fight back into the center of the barn.

Once more they circled.

Peter thought Tommy looked a little tired. His breathing a little labored. Shoulders a little lower.

"Give it up, Tommy," Peter said. "Give it up and I'll let you go. Escape on your own. I'll make sure no one comes after you for at least a week."

"Bullshit. The second you untie them, they'll make the call."

"Just go, Tommy."

The other boy glanced out of the barn. At the table full of weapons on the far side of the yard.

"Don't," Peter warned.

Tommy glanced back at him. Scowled. Made a run for it.

Peter went after him, but stopped at the entrance. A three-pound club hammer sat on the ground. He picked it up, eyed the growing space between himself and Tommy, and sent it arcing across the yard after him.

It landed on his leg, Tommy letting out a short sharp scream. All the hammer's weight thumping down on his calf and breaking both the fibula and tibia bones. The leg kinking, it threw the teenager onto his front so that he landed face first in the mud. The table only a few meters away.

When he raised his head, he found Peter standing over him.

Fury erupted in Tommy then. He went to stand, but Peter placed a foot on his back and pressed him into the ground.

Tommy lurched forwards. Grabbed Peter around the leg. Mouth wide open, he held the leg tight and bit into it. Forcing his teeth through the cargo trousers and into the flesh.

"Stop it, Tommy," Peter said without flinching.

Tommy began ripping his face from side to side like a mauling pit bull.

"I said stop it."

As blood dribbled down Tommy's chin, the pain began to creep in from the corners. Raising his other foot, Peter brought it down on the side of Tommy's head—once, twice, repeatedly, until he was forced from the limb.

He went to stand.

Peter let him get halfway up then swept the good leg away with a hook-kick. Tommy screamed again as he pressed his weight onto the broken leg in an attempt to keep his balance. Crumpling into a heap as a result.

"You can't fight with one leg, Tommy. Give it up."

Tommy, far from ready to give it up, swept his body along the ground, hands grappling and searching the mud. He found what he was looking for.

He flipped around and threw a rock.

Peter blocked it easily with an elbow.

It hurt, the arm ringing. But he didn't show it.

Tommy searched for another. Found one. Threw it.

Turning his body sideways, Peter took it on the shoulder. The rock skittling up and almost striking his face.

"Tommy. Please stop it."

Another rock hit him in the ribs. It almost winded him.

Tommy didn't get a chance to throw another. When he spun around on the ground to aim at Peter, his foe was right there.

Peter grabbed the rock. Ripped it from the hand. Tossed it away. Then he took hold of Tommy by the scruff.

Tommy reached up and grabbed Peter's forearms. His thumbs began probing for Peter's nerves. The ones that would cramp his fingers into letting go.

"Stop it, Tommy."

Tommy answered this with a stream of spit that flew from his mouth and splashed between Peter's eyes.

"Fuck you."

Peter struck him in the face, almost losing his grip of the shirt.

"Fuck you!" Tommy shouted. His cheek already swollen.

Peter hit him again. Split the cheek.

Hit him again.

And again.

And again.

He lost hold. Picked Tommy back up from the dirt.

He was still conscious. Mumbling something about being double-crossed and how he'd kill them all.

So Peter hit him again.

Again.

And again.

Until Tommy was unrecognizable and slurring nonsense out of his battered mouth like some Saturday night drunk sleeping it off in the tank.

"We gotta stick together... Can't trust nobody..."

Peter held him by the scruff. His right hand throbbing. The knuckles covered in blood. Some his own. Most of it Tommy's.

He spent a few seconds staring at the face of his mutilated brother. Then he hit him one last time. A huge blow that stopped the muttering and finally sent Tommy into unconsciousness.

He didn't immediately untie Mother and Magda. He left them in the barn. Instead, Peter tied Tommy up, shoved him across the back of his Yamaha like some butchered deer, and drove him as far into the woods as he could.

After two hours riding, he found a tight little gorge lined with rocks. There, he stopped and carried Tommy to them.

It wasn't until he was cutting the rope from him—

unable to leave him completely at the mercy of the wolves and bears—that Tommy started to come around.

"Pete?" he croaked like a waking child. "Pete? What are you doing?"

Peter was already on the bike, the ropes cut. He said nothing as he kicked it over, the engine rattling into life.

"No, Pete." Tommy sat up, the broken leg laying crooked in front of him. "No. Don't leave me here."

As Peter dumped the clutch and sped off into the trees, Tommy called after him.

"Peter, don't leave me! Come back! Come back!"

THIRTY-SEVEN

ALASKAN WILDERNESS, 2021

SITTING IN THE PASSENGER SEAT OF AN Ultramarine twin-engine helicopter, Ibliss uses a pair of Braveking1 night-vision binoculars to scan the endless trees they glide over.

When she graduated twenty years ago from the Fallen Angel program, she'd hoped never to have to see this place again. Alaska and all its desolate vastness had chilled her to the soul as a thirteen-year-old arriving from the juvenile detention center where she'd spent the previous two years.

When they had said "farm," her teenage mind had imagined some easygoing place in Nebraska or Kansas. Tending to the animals and learning to ride a horse. It would be easier than prison, that was for damn sure.

How terribly wrong that silly girl had been.

And how any semblance of silliness had left her soon after arriving. Probably around the time she'd learned all the major arteries of the human body and how to inflict fatal damage to them using anything ranging from a fork to a pen. Carotid and femoral were easiest; the neck or the inside of the thigh a cinch to get at.

At the farm the same skills that had got her through a life on the streets were molded, tamed and turned into the skillset of an *asset*.

A *hard* asset.

It had led to sixteen years in the Fallen Angel program. Four more than the asset nearest to her in length of term. And as far as she knew, the longest run of any agent *ever*.

No one had been an angel longer than Ibliss.

Not even Azrael.

When the program had fallen and she'd escaped the Russians, she had thought she was free. But an asset is never free.

"You do know that people are gonna be looking for me," the pilot tells her through the headset. "I got family. They gonna be wondering why I ain't home."

His name is Clive. Clive Brandon Harris the Third. She had only asked for his first name, but he'd blathered the whole thing out during an episode of nerves. Probably something to do with the gun she had pointed at him.

"I don't care," Ibliss says absently.

"This is kidnap, lady."

"It will be murder if you don't shut up and do as I say."

Clive looks about ready to burst into tears.

Ibliss's cell phone vibrates on her lap. Removing her eyes from the binoculars, she glances down at it.

Her heart drops instantly.

"Harry?"

"Hey, babe," a man's voice says on the other end. "How's the conference going?"

"It's finished for today."

She feels so sad having to lie to him.

"Where are you now? Sounds like you're in the bar."

"No. I'm back in the hotel room."

"Then what's that sound?'

"What sound?"

"That loud humming."

He's referring to the helicopter.

"The hotel is close to the subway," she lies. "It's pretty busy."

"Typical of that crummy firm you work for. Putting you in some stink hole next to the subway. They've got no respect for you, Sara. All the work you put in. Like, take this weeklong conference for example. They only tell you about it on Monday. Not even a day's notice."

"I know. It's bad. But with HR getting rid of so many people this year, I've got to put in the extra effort just to keep my job."

"It's unfair," Harry complains on her behalf. "Those assholes in the boardroom with their shareholder meetings. Treating people like underlings while they reward themselves with fat bonuses."

"That's the world, I'm afraid," Ibliss says as she spots smoke in the distance. "Dog eat dog."

She quickly checks the tracker on the phone.

"Shit!" she exclaims.

The red dot is gone.

"What's up, hun?"

"Sorry, Harry. Not you. I just got a text. They need me

to go downstairs and meet them for drinks with one of our clients. They're insisting."

"Jeez. Can't they leave you alone for one night?"

Ibliss doesn't answer straight away. She's reloading the tracker. But each time it comes up dead.

"I'm sorry, Harry, but they're trying to reach me. I need to hang up."

"Okay, babe."

She goes to put the phone down.

"Hey, babe?"

She pauses her finger. "What, Harry?"

"I love you."

"I love you, too," she replies.

The call ends and she points at a thin tendril of smoke that rises from the trees.

"I need you to fly there," she tells Clive.

THIRTY-EIGHT

FAIRBANKS, 2021

IT IS WHILE LUMBERING ALONG THE FOGGY STREETS of Fairbanks in Kitten that Michael and Peter are passed by several speeding police cars. Their lights flashing, sirens screaming.

The two look at each other from across the cab.

"Are you thinking what I'm thinking?" the kid asks.

Peter says nothing. He simply follows the direction the cops are going. Gradually, they creep up on the airfield. It sits in a valley of low ground. Coming from the direction of hills, they stop on a street that overlooks the strip of flatland and gaze down at it through a gap between two houses. The airfield is swarming with red and blue lights that blink in the dark like fireflies.

"It has to be them," Michael says.

Sighing, Peter puts the vehicle back into gear, turns it around 180 degrees and continues in the opposite direction.

"What are you doing?" the kid exclaims. "We should be going down there to see what's up."

"No. We should not. We need to exchange vehicles."

"*Then* we go down there?"

"I said no, Mikey."

The kid turns a hurt look on him.

Peter tells him, "We have to think of ourselves now. Whatever has happened down there is too much for us to handle."

"But what if she's dead? We have to at least find out."

Michael continues to shine that sad look on Peter.

The master assassin can't help seeing it in the reflection of the windshield.

He gives in.

"Okay. But first we change vehicles. We're gonna stick out like a sore thumb in this."

THIRTY-NINE

ALASKAN WILDERNESS, 2021

THE ULTRAMARINE HOVERS OVER THE FOREST canopy like a hummingbird drawing nectar from a flower. Its spotlight illuminates the wreck of the Cessna.

Sitting on the ledge of the open door, Ibliss's feet balance on the wet landing skid as she surveys the wreckage below.

A four-hundred-meter trail of broken trees led them to it. The Cessna's wings are smashed off but the fuselage is relatively intact. Semyon has managed to land it well. All things considered.

Inside the back of the Ultramarine is a rescue hoist. Ibliss is wearing the body harness. A line of double-braided polyethylene fiber is clipped to the back of it. The other end pokes out of a winch controlled by the pilot.

"Get us closer," she tells Clive through the headset.

"Sure thing."

The helicopter gently lowers several meters, then holds

its position. Ibliss takes hold of the line hanging from her back.

"Give me three meters."

The winch cranks into life and feeds out the requisite amount, the line looping from her fist. That done, she turns to the pilot.

His sweat glossed face watches her from the front.

"I'm going to head down there now," she tells him in a threatening undertone. "And I just want you to remember one thing."

"Uh-Huh."

"I can shoot you from down there. Put a bullet straight through the floor of the cockpit that'll go up through your seat. Enter your body through your asshole. And come out the top of your skull along with your brains and your shit. That understood?"

The pilot swallows and nods.

"Now switch the searchlight off."

The forest goes pitch black, then dark blue as her eyes adjust. Ibliss drops off the skid, plummeting three meters through the canopy until the rope goes taut and she pulls up.

Dangling there, she takes the Heckler & Koch G36 close combat assault rifle from her back, trains it on the crash site and lines her eye up with the night-vision optics.

"You can start lowering me."

She descends slowly into the forest. Delicately shifting her weight in the harness, she is able to rotate herself on the end of the line. It enables her to scan the surrounding trees.

Touching down on terra firma, she unclips the line from

the harness and drags it toward the fat trunk of an ancient spruce.

"Give me another two meters," she tells Clive.

The line slackens and she loops it around the spruce, before clipping it. Tethering the Ultramarine to the tree.

"Hey! You shouldn't do that," Clive tells her through the headset. "You'll cause me to crash."

"Then you'd better stay alert and careful. No running away."

Ibliss investigates the Cessna, an eye trained to the night-vision optics. The barrel of the G36 trained on the Cessna.

She approaches the plane from the rear. It is wedged between two giant spruces. The pilot-side door lies wide open and is partially ripped off. She rounds the Cessna. Keeping an eight-foot perimeter. Coming level with the door, she finds the cockpit empty of passengers. But not empty completely.

A piece of folded paper sits on the pilot's seat, weighted down with an AK bullet.

Ibliss breathes slowly out her nostrils. Weighs up what to do.

Why not?

She begins moving cautiously forward through the waist high scrub, one slow-motion step at a time.

Her caution is vital.

It saves her life.

She feels the wire against her shin. It is highly strung. The click of the grenade pin comes soon after.

Ibliss repels herself into a backwards somersault. Only the periphery of the blast catches her, but it is still enough to throw her through the air. She lands heavily several meters away. Where she is soon pelted with mud, splinters and other debris.

"You okay down there?" the pilot's voice crackles in her ear.

He's obviously more worried about being tied to the tree until his fuel runs out than her being hurt.

"Yes," she says in a jaded tone. "I am okay."

There are no more traps. When she reaches the Cessna through the smoke, she snatches up the note and reads.

Boom!

FORTY

Peter has a lockup in an isolated part of Fairbanks.

Of course he has.

On the outside it resembles any of the other fifteen garages that line a dirt lot surrounded by wreckers' yards.

But it's not.

Lockup number six is very different. For one, its door may look like a regular garage door, but underneath the thin layer of red fiberglass are two steel plates clamped over a sheet of ballistic nylon and steel polymer mesh. As for the brickwork, well, that's reinforced with the same mesh as the door, along with a steel cage sunk into the masonry. It makes the space inside slightly smaller, but being that there's an underground room beneath the main part, there's plenty of storage.

"Here. Take this," Peter says to Michael, handing a backpack up to Michael through a round hatch that links the basement and the upper garage.

"What is it?" the kid asks as he takes it.

"It's a portable StingRay and a laptop to operate it."

"What's a StingRay?"

"It's for listening in on cell phones and police radios."

"You mean like the thing you had built under your house in Monterey?"

"Yeah. Just on a smaller scale."

"You want me to put it with the money?"

The money was in a hidden compartment beneath the trunk of a completely *clean* olive green 1995 Range Rover. Their getaway.

"No. Put it on the backseat. We'll need it soon enough."

Gathering up the guns he's going to take, Peter climbs the ladder into the upper garage.

"Is that all you're taking?" Michael asks when he emerges from the basement.

The only weapons he has are his HK45 and a Mossberg Patriot Long Range Hunter rifle. A couple of packs of 6.5mm Creedmoors.

"We're not going to war, Mikey."

"But all that stuff down there, and you bring those?"

"We have to make our way down south," Peter explains as he loads the hunting rifle into the trunk. "We'll be driving into Canada. All that is gonna be a lot harder if we're packing illegal firearms. I have a permit in the name of David Rutledge for this pistol and the hunting rifle. Both of which are widely available on the domestic market."

The kid looks at him dumbfounded. Like he's only just

getting that you can't walk the streets with a military grade assault rifle.

Peter taps his temple with a finger. "You gotta think, Mikey."

"But how we gonna get Mother back with those?"

Peter doesn't say anything. He merely shuts the trunk, walks to the front of the Range Rover and gets in.

"Come on," he says. "Let's go find out what happened at the airfield."

FORTY-ONE

ALASKAN WILDERNESS, 2021

EVEN THOUGH THE NIGHT IS COLD, SWEAT STILL drips down Semyon's back. In the impact of the crash he has bashed his elbow. It throbs while he carries the old woman piggyback, her arms looped around his neck, legs dangling by his sides.

"I don't understand, Misha," she says breathlessly, "where all my energy has gone. I feel so tired."

"I keep telling you. It was when I disabled the tracker," he explains in a weary voice.

She removes an arm from around his neck and rubs the side of her head. "Maybe. It hurt a lot."

"Not enough," Semyon mutters under his breath.

"What was that?"

"Nothing. Now be quiet. We have a long way to go."

"Where?"

"I told you. The extraction point. Now shut up. It exhausts me to talk."

Semyon marches on through the woods. The old woman on his back. The heavy sports bag of ordnance hanging down his front. The strap pressing into his neck. His boots pressing into the mud. He is like a machine. Going on and on.

In total, he carries around 250 pounds. It is close to his own body weight. Yet it hardly bothers him. Because Semyon has always been stronger than most.

Even in the womb.

A little known fact about Semyon Mikhailovich is that he is a twin. One who was the winning recipient of feto-fetal transfusion syndrome. The condition in which one twin feeds on the placenta of the other, thus getting more nutrients. Where his brother had emerged withered and a third of his bodyweight, Semyon had been born big and strong. An apex predator even in the womb.

FORTY-TWO

FAIRBANKS, 2021

A SLEAZY ROADHOUSE SITS ON TOP OF A CLUMP OF hill overlooking the airfield. A blinking bar light advertises Budweiser. Another advertises the pool tables and a jukebox. A mingle of voices, country music and clacking pool balls emanates from within.

Pickups fill the frozen puddles of its dirt lot. In the corner closest to the airfield, Peter and Michael sit on the hood of the Range Rover. They have the perfect view through the fading mist. Police vehicles cover the frozen tarmac. Using binoculars, they spot plastic crime scene cards next to bullet casings, as well as a dark patch of blood.

The two of them look like plane watchers.

Peter places the field glasses down and grabs the StingRay antenna.

"Here," he says to Michael.

The kid looks away from his own binoculars.

"Take it," Peter adds.

Soon enough Peter is hunched over the laptop while Michael holds the antenna in the direction of the closest cell phone tower. As he does, Peter searches the list of cell phones it picks up, the antenna intercepting their activity as they communicate with the tower.

A piece of standardized spyware used by most governments across the planet to monitor its citizens, the StingRay IMSI-catcher (international mobile subscriber identity-catcher) gives Peter access to the details of every cell phone within a seven-hundred-meter zone. It also gives him the names on the airtime contracts associated with each phone.

Checking the names against a list of officers from local PD, Peter finds the phone belonging to the chief of Fairbanks, Don Rupee. He hones in on it and takes control remotely, activating its microphone and camera.

The phone is in Rupee's pocket, so no picture. But voices can be heard. Michael and Peter listen in on headphones like a couple of Stasi officers. The sky is now clear, the wind dead, and the stars stretch out before them as their feet dangle over the grille of the Range Rover.

It takes ten minutes of listening in on the cops to get exactly what happened. There was a shootout on the runway. Police are searching for a plane that they believe has gone down in nearby forest. Search and Rescue helicopters haven't had any luck yet, blaming low visibility: the fog still thick where the ground is higher.

Peter is pinching his brows together when he peels the headphones off. After spending a moment staring into the distance, he packs the laptop down and says, "There's nothing we can do. You heard. The plane must have crashed."

Michael sits frozen at the edge of the hood. It is only when Peter goes to take the antenna from his hand that the kid jumps to life.

"She's alive," he says sharply.

Peter sighs. Tugs the antenna from his grip. "Look, Mikey," he says, packing it all away into the rucksack, "we gotta move. It's a long way to Anchorage."

"We have to save her."

"We don't even know where she is."

"In trouble, Peter. That's where."

"Please, Mikey. We have to think of ourselves right now. We're homeless. We need to prioritize. Okay?"

Peter zips the bag up and jumps down. As he gets into the driver's side, Michael slips off the hood and follows him. Peter closes the door and the kid stands there at the open window.

"Get in," Peter tells him.

Michael shakes his head from side to side.

"Please, Mikey."

"If you won't help me find her. I'll do it myself."

"Really? What're you gonna do—hike through the woods?"

Michael takes off. Fists curled, head down, feet crunching across the gravel. Peter clenches the steering wheel. Exhales through his nostrils. Gets out.

Michael is almost at the street when Peter catches him by the shoulder of his jacket.

"Hey!" he snaps, spinning the kid around. "We *have* to leave."

"Not without her."

"And how're we gonna find her, huh? Commandeer a helicopter?"

"We should try at least."

Peter breathes a withered sigh. He looks off into the middle distance. Then, eyes back on the kid, he says, "I know it's hard, Mikey. It's not even a year since you lost your mom. You just lost Magda. Now you're losing Mother. I get it. It's hard. But *this* life—the one that you want to join me on—is full of hardship. You have to make decisions that hurt you to make. But if you are to survive, you *must* make them. And make them well. Otherwise you're dead. You understand?"

He looks deep into the kid's eyes.

Nodding, Michael gives in. "Okay."

"Good. Now let's go. We've got a long drive ahead of us."

FORTY-THREE

ALASKAN WILDERNESS, 2021

THE DRIVER OF THE FAIRBANKS TO ANCHORAGE locomotive is leaning back drinking his morning coffee when he spots the fallen tree covering the tracks about three hundred yards in front.

"Ah, shit," he grumbles, sitting up and taking ahold of the radio.

His voice fills the carriages behind him, many of the passengers eating breakfast in the restaurant cart. *"I'd like to ask each passenger to brace themselves for braking. I repeat: brace for braking."*

He clips the receiver back on its peg and pulls the brake lever. The train jolts as each of the carriages slam on the anchors, everything screeching and hissing and jarring as they come to a gradual stop a couple of feet from the broken tree.

The door to the engine room opens behind the driver. The co-driver's head leans through it.

"What's up?" he asks.

"Another god darn tree, Frank. Radio a couple of the guys to help get it drug off."

"Okay, Al."

While Frank radios the others, Al puts his high-visibility vest on over his jacket, grabs his cap, and jumps out the cab. His feet crunch across the stones and soon he stands over the tree.

He's confused.

It doesn't look like it fell on to the tracks. The trunk's too short to have reached here from the trees bordering the edge. To Al, it could only have gotten here if it had been dragged up the bank of stones.

"What's up?"

Al turns to find Frank.

"The others coming?" he asks.

"Yeah."

Al's attention returns to the tree.

"Someone drug it here," he says.

Frank frowns. "You serious?"

"It couldn't've fallen here."

"The wind was pretty bad last night."

"The wind don't drag trees up banks of stones."

"So what: a bear did it?"

"No. A man."

"Who the hell's all the way out here?"

While they stare at the tree, Semyon and Mother sneak to the train in the background. Quickly, he helps her up into the open door of the engine. Then, with the old woman inside, he grabs the sports bag and hefts himself and the ordnance up there.

"This way," he says, nodding in the direction of the carriages.

They step into the humming drone of the engine room. A thin aisle leads them past an electrical board covered in blinking lights. As they reach the end of the aisle, the door opens: revealing a train conductor.

"What are you doing back here?" he asks sternly.

"My dear old grandma," Semyon says in a perfect Midwestern accent, taking Mother by the elbow. "She got lost. I had to come all this way to find her. I do apologize. Sincerely, I do."

Semyon's friendly tone placates the conductor and the man's voice softens.

"Well, passengers aren't permitted back here."

Mother gazes at him with blank-eyed confusion. She looks like the type of grandma that would bake you the perfect apple pie. As opposed to the type that would gift you a garrote.

"I'm so sorry, son," she says in a frail and timid voice. "I get so muddle-headed. It's all my fault."

She looks about to cry.

The conductor's demeanor is completely loose by now. "That's okay, ma'am," he says softly. "Just remember you can't come back here. You've got to stay with your grandson."

"I'll do my best. Thank you so much for your kind understanding."

"Good day to you both."

"Good day."

With a gentle nod, the conductor is on his way to join the others in dragging the tree from the rails.

Mother turns a sore look on Semyon before playfully striking his chest with a hand. "Your grandmother?" she says peevishly in Russian. "You really aren't funny sometimes, Misha."

"It worked, didn't it?"

They continue through the train, into the carriages. The smells of the restaurant cart—bacon, sausage, buttery scrambled egg—makes both their stomachs jolt.

"We should eat," Mother says.

"First we need tickets."

As they pass between two carriages a man emerges from a bathroom. The second Mother sees him, she lurches forwards and grabs him by the shoulders. Headbutts him back into the toilet.

She's so quick, Semyon doesn't have a chance to process what's happening, let alone stop her. She rushes the guy into the closet-sized bathroom and slams the door behind them.

The muffled sounds of a struggle emanate from within. Semyon's eyes search up and down the carriage. That section is given over to baggage racks and bathrooms. It is deserted and no one is around to listen to the scuffle as it dies down.

The door opens a few inches and Mother peeks her face out.

"You have ties?" she asks.

Semyon nods. He places the sports bag down, unzips it, and takes out a baggy of thick plastic zip-ties.

"Something for his mouth, too," she adds when he hands them to her.

Semyon removes a roll of duct tape from the hold-all.

"Thank you," she says, before shutting the door once more.

Less than a minute later she is emerging.

"Do you have a...?"

There's no point finishing the sentence. He is already holding up a flathead screwdriver. She says thank you and turns back to the door with it, locking the bathroom from the outside.

When she is once more facing Semyon, she removes two rectangular slips of laminated card from a pocket and holds them up to him.

"There," she says. "Two tickets."

FORTY-FOUR

DENALI STATE PARK, ALASKA, 2021

IT HAS BEEN A LONG TIME SINCE PETER LIVED IN the field. A long time since he was required to stay awake for days on end. Recently he has gotten used to the luxury of eight hours sleep.

Fatigued, the tree-lined road meanders in his sight.

"I can drive if you want," Michael offers as Peter blinks his eyes and leans heavily on the steering wheel.

"It's okay."

"No. You sleep. I got enough after Fairbanks. I'll drive. I mean, it's not like I can get lost."

With a sweep of the hand the kid intimates the endless band of gray that disappears at the horizon as though it drops right off the edge of the world.

"This isn't a racing simulator, Mikey."

Michael turns to Peter from the road. "So you watched me doing that, too?"

Peter says nothing. But, yes, he had spent many nights on his balcony in Monterey, watching the kid play video games in his bedroom.

"Come on," the kid goes. "Let me drive."

Peter weighs it up. "I suppose I could do with some rest. But this is a little more complicated than a dirt bike or a simulator."

"What can be so complicated about driving in a straight line?"

A minute later the Range Rover idles at the side of the deserted road. Nothing but the trees and mountains for company. Michael sits in the driver's seat. The chair pushed forward so that his feet reach the pedals.

"You know what the clutch is?"

"Obviously."

"And you know what it does?"

"Disengages the engine so that you can change gear."

"And you know which pedal it is?"

Michael rolls his eyes. "The one on the left."

"What about the gas?"

Michael turns to him with a dry look. Instead of answering with words he revs the engine.

"Okay, smart ass. So you also know the brake's in the middle."

"If," Michael says pointedly, "you'd paid attention while spying on me, you'd know that my driving simulator was exactly like a real car."

"Did you drive many Range Rovers down the backroads of Alaska on your simulator?"

"No. But I've driven a Ferrari Testarossa around the Nurburgring. So this should be a piece of cake."

"What about cops? Many of them on your simulator?"

"There weren't. No."

"Well, there are here. So in order to keep a low profile, you'll have to stick to the speed limit and drive carefully and responsibly."

Michael rolls his eyes.

"You ready?" Peter asks.

"Sure am."

Michael plunges the clutch down and grabs the stick. He slips it into first and revs the engine. The needle flicks to the side as the vehicle grumbles.

"Not so much gas. It's a diesel engine. It'll roll out on barely—"

The Range Rover staggers forward and stalls.

"Any gas," Peter finishes.

"What happened?" Michael asks, confused and staring down at the steering wheel as if it were the Rover's fault.

"You dumped the clutch," Peter explains. "Like I said, Mikey: it's not a Testarossa. Which, by the way, I've driven for real. So you can let your head shrink back to normal. Now. You need to give it just a little gas and release the clutch real slow. Then you're gonna want to ease it up through the gears. Remember to be real gentle with the clutch. You got it?"

Michael nods.

"Now restart it."

The four-by-four jumps forward again. The engine chugging and clunking to a stop.

"It's still in gear," Peter says coolly. "You need to keep the clutch in if you're going to start it in gear."

Michael looks frustrated.

Peter changes his tone. "You can't get everything right the first time, Mikey. It takes patience."

The kid breathes in and out, gently and slowly. Calms his temper. Then he starts the engine and eases the Range Rover forwards.

"That's it," Peter says. "Up into second... Okay. Not too much gas."

A huge beaming grin opens up on the kid's face. "I'm driving," he says excitedly, turning to Peter. "I'm really driving!"

"That's right," Peter says, a worried look on his face. "You're driving. Really slowly. In second. And moving a little too much in the road, if I'm honest. But you are, indeed, driving. Now bring it up into third."

Once they're in fourth, Michael's confidence grows. He brings it up into fifth, taking the speed to sixty.

"I told you about speeding, Michael," Peter says, eyes moving between the road and the speedometer. "The limit's fifty-five."

"Just let me have a little fun first. Then, when you sleep, I'll stick to the speed limit."

They come up on a big Scania hauling logs from Denali down to the docks of Anchorage. The speeding four-by-four is like a jackal chasing a buffalo.

"Michael, there's a blind turn up ahead. You need to wait till the turn is over before you overtake. Please, Mikey. Just WAIT UNTIL THE CORNER'S..."

Michael accelerates the Rover around the truck and enters the opposing lane. Immediately the headlights of another huge rig burn their retinas as it hurtles toward them from around the corner.

"Cut in!" Peter cries out. "CUT IN!"

Michael swerves the Range Rover in front of the Scania just in time. The other truck steams past on their left. The Scania mere inches behind. The four-by-four wobbling on its wheels as the kid straightens it up.

He is all smiles.

Peter is all white. Fingers sunk into the dash.

"We made it!" Michael says as the flashing headlights of the Scania fill the cab.

"We sure did," Peter agrees as he picks his fingers from the soft plastic of the dashboard. "We sure did."

FORTY-FIVE

ALASKA RAILROAD, 2021

HAVING EATEN BREAKFAST IN THE DINING CART, Semyon and Mother work their way to the rear of the train where the seat numbers on their stolen tickets are located. The carriages are filled with tourists. Many of them line the windows, holding smartphones and cameras. The train is passing through a wide valley of grassland. Not far from the tracks, a herd of caribou graze on the thawing vegetation. There is an elk, too, some way off from the reindeer, his huge antlers glistening in the morning sun.

Halfway along the carriage, a particularly large group of foreigners block the aisle.

"Get out of the way!" Mother snaps.

A tall man turns to her and frowns. He hasn't understood what she said, but he understands her tone to be offensive.

"I said out the way!"

The man shrieks and jumps to the side, almost knocking his wife and elderly mother over. While he hops on one foot, he holds the other by the toe: where she'd stamped her heel.

Semyon smiles as he follows her around the sneering faces of the tourists. *I might actually grow to like her*, he thinks.

Upon entering their own carriage, or at least the one on the tickets, they hear the sounds of an argument. A woman is complaining while an officious-sounding man scolds her. They slow their approach to a creep and gradually come within a few feet of the disagreement.

A middle-aged woman with sandy-colored hair and a red face is arguing with the conductor they came across earlier.

"But I keep telling you," the woman goes. "My husband has our tickets."

"Then you must get him, ma'am. Because without a ticket I cannot let you remain inside this cabin."

"But I told you: he's gone missing. And *you* won't help me find him."

"I'm a conductor, ma'am. Not a missing persons detective."

"He said he was going to the bathroom. That was an hour ago."

"Have you checked the bar?" He glances at his wristwatch. "They've been serving alcohol for almost an hour now."

Her face went even redder. "My husband doesn't drink," she splutters. "This is all—"

"Look, ma'am," the conductor interrupts, spotting Semyon and Mother over her shoulder. "You're disrupting things for the other passengers."

Right on cue, Semyon steps forward with the tickets, Mother holding on to his elbow.

"I see you got her safely back," the conductor says as he takes the tickets and stamps them, the red-faced woman waiting impatiently to the side.

"Yes," Semyon says. "But now it is time for her nap."

Semyon thanks the man, takes the stamped tickets back and guides Mother into the cabin. They shut the door on the argument and draw the curtain.

Semyon places the sports bag in the overhead compartment then pulls the curtain across the outer window of the carriage. They are momentarily left in darkness. He switches the electric lamp on, turns around—

She's right there.

Big gray eyes glint in the dim electric light. She takes his shoulders gently in her old hands. Tells him: "I had lost hope, Misha. So much hope. Out there on that farm. Doing..."

The words fail her as she grimaces at the recollection.

Before finally managing the word, "Things."

"What types of things?" he asks mischievously.

Her eyes fade.

"I once killed a boy," floats from her lips.

They stand frozen for a while in the middle of the cabin, swaying a little with the movement of the train. Semyon watches the memories twitch and flicker the muscles of her wrinkled face.

Her eyes come alive. Settle on his striking visage. And a smile trembles her lips.

"I am so glad you found me, Misha."

She drops her head to his chest, resting it over his heart. Semyon stands there stiffly, the old woman draped over him.

"We need to sleep," he tells her.

"Why don't you place your arms around me?"

Semyon reluctantly lifts his hands and places them against her bony back. She begins to peck his torso with little kisses.

"Hey, cut that out," he tells her, removing his hands and stepping back.

It frightens him—the man who cannot be frightened—this woman's affection. Even if it is nothing more than some kink in her dementia. Even if she appalls him more than anything. The affection she shows him—Misha, whoever—it scares Semyon.

"Stop it!" he snaps, tearing her away as she tries to retake him in her arms.

A forlorn expression floods her face. She looks hurt.

"We are on a mission," he says. "We need to act like it. Reserve our strength."

"It never stopped you before."

"You—*we*—were younger."

The wrinkles at the edges of her eyes spread out like ripples. "Younger?"

"I'm tired," he says, genuinely so. "Please. Let's rest."

Her expression smooths out and she nods. "Okay. We will sleep."

Semyon takes the window. He removes his boots, pulls his socks off, and rests his feet on the seat opposite. Settling back, he flicks the light switch, drenches them in darkness, and closes his eyes.

FORTY-SIX

DENALI STATE PARK, 2021

PETER WAKES GRADUALLY TO TEPID DAYLIGHT. HE flicks the sunshield down. Stretches and yawns. A strong wind sweeps across the road. The tall pines that border it rock from side to side and tree debris skittles across the lanes. There's ice in the air. Swirls of it wash over the windshield.

The weather doesn't bother Michael. He is relaxed in the driver's seat, one hand on the wheel, an elbow on the door. Peter glances at the speedometer. The kid is sticking to fifty-five.

Checking the time, he sees that he's been asleep for four hours. It is enough.

"You talk in your sleep," Michael points out.

"Do I?"

"Yes."

"What did I say?"

"You kept apologizing to Tommy."

Peter goes cold.

"How did you kill him?" Michael asks.

"Is it okay not to talk about it?"

"You regret it, though. At least that's something."

"Please, Mikey. I just woke up."

The kid challenges Peter more than anything ever has. Not since that week in Greece fourteen years ago with the boy's mother has Peter ever been with someone who pushed him so much to be human.

"Sure," Michael says. "I'll put the radio on."

He presses the button.

"*This is KSKA public radio with an urgent weather bulletin. I'm afraid, folks, we got a doozy of a cold snap coming in from the west. A big mean snowstorm that's gonna bring chaos to the roads. The state governor has just this minute issued a stay-at-home order and for anyone on the roads to make sure they're somewhere safe before five tonight. Because it's gonna be one heck of a storm.*"

They come upon several billboards. One advertises the nearby town of Talkeetna. Population 1030. Pretty crowded for this part of the world. The next advertises Jack's Diner. 7 miles.

"You hungry?" Peter asks.

"Oh, yeah."

"Good. We'll get breakfast."

FORTY-SEVEN

ALASKA RAILROAD, 2021

IT IS AN HOUR LATER WHEN SEMYON WAKES IN A
panic. He is sweating all over. Jerking breaths into his lungs.
Chest heaving.

As he stares into the darkness, he feels a hand rubbing
his back.

"It is okay, my love," she coos into his ear.

He flicks the lamp on. Recoils when he sees who it is.

Mother holds out a water bottle. "Drink, Misha. Drink."

He snatches it angrily and chugs the liquid down.

"Ugh," he groans afterwards as he lies back in the seat,
getting his breathing under control.

"I know how it feels to have nightmares," she says after a
while.

"I bet you do."

"It is this job of ours, Misha. It fills us with horror."

"The world is horror."

The two are silent for a while. Nothing but the gentle clanking of the train moving along the rails.

"Why didn't you make it that day?" she asks.

"What day?"

"In Shoyna."

"You mean the day of your defection?"

"No. *Our* defection. But you never showed. We had to leave without you. What happened?"

In a tired voice he tells her, "Maybe I decided it would be better for my health if I didn't become a traitor."

"I thought maybe you'd been caught. That Parfyon had found out."

"Parfyon Rogozhin?"

"Yes." She goes silent a while. Then she asks, "Where is he now?"

"Dead," Semyon assures her.

Best not to spoil the surprise.

"Good. He was an evil man."

"I think in our line of work we have to look beyond good and evil."

"Not when some are evil for their own ends."

"And how was Parfyon like that?"

"You know, Misha."

"Do I?"

"Yes."

"About what?"

"About him forcing women into sleeping with him. Threatening to denounce them to the Party if they refused."

"Did he do this to you?"

She swallows and her eyes go dull. When she speaks her voice is no more than a whisper.

"You know he did."

FORTY-EIGHT

TALKEETNA, 2021

THE DIRT LOT OF JACK'S DINER IS MOSTLY FILLED with trucks hauling lumber. Some RVs. A couple of four-by-fours that probably belong to hunters. The diner itself is a one-story log cabin with panoramic windows.

To one side of the entrance is a very old stuffed bear, its fur covered in bald patches. The piece of taxidermy stands on its hind legs looking fierce.

On the other side of the doors is a seven-foot-tall Native American chief. He isn't stuffed. Just carved out of wood. Standing in full headdress with a great big tomahawk in his hand.

"That's wrong," Michael says as they're about to enter.

"What is?"

"The Native American. He's a Sioux."

"So what?"

"The Sioux were never this far north. In this region it's the Dena'ina."

"The bear's probably Russian, too. So what?"

Michael glances at the gnatty thing. It's browned claws look ready to drop out.

"I guess," the kid says.

Michael goes to step inside when Peter catches his arm.

"You go in and order for me," Peter tells him.

"What are you gonna do?"

"I need to make a call."

Inside, the weather bulletin is bleating on the radio behind the cashier stand. "*Hey there, folks,*" the forecaster's voice resounds. "*That big storm has just made landfall at Nome. With heavy winds driving it down south there's gonna be thick snowfall in Anchorage by this evening. I don't wanna sound alarmist, but this one is gonna be a biggy. So get your behinds inside, people, and batten down the hatches.*"

Michael picks a table by the window and orders breakfast.

In the meantime, Peter strolls over to an abandoned corner of the diner and pulls his burner phone from his jeans. Dials one of the few numbers on it.

The call takes a while to answer. There is no voicemail and it is a full minute before it's picked up.

"Hello?" a female's voice says.

Peter takes a while to answer. He can hear two young girls playing in the background.

"Hello?" the woman repeats.

"Marta," Peter finally says.

She sighs down the phone. "Please say you don't need my help."

"I'm afraid I do."

"I thought we were all done."

"For old times?"

She breathes into the phone. "Old times, you say? Like the old times that cost me a husband and my daughter a father? Those old times?"

"I can assure you this has nowhere near the risk factor. It honestly shouldn't take up too much of your time."

"It already has."

He senses that she is about to put the phone down.

"Marta, please?"

"What?"

"All I need are documents. For me and the kid."

There's a brief pause. Then. "So he's still with you."

"Yeah. But we're homeless."

"I thought you said Alaska would be safe for as long as you'd need it."

"Something happened. Something I couldn't have foreseen. Now I need documentation to get us to Europe."

"I thought you had people."

"*Pat* had people. All my guys stateside are burned."

"And you want me to risk everything I have left to get you those documents?"

"Please, Marta. I'm begging you."

The sound of a long sigh hisses in his ear. "Okay. I'll do it. But this has got to be the last time. I have a nice little life with my two daughters now, Peter, and I really don't want it interrupted. You got that?"

"I got that."

"Can you get to California?"

"Yeah. I've got ID for me and the kid to get across the Canadian border. Just no passports."

"Okay. When you're in California, call me."

Peter joins Michael in the diner.

"I ordered you pancakes with a side of bacon," the kid says.

"Maple syrup?"

"Of course."

"What did you get?"

"The special. With a side of ice cream."

FORTY-NINE

ALASKA RAILROAD, 2021

As Semyon and Mother sit in the cabin the tannoy comes on.

"*This is the chief conductor. I'd like to remind you that this train will shortly be arriving at Chase. After that we will be stopping at Talkeetna, Wasilla and Anchorage, where this train's journey ends. Estimated time of arrival at Anchorage is currently three-fifteen p.m.*"

The train begins slowing, the brakes scream, the carriages jolt. Semyon pulls the curtain to one side. Chase train station consists of a concrete platform in the middle of vast wilderness. Nothing but a road, a flat valley of grassland, ice and snow.

Mother begins fidgeting.

"I need to use the bathroom," she tells him.

Semyon watches her leave the cabin. Convinced that she

really does think he's someone else, he trusts her to come back.

It is then, as he sits alone in the cabin, that a strange thing happens inside of Semyon Mikhailovich. Her absence begins to make him feel oddly desolate.

He ponders this reaction for a minute, but doesn't get to do so for a second. The door to the cabin opens and in walks a very attractive female dressed in a tight catsuit. She takes a seat opposite, and, as their eyes meet for the first time across the compartment, Semyon realizes, instinctively, that *this* is what attacked him at the airfield.

"Where's the old woman?" Ibliss asks.

Semyon smiles. Glad the two women hadn't passed each other in the aisle.

In the ex-Fallen Angel's fist is a compact Ruger LCP pistol, the barrel pointed at Semyon.

The GRU assassin remains calm. No increase in heart rate. His eyes take a quick glance at the sports bag of guns in the overhead compartment above her.

He'll never make it.

"Wow," he says coolly, eyes back on Ibliss. "So the Americans really do give a shit about the she-wolf."

"It's more about *you*, if I'm being honest."

Semyon narrows his eyes. "You are Ibliss, right?"

She narrows her own.

"We fought in Vienna," he adds. "I chased you along the rooftops of the opera house. You did very well that day to escape me."

"Yes," she replies in her own dry tone. "I enjoyed killing the three-man wet team that was with you."

This makes Semyon smile.

"Where's the old woman?" she asks.

"I thought you only wanted me."

"Where is she?"

"She's old. Where do you think?"

"The bathroom?"

The grin widens on Semyon's face. "So what," he says, relaxing back into his seat, "you're still running errands for the CIA? I mean, correct me if I'm wrong, but didn't the agency put a hit on every Fallen Angel that managed to survive my purge on you."

"I thought it was the GRU's purge."

"Who cares. Now there are only three of you left. Though," he adds in a dubious tone, "you are the first of those three to confirm to me that you are indeed still alive."

Her jaw tightens.

Semyon leans forward—slowly, with careful movements, always aware of the pistol facing him. In a cold voice, he tells her, "Of course, it was more than three that escaped our hit squads. Eight of you were skilled enough to escape. But only three of you escaped the subsequent death squads sent by your own people."

Never breaking eye contact, Ibliss tells him, "Honestly? I don't give a rat's ass. I'm here for *you*. That's all I care about. The here and now."

She peels a pair of handcuffs from her utility belt and tosses them across. They land heavily on his lap.

"Put them on," she tells him.

He rolls his eyes.

Cocking the hammer of the pistol, she snarls, "*Put* the cuffs on."

They're not hinged. They're chained. Semyon is glad of this.

"Sure," he says casually.

Picking them up from his lap, he closes them over his wrists, one and then the other. Holding them up, he tugs his hands apart to show they're secure.

"Now get up," she orders. "You're gonna take me to her."

In the aisle, Ibliss places him directly in front of her and holds the gun to his lower back.

"Lead on."

He does as he's told. As they venture through the carriages, making their way toward the bathrooms, the tannoy crackles into life. "*Passengers for Talkeetna should gather their belongings now. The next stop is Talkeetna. I repeat, folks, the next stop is Talkeetna. After that, Wasilla and Anchorage, where this train's journey ends.*"

Crossing over into the next carriage, they are hit by an icy blast of air that blows at them the second they enter the aisle. It comes from the other end, where a door must be open somewhere further on.

"Which bathroom is she in?" Ibliss asks Semyon.

"The one at the end."

They continue slowly. The draft ruffling their hair.

"What do the Russians want with her anyway?" Ibliss asks.

"She's a traitor."

"But why alive?"

"Beats me. I'm just like you: a messenger."

"Where were you heading?"

"I'm unlikely to tell you that now, aren't I?"

"Doesn't matter. You won't make it."

"I beg to differ."

"You can beg all you—"

Something moves to their right. Before Ibliss can wheel around with the pistol, she is being shoved hard in the chest and toppling backwards out of an open door.

Panting and out of breath from the effort, Mother stands holding onto the edge, watching Ibliss roll down a grass bank and out of sight.

"Good work," Semyon says as he comes beside her.

"I saw her in the cabin...with you," Mother says. "Who is she?"

"It doesn't matter. Let's get back and get these handcuffs off. I have a pick set in my bag. After that, we need to move. This train is no longer safe."

FIFTY

TALKEETNA, 2021

WHEN THEY'D LEFT JACK'S DINER, MICHAEL HAD insisted on driving.

It's early afternoon when they enter the small town of Talkeetna. Sitting on the banks of a wide stretch of the Susitna River, it serves as a base to those hiking the Denali Nature Reserve or venturing out to the local mountains. Downtown Talkeetna is a collection of craftsman bungalows and wood cabins. Not a hint of concrete exists in any of it. A mom-n-pop coffeeshop sits on one corner of an intersection. There's a shoe repair store. DIY place next door: Fred's Lumber. A general store. People waving to each other. Stopping to chat in the street.

"It's refreshing."

Peter turns away from the view. "What was that, Mikey?"

"I said, it's refreshing. You know, not to see a Walmart or a Starbucks. I guess this must've been how it used to be."

"Maybe."

The wind is real strong now. Michael brakes sharp when a sign from outside a barber's shop falls into the road. It carries on across, making a terrible clattering sound, the weather dragging it all the way to the other side, where it flips up at the curbside and hits the front doors of a bakery.

At the end of the strip, the sky is practically black.

"You think we'll make it to Anchorage in time?"

"We should do," Peter says, checking his wristwatch and then the sky.

He isn't sure, though. The radio buzzes in the background. More severe weather bulletins.

"Batten down those hatches, folks."

FIFTY-ONE

ALASKA RAILROAD, 2021

It feels like evening but is only afternoon. A giant, sky-eating cloud rolls toward Talkeetna like an upside-down tsunami and the first flakes already sprinkle down, striking the windows of the train as it moves toward the town's modest station.

Semyon and Mother move through the carriages. If people are waiting for them, then it would be best to leave via the engine at the front. Get away via the railroad.

"Misha, wait."

Semyon stops. He is in front, the sports bag hanging from his shoulder. When he turns, she is leaning heavily against a wall of the carriage.

"What's up?" he asks.

Panting, she tells him, "I cannot seem to catch... my breath."

Semyon goes to speak but is interrupted by the tannoy.

"Passengers for Talkeetna should gather their belongings now. The next stop is Talkeetna. I repeat, folks, the next stop is Talkeetna. After that it is Anchorage, where this train terminates."

"Come on," he says impatiently. "We have to get to the engine. It's only another four carriages."

"I can't," she insists. "I must sit down. I feel... sleepy."

With some effort, she raises her gaze to meet his. Her bloodshot eyes are practically hanging from the bags on her face.

"I've never felt so old," she remarks in a frail voice.

Semyon checks his wristwatch. Nods. "Okay. Have a little rest."

He guides her to a seat that pokes out of the carriage. It is next to a door. He opens the window on said door, pulling it down. Cool air rushes in and washes over her face. The train starts to slow. Semyon stands on the opposite side of the carriage with his back to her. While she catches her breath, he watches the outside and considers their current situation.

Though thankful for Mother's decisive actions, he is also upset that she wasn't armed with something that could have gotten rid of Ibliss for good. He is sure that the fall has only damaged her. Nevertheless, it's not the Fallen Angel he's immediately concerned with. It's whether she has others in the vicinity.

He thinks about it. Normal procedure, in his experience, would have been to send a wet team onto the train. Do it while it's stopped in a station: like now. There would be two teams. One remaining on the platform. The other on the train. A single person getting on and joining him in the cabin would be too risky.

Unless that was all they had.

Semyon slowly comes to the conclusion that Ibliss is alone. At least for now.

The thought makes him give up the idea of climbing out the engine and making a getaway. In fact, as the train approaches the Talkeetna train station, he wonders whether they shouldn't just stay onboard all the way to Anchorage.

"This train now stops at Talkeetna. All onboard for Talkeetna, this is your stop."

Another train is already in the station. The Anchorage to Fairbanks service going the other way. They pull alongside it. No more than a foot gap between the two trains.

While they slow to a crawl, Mother watches the windows of the other train. She is in a daze. The faces go past in a blur. Her muscles are so sapped she wonders if she is ill. Poisoned. Surely something must've debilitated her.

She turns to Misha.

He takes partial cover at the edge of the opposite door. His hawk-eyes scanning the station through its window.

Talkeentna Train Station is nothing more than a one-hundred-meter-long length of concrete with an old one-story wood-slat station house in the middle. A clocktower poking out the roof tells the wrong time.

Semyon's anticipation piques when his burner phone vibrates in his pocket. Plucking it out, he expects it to be Parfyon.

It's not Parfyon.

"We are watching you," an artificially deep voice says.

Whoever it is is using an electronic vocal distorter.

"Oh yeah?" Semyon replies.

"*We are watching and we know where you are.*"

"Is this Ibliss? Why the change of voice?"

"*We are waiting for you.*"

Semyon slowly drops the bag to the floor. Unzips it. Pulls a Makarov from within. Keeping the small pistol down by his side, hidden from the other passengers.

"Waiting for *me*?" Semyon asks.

"*Yes.*"

"Then you should be able to tell me where I am."

Without missing a beat, his interlocutor replies, "*You are currently on the southbound Alaskan Railroad service for Anchorage. You're at Talkeetna station.*"

"You only need a train timetable to know that, Ibliss."

"*You are standing beside the middle exit on the western side of carriage thirty-seven.*"

Semyon looks up. Goes cold. They're right: this is carriage thirty-seven. He's standing beside the middle exit on the western side.

The Hunter tucks himself in further. His eyes search the people hustling to the other doors. Gripping the pistol as he holds it out of sight.

"This *is* Ibliss, isn't it?"

"*No. This is the man watching you from the platform.*"

Semyon peeks.

Only a few people dot it. None of them look like anything other than what they are: potential collateral damage.

The doors unlock. The bolts clicking. Passengers begin opening them and leaving the train.

"*Can't you see me?*"

The five people on the platform have all gotten onboard via different carriages. None of them get on this carriage. The platform is quickly clear and the train waits for departure.

From his tucked-in position, Semyon studies his surroundings like a machine scanning for life. With the phone clamped to his ear, he gradually smiles.

"You're just fucking with me."

"*Am I?*"

"Yes."

"*Then why are you hiding in cover?*"

Semyon's nerves tingle. He searches for possible sniper nests. The railroad sits on the highest point in a sparse area that's essentially nothing but dirt lots and crisscrossing roads. To the west a freeway rolls by on concrete legs. But all of that sits on lower ground. Not great for getting a clean shot at the train. As for the station house, the roof is clean.

"You're full of shit," Semyon tells his interlocutor.

He waits for a reply but gets nothing.

"Hello?"

The line goes dead.

Semyon eyes the carriage. Up and down the aisle. Only a few seats are occupied. The passengers gazing about disinterestedly.

He considers things.

Time to move.

He tucks the pistol in the front of his jeans and pulls his sweatshirt over it. He zips the bag up before lifting it to his shoulder. With one hand on the door handle, he gets ready to leave, but as he twists it he turns around to Mother and his stomach drops.

She is gone.

The window of the door she was sitting next to is wide open. So is the one on the door of the northbound train exactly opposite, the opening acting as a portal between the two.

"Misha?!"

Semyon glances in the direction of where the cry came from. Three windows along, he spots her being manhandled along the aisle of the neighboring train.

"LET GO OF ME," Mother cries at her kidnapper.

Whoever he is, he's strong. He contains her easily while hurrying her toward the back of the train. She decides to fight dirty. She bites him. Latches onto the top of his arm.

"Stop that," he says, the pair of them coming to a halt.

She draws blood. The crimson oozing from his shirt.

"You taught me to push pain into the corners," he tells her. "So biting me with those false teeth will do very little."

She removes her bloody mouth from his arm and looks up.

"Ugh!" she groans. "It is you."

"Yes," Peter replies. "It is me."

"The man without a face."

"Only the one you gave me. Now come on. Peter is waiting."

Her eyes brighten. "The boy is here?"

"Yes."

"But we must wait for Misha."

"That isn't Misha. Now come on."

He goes to tug her away but she stubbornly refuses. Grabbing onto the back of a seat, she locks her fingers.

Peter has had enough.

"There's something else you taught me," he says.

"What?"

He plunges two fingers into a pressure point behind her left ear. The sharp poke cuts the blood off for just long enough to send her temporarily into unconsciousness. That done, she is much easier to handle.

Peter throws her over his shoulder and marches toward the end of the train. When he reaches it, he flings the emergency door open and climbs out. Michael is parked there in the Range Rover. The back door is already open and Peter lays Mother across the seat.

"Is she okay?" the kid asks.

"Yeah. She's—"

Machine gun fire erupts and Peter throws himself into the back of the car over Mother.

"Drive, drive!"

The kid crunches the Range Rover into gear and pulls them out of there as a stream of bullets hits the tailgate.

SEMYON DROPS down from the train. The gun clicks in his hands. He has taped his magazines together. He pops one from the well, flips it around, snaps in the other.

He doesn't take any more shots, however. Not with the vehicle now out of range.

He merely watches it turn sharply at a crossing and head in the direction of the freeway. All the time thinking:

Who was that?

FIFTY-TWO

TALKEETNA, TEN MINUTES EARLIER

AT THE MOMENT SEMYON AND MOTHER WERE working their way through the train, Peter and Michael were coming up on a railway crossing that passed over the main drag at the southern end of downtown Talkeetna.

The lights began flashing red.

"You think we'll make it?" Michael asked, accelerating the Range Rover and taking hold of the stick.

"Don't," was all Peter said.

The kid rolled his eyes and released the peddle.

They came to a stop in front of the falling barriers. As the train rumbled slowly by from right to left, the windows of the carriages passed by like a movie reel and both gazed disinterestedly through the windshield at them.

Peter was thinking about the storm when—

"Mother!"

"What?"

Michael was pointing at the train. "Mother. It's Mother. She's on the train."

The kid's eyes followed the window all the way.

The train crossed, the barriers began to rise. Michael dropped the clutch and steered onto the tracks. The next thing, they were racing down the railroad, the Range Rover shaking violently as they came up on the train.

"Michael, what the hell are you doing?"

"You can get onto it," the kid said. "If I can get us close enough, I know you can."

"Michael, it might not have been her."

"It *was*. I'm sure. She's with *him*."

The kid got them right up to the back of the last carriage.

"Mikey, come on. This is really dumb."

Michael turned to him. "Don't tell me you don't care about her. Because you do. I know you do. Now come on."

Groaning, Peter gave in. "Let me think."

Michael's eyes flittered between Peter and the train. The assassin had his eyes closed and was still. Hardly the actions Michael was hoping for.

Peter's eyes snapped open.

"Okay. I got it."

He reached into the back and grabbed the rucksack containing the laptop and the Stingray. He set it up on his lap.

"What do you need that for?" Michael asked.

"I'm sure he'll be using a burner phone to contact his people when he needs them. I bet it's the only burner phone on that entire train. So it should be easy to spot which one it is."

"What are you gonna do when you find it?"

"Call him. Talk to him."

"What do you want to talk to him about?"

Peter turned sideways to the kid.

"Subterfuge, Mikey. Simple subterfuge."

"You mean distracting him?"

"Exactly. Like a magician or a pickpocket before they trick you."

Peter found the phone. Just like he said, there was only one phone on that train which had no details attached to it.

"Okay, I got him," Peter said, collapsing down the laptop. "Now," he added, eyes on the locomotive in front, "this train will be stopping at the station soon. When it does, all I need you to do is wait for me to come back with her. You got that?"

"Not much to get. So yeah."

FIFTY-THREE

A FEW MILES OUTSIDE OF WASILLA, 2021

AN HOUR LATER, BEATS OF SNOW FLITTER DOWN, brought over from the biblical storm cloud that moves silently after them. Now on the freeway, they have another hour to Wasilla before it's a further forty-five minutes of driving to Anchorage. Once there, they'll have to get out of the storm for the night.

Peter has taken over driving duties while Michael sits in the passenger seat.

"I don't like her being tied up like that," the kid says.

"It's safer that way."

Mother is laid out across the backseat. She is gagged with duct tape and bound with zip-ties. Both her wrists and her ankles to be on the safe side.

"But how are we gonna get her across the border?"

"Underneath a blanket," Peter says.

"It feels wrong," the kid tells him.

"And how else do you think we'll get her into Canada? I've only got ID for the two of us. Not her. She was never part of the plan."

Peter is cursing their luck. He *just about* had a plan with the two of them. But now they have a senile old woman with a violent temper accompanying them, the original plan is done. What would he say to Marta? I need another passport made? Get Mother over to Europe with them?

It couldn't be done.

No. He has no other choice but to dump her somewhere the first chance he gets. Leave her at a hospital. Or some other place. Maybe an asylum. Try and persuade the kid it's the best thing.

"*Breaking news!*" the radio bleats.

Peter turns it up. Expecting it to be about the storm. But it's not.

"*This just in,*" the newscaster says. "*Police are searching for several individuals after shots were fired at vehicles in Talkeetna earlier today. Here's our on-the-ground reporter Rose Tyler with more.*"

"*Thanks, Jim. I'm here at a railway crossing close to the Talkeetna train station where witnesses describe seeing a scene straight out of an action movie.*"

The raspy voice of one such witness comes on the airwaves. "*I was just driving over the crossing and out of nowhere this four-by-four comes racing at me. I thought it was gonna hit my car, but he swerves just in time. That's when I hear the pop-pop-pop of a machine gun going off and there, bold as darn brass, is some guy holding what I think was an AK.*"

"She's waking up," Michael says.

Peter glances up at the rearview mirror. Indeed, Mother's gray eyes are open.

"Can I give her some water?" Michael asks.

"Okay."

Michael removes the piece of duct tape from her mouth and feeds her water from a bottle.

"Oh, Peter," she says softly when she has finished drinking. "Get me out of these ties."

"He won't let me," the kid whispers down to her.

She frowns at him. "You don't take your orders from him, do you?"

"No. But... Well... it's..." He turns to Peter. "Can't we just take them off?"

"No, Mikey," Peter says bluntly.

"Don't worry," the old woman whispers. "Misha will soon come and save us."

"That wasn't Misha," Michael says to her. "He was from the Russians."

"Yes. Misha is Russian."

"But he wasn't Misha. He was someone else."

She studies the boy with a dubious expression.

"What did he want with you, anyway?" Peter interjects. "I mean, where was he taking you? And *why* was he taking you? The Russians usually take nothing with them. They just leave a dead body."

"Misha was taking me back to Russia," she replies. "Back to my home. Away from bastard CIA like you."

"Somehow I don't think he was taking you home," Peter puts to her.

"Then where was he taking me, then?"

"A GRU torture chamber probably."

Up ahead are the red glow of brake lights. The frozen air is thick and visibility is becoming poorer by the second. It forces them to slow down as the traffic presses together. Until they are eventually trapped in a traffic jam.

"This is all we need," Peter complains.

FIFTY-FOUR

TALKEETNA, 2021

"Oh, Eddie," his wife says over speakerphone. "That storm's almost here. You need to get your ass home and off that road."

The aforementioned Eddie is currently driving his Dodge Ram along the Talkeetna Spur Road.

"I aim to, Cathleen," Eddie replies.

The septuagenarian has one eye on the road while the other studies his wing mirror; focused on the rolling wave of white that sweeps down from the mountains like a pack of marauding horses.

The rest of the sky is black and his wipers knock away the flakes that are getting larger by the minute. The radio muses in the background. The storm prominent amongst the disc-jockey's current phone-in discussion. "*Man, I'm out here in Chase and we already in the middle of it. You better tell folks to get inside, because the snow is already past my kitchen window.*"

"I'm so worried, Eddie," his wife goes on.

"I'll be back in time, sweetie. Don't you worry. Just trust me. I'm only ten minutes away from the ranch."

"Well, I got Beth and the boys here. We're all snug as a bug in a rug. We're just fretting about you is all. They say it might put the power out."

"Don't you worry about me. You heard from Robbie?"

"Robbie is at the plant. It's too dangerous to try and come back. Hour and a half drive ain't the thing you wanna do in a blizzard. Specially on mountain roads."

"No. It ain't. So where's he gonna stay?"

"They're all gonna sleep in the lunchroom. He says there's plenty of food and they got a generator there in case they lose power. So all is good. It's just you, Eddie, that's got everyone upset."

"What in the hell?"

Eddie is sitting forwards in his seat.

"What's up?"

"There's someone in the road."

"Someone in the road?"

"That's what I said weren't it."

There certainly is. A man dressed in black stands right in the middle of the lane Eddie travels down. As still as a statue, hands behind his back, a huge sports bag at his feet.

"I mean," Eddie mutters half to himself, "what in the hell kinda stupid you gotta be to be out on your own with a blizzard coming?"

Eddie pulls beside the stranger. Rolls his window.

"Hey, there, partner. You need a—"

The second he sees the Margolin MCM it goes off.

Blasting a .22 bullet into his face just below the eye, obliterating his left frontal lobe, passing through the crown, and burying itself in the roof of the pickup.

"Eddie? Eddie, what was that? Eddie?"

Semyon opens the door, pulls the corpse out and drags it into brush at the edge of the road. Then he loads the bag of guns onto the passenger seat, gets in the Dodge Ram and drives off.

"Eddie? Eddie? I can hear you driving. Eddie?"

Semyon cancels the call and tosses the cell phone out the window.

FIFTY-FIVE

WASILLA, 2021

THERE'S NO LONGER ANY NEED TO OUTRUN THE storm. They're already in it.

Fat snowflakes plummet from the sky. Heavy wind blows it about in whorls and the air resembles a swarm of hungry insects. The wipers move rapidly to clear a space for Peter to see out—a small semicircle onto the obscure snow-drenched world they slowly travel through.

Blue lights flash somewhere in the vague distance.

Must be an accident.

The road quickly becomes a collection of stuck cars. They pass a sedan flicking slush back at the people trying to push it. The wheels churning the snow, but getting no grip.

With the Range Rover in four-wheel drive, Peter steers around the stagnant vehicles and takes the hard shoulder.

"Get the blanket over her," he tells Michael.

"Can't we just sit her up?"

"It's the cops, Mikey. They see her hands and feet bound that's not gonna end well."

"Then can't we untie her?"

"No."

Peter glances sideways at him. His face is very serious.

The kid groans, leans forward and opens the glove box. He takes a gray blanket from it and unfurls it over the old woman, leaving only her face exposed.

Making eye contact with her through the rearview mirror, Peter tells Mother, "You care for your Peter, don't you?"

"Of course I do."

"Then you be good. Because if we are arrested, men will hurt him. Bad men."

"*You* are bad man."

"Worse men than me."

"Please, Mother," Michael says. "For me?"

She turns from the mirror to the kid, who leans over her from the front seat. "Okay," she says softly. "But only for you. Never for *him*."

They reach the front of the jam. A Kenworth W900 has jackknifed and spilled its forty-foot load of logs. The whole freeway is blocked. Four police cruisers, two fire trucks and an ambulance are in attendance. A firefighter uses a huge chainsaw to cut the logs blocking the way, while another two firefighters use the jaws-of-life to open up the crushed cab so they can pull the driver free.

Peter parks them a short way from the blockage.

A state trooper in a snow-encrusted coat begins making his way to them, holding onto his hat and leaning against the wind.

"Get her face covered," Peter says.

"Okay, Mother," Michael tells her as he leans into the back. "You remember, don't you? Keep quiet."

"Only for you."

Michael covers her face, then places their coats, some magazines and other stuff over her to make it look like the back seat is merely filled with random junk. As the officer reaches them, Peter gazes at the mirrors, searching the stormy road behind them.

Tick-tock. Tick-tock.

A knock at the window draws Peter's attention to his left. He rolls it down. The storm immediately invades the car, blowing the magazines about on top of Mother and filling the warm air with snowflakes.

The trooper ducks down. Brings a red-cheeked, blue-nosed face close up and shouts over the storm, "You folks got enough gas to keep the battery charged for the next few hours?"

"We do," Peter tells him.

The officer looks across the car at Michael.

"That your boy?"

"Yeah. We're on a hunting trip. Trying to get to Anchorage."

"Oh, you won't be getting to Anchorage for at least a day or two."

"Why's that?"

"They've closed the bridge after Wasilla. No one's going through until the storm is over. Weatherman reckons that could be another day depending on the wind."

Peter leans back in his seat, clenching his eyelids shut. Like with Mother, he hasn't planned for this.

"*Shit*," seethes between his teeth.

"Look," the cop goes on, "this part of the road should be clear in another couple of hours. After that, there's a snow plow to guide everyone to Wasilla. It's about four clicks from here. Once you're there, it'll be the city's emergency shelter, which is Wasilla high school, or a hotel if you're..."

The trooper trails off as his eyes catch sight of something on the rear of the Range Rover. He begins making his way to what he thinks is a bullet hole. Sure enough, it certainly appears to be one when he runs a finger around the edge of the dented metal. Searching the exterior of the car, he spots another. This one is long where the bullet has grazed the bodywork, the paint scratched off in a line, the metal torn. Following it round to the back, he finds a dozen or so spread across the rear fender and the spare tire. He starts to think. Earlier on, the shootout in Talkeetna. What was the description of the vehicle being shot at?

Green four-by-four, flashes through his head.

"Hands where I can see them," he barks when he returns to the window with his pistol drawn.

Peter does as the officer asks, placing his hands on the wheel, facing forwards, staying perfectly still.

Michael is watching closely from across the car. The kid's heart pounding in his chest.

"You and your boy there didn't happen to be in Talkeetna earlier on, did you?"

"I'm sorry, Officer," Peter says calmly, not taking his eyes from the firefighters cutting the truck's cab open. "Have I done something to offend you?"

"There was a shootout in Fairbanks last night. Then another in Talkeetna about an hour ago. Description of the car involved matches this. Now. I need you to get out the car real slow, mister. You get me?"

"I'm just a father taking his son hunting."

"Yeah? Then how do you explain those bullet holes in the back of your car?"

Peter swivels his head slowly to the left, making eye contact.

The trooper shivers. This is mostly a rural area. Peter bets that he's never had to shoot that gun, let alone killed someone with it. The man's eyes shimmer with terror. The gun shakes in his grasp. The cop can't help glancing at his colleagues, hoping to catch their looks. But the blizzard is too thick and only their outlines are visible.

"You got kids, Trooper James?" Peter says in a calm tone that belies the situation, having read the acetate name badge on the breast of the man's coat.

Trooper James frowns. "What kinda answer is that?"

"You do, don't you? Guy your age always has kids. You got a boy?"

The cop gets angry. Stepping back from the car, he shouts, "Outta the goddamn car. Now!"

Once more he looks for his colleagues. Spotting two of them close to the crashed cab, he whistles. But the sound is swallowed by the raging blizzard, and the other cops are too busy helping the firefighters open up the truck to notice.

Eyes back on Peter, who hasn't budged an inch, he takes one hand off the gun and removes a pair of handcuffs from the back of his belt.

"You come on out of that car now," he says in a trembling voice.

Peter's serene demeanor scares him. People who have guns pointed at their heads aren't supposed to be this calm.

"I bet you coach your son's little league team," Peter goes on, his voice almost hypnotic.

"Shut up and get out of the car. Now!"

"Eh, Peter?"

Michael sits watching the wing mirror with narrowed eyes.

"What is it?"

"I think there's something coming."

Peter takes his eyes off the trooper and looks in the rearview. Bright headlight beams burn through the storm, getting bigger and bigger until they explode.

"Hold on!"

The grille of a Dodge Ram smashes into their tailgate. The cop throws himself backwards to avoid the collision. The Range Rover lurches forwards and crashes into one of the spilled logs.

The two cops, the firemen and the paramedics all look that way, their attention finally won, and it is at that point the cops spot Trooper James getting up from the snow with his sidearm out.

"Watch them!" he shouts, jabbing a finger at the crashed Range Rover, its grille smoking into the cold, blustering air.

The Dodge Ram has come to a stop. Its fog lights are on. Set to the highest beam. They blind Trooper James as he makes his way cautiously to it with an arm partially shielding his eyes.

When he reaches the driver's side, he pulls the door open.

It's empty.

He senses movement to his right. Twists sideways.

Too late.

The buttstock of an AK-74 bursts at him. Striking his face with a sickening crack. The blow forcing his nasal bone inwards. Shards of which annihilate the frontal lobe. The blow killing Officer James instantly.

As he lies dead on the ground, a boot steps over him and the dark figure of Semyon Mikhailovich, the Hunter, emerges from the storm.

He opens fire on the Range Rover. Bullets crackle the bodywork. Stones in a metal drum. It is at this point that the remaining two cops start shooting. Forcing Semyon to concentrate some of that fire on them.

The people in the cars start to panic. A woman's scream sounds somewhere. Cars begin reversing out of there. A station wagon crashes blindly into a pickup. Roaring engines. Spinning tires. Pandemonium.

Of the two remaining troopers, one is already dead. Caught in the open, he now lies on his back in the snow, a stitch of bullet holes across his chest. The other continues to fire from the edge of the Kenworth's cab where he's taken cover.

"All units, all units, I need backup out here," he gasps into his radio, trying to get the other six troopers who are helping trapped drivers further along the jam.

"*Hey, Cody. What's up?*" crackles from his radio.

He places it to his mouth. "I'm under severe fire. Two men already down. They got James and Riley. Repeat. Men down!"

"*We're about a minute away, bud. Hold on.*"

"You gotta be quicker than that."

"*We're about a hundred meters off your position. Just hold on.*"

Trooper Cody puts the radio down. His eyes desperately search the snow. The figure had disappeared into it right after shooting Riley. Just faded into the storm.

Snow crunches to his left. He turns sharply. Sees the gray air light up with muzzle flash.

A single burst of fire sends ten 9mm bullets through Officer Cody's chest. He's dead before he even hits the ground.

Semyon steps over the body, presses the AK into his shoulder. Lines the scope up with the Range Rover. Resumes pummeling it while moving slowly toward the passenger side.

When he reaches it, Semyon finds the car empty. The driver's side doors are both wide open. Three sets of footsteps lead off into the white. And something else:

Blood.

One of them is hit.

Semyon smiles like a hungry wolf tracking an injured deer.

Following the blood, he is led across the northbound lane and into the woodland that lines the edge. He moves cautiously through the frozen mist. Trees emerge from it and move toward him. Branches whip at him. Debris strikes him. But all the time his eyes focus on the blood drops leading him on.

He freezes.

The trail ends. Veering right, it appears to finish on the other side of a wide spruce.

He spots the shoulder of a jacket poking ever so slightly out from the trunk.

Semyon shows his teeth.

He fans around the tree in an arc. The plan is to come around it and shoot his enemy from the side.

But he doesn't get that far.

Before finding out that the shoulder belongs to nothing more than Peter's coat, a snap of branches to his right makes him wheel round.

A foot kicks the AK high out of his hands.

A whorl of fists and feet follow. Moving at him from the storm. A sweep kick at his knee. An elbow aimed for his face. Semyon avoids the first. Blocks the second. He enters a dance of limbs amongst the trees. Combination attacks flow into each other in a raging river of relentless motion. Blocking, dodging, the Hunter is forced into a retreat. Peter keeps coming. The self-made cut on his palm now bandaged. He doesn't give Semyon time to think. To weigh his opponent up. Only to deflect, push back, look for a gap.

Then, as they surge and counter-surge, the two moving in and out the trees, Semyon begins to feel a level of familiarity with the fight. With the opponent.

Peter parries a cross-punch with his right and attempts a left hook to Semyon's ribs. But the Hunter twists his body away in time and Peter's knuckles only graze him.

Peter is also feeling a level of familiarity with his foe.

Semyon recovers his balance. Peter has stopped advancing.

The two stand six yards apart. Their breaths stretch into the air. The storm beats everything around them. The trees rock and creak.

Semyon narrows his eyes. "Azrael?"

Peter says nothing.

Semyon, mouth agape, is stunned.

It almost costs him.

Peter charges. A fist flicks toward Semyon's left eye. It is a feint. Peter's real attack comes in the form of a knee thrust. Semyon drops back and lashes out with a foot, blocking Peter's follow-up box kick when he misses with the knee.

Something sparkles in Peter's hand. A US Army-issue bayonet. He attacks with it, the blade dancing through the air like a silver fish caught on a hook. Semyon lets him come forwards, parrying his arm and avoiding the blade.

He finds a gap.

As the knife cuts sideways through the air, Semyon pivots, sweeps under the outstretched arm, takes it by the elbow, and drives it into the nearest tree, burying the bayonet to its hilt. Peter's hand slips when he goes to tug it out and he is once more unarmed.

The two pause. Stand apart. Stare into each other's eyes.

"It really is you," Semyon says. "Don't you recognize me?"

Peter's heart freezes. He is caught in a flux of emotions.

Then.

"Hands in the air!"

Semyon wheels around. A trooper emerges from the storm aiming a shotgun at him.

"Just you wait there, you son-of-a-bitch cop killer."

Turning around, the trooper cups his mouth to holler for the others.

He never gets to.

Semyon rips the bayonet from the tree and sends it spinning through the air. It hits the side of the trooper's head before he even musters his voice.

The blade buried four inches into his brain, the trooper looks stunned. He reaches a hand up to touch the knife. Then he drops to his knees. Comes to rest like that in the snow as his eyes go dead.

When Semyon turns back to Peter, Azrael is gone.

PETER EMERGES from the trees onto the northbound lane of the freeway. Gunshots reverberate behind him. He staggers to an abandoned Toyota RAV4. The passenger door opens as he reaches it, Michael jumping out.

"Get back in the car," Peter tells him.

The kid nods. Does as he's told. Peter jumps into the driver's seat. Mother is in the back. His return appears to have disappointed her.

"What happened to your hand?" she asks dryly. "Did he cut you?"

"No," Peter replies, feeling underneath the steering column. "I cut my," he yanks the plastic covering away, "self."

"Ah, the injured wolf trick," she remarks.

"That's right. One of yours."

The dull crackle of more gunshots makes it through the storm as Peter attempts to hot-wire the Toyota.

"What are we gonna do without guns?" Michael asks.

Their weapons are still hidden in the Range Rover. Along with the money and the StingRay.

"I'm not bothered about the guns," Peter replies. "It's the money that bothers me."

"Maybe we should go back for it."

"We will as soon as I get this car started."

"They'll be waiting," Mother interjects from behind them.

"What about the guy?" Michael asks. "Is he gone?"

"No."

Peter observes Mother smiling in the rearview mirror.

"What happened?" Michael asks.

"Yes," Mother puts in. "What happened to Misha?"

Peter makes eye contact with the old woman through the mirror. "That wasn't Misha," he tells her. "That was—"

"Hold it right there!"

A woman cop stands at Peter's window, pointing her gun at the side of his head. Something hard taps Michael's window on the opposite side. The kid turns to find another cop.

They must have followed Peter out of the woods.

"Place your hands on the dashboard where I can see them, kid," a muffled voice commands Michael.

The thirteen-year-old turns to Peter.

"Do as he says," Peter tells him.

The kid places his hands on top.

"Get out the car!" the woman screams at Peter.

With slow movements, Peter reaches to his left, pulls the handle, pops the door. His hands are raised as he steps out into the snow. A third cop emerges. Coming in from the rear carrying a Remington 870 shotgun and aiming it at him. Ready to turn Peter into pink mist if he has to.

The three cops form a triangle around him.

"Face the car and place your hands on top of the vehicle," the woman orders.

While Peter slowly turns to face the Toyota, he scans his surroundings. He just so happens to be the owner of fantastic peripheral vision. He can practically see what goes on behind him. Taking in the three cops' positions, he calculates that there is easily a seventy percent chance he can dispossess the female as she comes up behind him with the handcuffs. Use her as a shield. Pivot around while holding her out in front. Kill her two partners with her own sidearm. Before finally putting a bullet in her.

But as she closes in on him and he gets ready to strike, Peter looks down into the Toyota and spots Michael gazing up at him with big eyes. Something in the kid's look tells him not to do it. To let these people live.

So when the cop tells him to place his hands at the back of his head, Peter does exactly as she says.

FIFTY-SIX

SEMYON MATERIALIZES FROM THE STORM LIKE A demon sent from hell to retrieve dead souls. Having escaped the police through the woods, he comes upon a sprawling single-story ranch house. It sits miles from its nearest neighbors and stables line the land to the rear of the property.

An American flag flutters on the end of a pole beside the porch door. Lights are on inside. Shining at the edges of the drawn curtains.

Semyon places the heavy sports bag down, unzips it, and removes a SIG Sauer M17. Twists a MODX-9 silencer onto the end.

When he reaches the porch, he can hear the bass murmurs of a television set coming from inside. In the living room, and completely oblivious to the murderer outside their home, an elderly couple sit on a couch watching *Jeopardy.*

"What is the USSR?" the wife answers while taking a fistful of popcorn from the bowl on her husband's lap.

"*What is the USSR is correct*," the TV announcer says.

"Yes," the wife hisses, pumping her fist.

Semyon is already in their hallway. A large Alsatian dog sits up from its bed. It doesn't bark, but it does growl. Semyon tucks the gun in the waistband of his pants and crouches level with the dog's height. With hair raised all along its spine, it gets up from the bed, and slowly makes its way to him in a low position.

Inside the living room, the wife goes to sip her drink but finds the glass empty.

"You want another soda, George?" she asks her husband as she gets up off the couch.

"Sure. I'm almost out, too."

She heads out of the room into the hallway. Gasps and drops the glass when she practically bumps into Semyon standing beside the dog.

The sound of the smashing glass makes her husband twist around on the couch. His heart goes cold the second he sees his wife being led into the room at gunpoint, the silenced pistol pressed to her cheek, a thick arm around her chest.

"Don't do anything stupid," Semyon tells the husband. "I only want food and a car."

"Mister," the husband says in a trembling voice. "Take what you want. Just don't hurt her."

"I need you to get up from the couch.," Semyon says forcefully.

The man notices the dog. "Bruno," he shouts, "get him!"

The dog does nothing. Just tips its head to the side as it sits beside Semyon panting.

"All I want is food and your car," the Hunter repeats. "I will tie you up. But that is all. Now stand up from the couch and place your hands above your head."

The husband stands slowly. His hands hovering above his shoulders.

Semyon shoots him between the eyes.

The wife lets out a piercing scream.

Semyon shoots her as well.

With the dog watching, he drags both bodies into the basement. Then, as the snow hits the windowpanes, he sits in a leather armchair petting the dog and making a call on the burner phone.

"May I speak with Parfyon, please?" he says in Russian the moment it is answered.

Parfyon comes on.

"Semyon," the old man wheezes.

"I have unfortunate news. The package was stolen from me."

"By who?"

"Azrael."

Silence swallows the line for a few seconds.

"So the rumors are true," Parfyon eventually says. "Azrael *is* alive."

"I could not have foreseen that he would come after her. But it makes sense. He always was a sucker for that old she-wolf."

"She does have that type of allure on men," Parfyon comments. "Nevertheless, our people here are one step ahead of you. They have located them."

"Where?"

FIFTY-SEVEN

WASILLA POLICE DEPARTMENT, 2021

WASILLA POLICE DEPARTMENT IS A ONE-STORY building on the edge of the tiny city. It contains twenty-eight state troopers, and, because of the storm, all twenty-eight are on duty. This makes the smallish building pretty cramped.

The three of them have been separated. Michael sits with a child services worker named Candy in the Detectives' Office. Mother sits in an interview room, muttering to herself, a trooper sitting with her. And in the next interview room, Peter sits alone, his hands cuffed and attached to the table by a chain. Forcing him to sit hunched forwards at all times.

Outside in the corridor, two detectives sip coffee from Styrofoam cups as their eyes study Peter through a one-way.

Peter faces the mirrored glass, perfectly still, staring straight ahead. As if watching the men outside.

"He gives me the creeps," Detective Gates remarks.

"I agree with you on that," his partner Detective Murphy replies.

It's at that moment that a third detective, the entirety of their Detectives' Office, rocks up and tells them, "The fingerprints came back."

"So what we got?"

"The kid is definitely Michael Henderson."

"Jesus Christ," Murphy says, shaking his head. "He's been out here all that time. God knows what's been happening to the poor kid."

Gates nods at the window. "What about *him*?"

He means Peter.

"The prints on Paul Adams's file don't match this guy. *This guy* matches no one. Like he never existed. And the woman: well, her file came up classified."

"Classified?"

"Yep. When I put the prints through the system I got shut out. She must be real high level."

"Then who in the hell are these people?"

MICHAEL SITS ALONE IN THE DETECTIVES' Office. It's a small room with only three desks. On one of them sits the StingRay and the laptop, which the detectives have been going over. The Money and the guns, he gathers, are in the evidence lockup. At the back of the room is a window. A shutter is closed over it on the outside and the storm rattles the metal as it whips the building.

The door opens. Candy and a tall, whip-thin detective step inside the room. The social worker, furnished with a cup of hot chocolate, takes a seat opposite Michael and passes it across the desk.

The kid gives the chocolate a derisive look. Then. "What am I—seven?"

Candy tries to smile it off. "Michael, this is my friend Detective Gates."

Gates gives a little wave as he stands in the background holding his smartphone.

"We'd like to take some pictures," the social worker adds. "Do you mind taking your top off for us so we can take a look at your torso?"

"Why?" the kid wants to know, eyeing Detective Gates suspiciously.

"I noticed you've hurt your hands. How did that happen?"

Michael lifts the backs of his hands up to his eyes. They're scraped, swollen and bruised. He gets a flashback. The cold, musty barn. The outlines of a man on a wooden wall. Mother giving him numbers. Which punches or kicks to use. Quicker and quicker.

"And the bruise on your cheek. How did you get that?"

Michael lifts a hand to his face, feels the cheek. The flashback continues. "Wrong!" Mother shrieks as the cane sails through the air and catches him.

"I got it playing," he tells Candy.

The social worker makes a face. Like she's calling bullshit.

"See," she says through her nose like the British upper class, "I don't think that's true. I think someone hurt you. Have you got bruising elsewhere?"

Michael instinctively feels his ribs. Looking up, he says, "No."

The detective pipes in. "How'd you get those calluses all over your hands?"

Michael stares down at them.

"They been forcing you to work for them?"

Looking up from the hands, he frowns at Gates.

Candy leans across the table. "Look, Michael," she says, "we know that you've been hurt. After all, this is the man responsible for your parents' deaths."

"He didn't kill my parents. He tried to save them."

"If it wasn't him," Gates pipes in, "then who did kill your mom and dad?"

"Men sent by Fred Wilson."

The detective narrows his eyes. "You mean Paul Adams was involved with Wilson and all that stuff they found in LA?"

"Yes. I mean no," Michael splutters. "Paul Adams doesn't exist. Fred Wilson was trying to get Peter to—"

"Peter?" Gates interrupts. "That's the guy we found you with, right?"

Michael says nothing. He just sighs.

"What about the woman?" Candy asks. "The one you said you call Mother."

The kid remains reticent. Candy thinks a moment. She slides a hand across the table and touches the top of his. Her look is soft and imploring. Giving off a *tell-me-all-your-secrets, kid* kind-of-vibe.

"Did he hurt you, Michael?" she asks in a motherly tone.

"No. Never."

"Then how'd you get those marks on you?"

"I told you. Playing."

"You don't have to be scared, kid," Gates assures him. "Ain't no one gonna hurt you here."

CARRYING with him a cup of steaming coffee, Detective Murphy comes into Interview Room Two. Mother is sat at the table staring into space. Her hands are laid on her lap and her lips twitch ever so slightly, as if she's chewing something with her front teeth.

"Has she asked for anything?" Murphy asks the trooper who sits with her.

"No," the woman replies. "She hasn't even spoken to me. Just keeps mumbling to herself."

Murphy steps across the room. "Evening, ma'am," he says, as he takes a seat opposite and places the coffee before her.

Mother's eyes come alive and narrow on him.

"I brought you some coffee," Murphy says.

She takes her eyes off him for a second to glance down at the steaming gray liquid.

Murphy goes on, "We've got someone from Senior Citizens coming to talk with you soon. But until then I'd like to ask you some questions if that's okay."

She says nothing. Her old eyes stay with him as he waits for an answer. The mumbling gets louder. He can almost hear it.

Murphy decides to lean over the table, bringing his ear right up to her whispering mouth.

Then he hears it:

"You are all dead, you are all dead, you are all dead, you are all..."

The hot coffee is in Murphy's face before he can do anything about it. As he staggers back in his chair, she whips a pencil from the breast pocket of his shirt. Rushes him. Plants it into his shoulder, right above the heart, just missing the pulmonary artery.

Trooper Kelly grabs Mother as she pulls the pencil out and goes to stab Murphy a second time. The detective manages to rip himself away before joining the trooper in subduing the old lady.

Two minutes later both Murphy and Trooper Kelly lick their wounds outside in the corridor, staring at the old woman through the one-way. Mother now chained to the table like Peter.

FIFTY-EIGHT

SEMYON SITS IN AN ARMCHAIR AT THE RANCH petting Bruno the Alsatian. The television is on.

"*Sensational news today,*" the CNN newscaster announces, "*as missing teenager Michael Henderson has been found alive and reportedly well in Alaska. As you know, Henderson was kidnapped six months ago by sex ring leader Paul Adams. Adams was, of course, a neighbor of the Hendersons. That was before he brutally shot and killed both parents and took Michael. Adams is also suspected in the kidnap and murder of a San Jose woman and her daughter...*"

"My my, Azrael," Semyon remarks to himself. "You have been busy. Hasn't he, Bruno?"

He turns to the dog and scratches its chin, making it raise its head and moan with pleasure.

The burner phone goes off.

"You requested assistance," Parfyon says down the line when he answers.

"I did."

"You are in luck. I foresaw the likelihood of trouble so have had a four-man team placed in your vicinity for the past two days."

Semyon's smile grows up his face.

"That *is* lucky," he hisses. "How long will they take to reach my location?"

"They should be with you within two hours."

"Good. Tell them to—"

The doorbell chimes. It makes Semyon cringe. Not from fear, from annoyance. He'd switched the old couple's cell phones off and disconnected the phone line. Hoping they didn't have anyone close by to check on them. It appears they do.

Too bad for whoever is pressing that doorbell.

"Parfyon, I will call you back."

Semyon opens the door. A tall, slender man in his forties stands on the porch with an anxious look. Semyon recognizes him from photographs inside the house. A Jeep Wrangler is parked in the driveway. A woman sitting in the passenger seat.

The snow bashes the man's red face as he stares at the strange man at his parents' door.

"I'm sorry," he says. "But who are you? And where are my parents?"

Semyon smiles ingratiatingly.

"Well, howdy there," he says in a cheery American accent. "You must be Paul?"

He'd read it on the back of one of the photographs he'd prized from its frame.

"I am. But who are you and where are my parents?"

"Your parents are inside," the Hunter assures him.

Paul turns over his shoulder to the woman in the car, clearly his wife. She stares back with a peevish expression.

"That must be Jenny, right?"

"Yes," Paul says, returning his narrowed eyes to Semyon.

"Your parents often talk about you both."

Suspicion written all over his face, Paul asks, "So who in the hell are you?"

"Well, I am hurt," Semyon says with faux pain in his expression. "I thought they would have at least told you about me."

"About what?"

"Well, as you know, your mom and pop are getting on now. They often times need help around the place."

"So what? You're their carer?"

"Exactly, Paul. I am their carer."

"And where are they now?"

"In the basement."

"The basement?"

"Yeah."

"Doing what?"

"Just hanging around, I guess. Come in and see."

Semyon turns and walks into the house.

"Okay, then," Paul half-mutters, removing his snow hat and following him inside.

Semyon leads the son across the hallway, opens the basement door, and stands to the side. With a motion of his hand, he says, "After you."

The smile puts Paul at ease and he walks as if hypnotized toward the top of the basement steps. When he reaches them and looks down, he is surprised to see that the light is off down there.

He turns to ask about it. Doesn't get any further than "Why are the—" before Semyon has put a bullet through his face and he's dropping backwards down the steps and disappearing into darkness.

Before he's even reached the bottom, Semyon is leaving the house and marching up to the Wrangler. The wife looks confused as he approaches without her husband. Maybe he's going to tell her to come inside.

He's not.

He reaches her door and makes the "roll your window down" motion with his fist. She presses the button and it lowers.

"Is everything—"

Semyon puts two bullets in her. She shudders from the impact and then stays perfectly still. The Hunter then walks around the grille and gets into the driver's side. The keys are still in the ignition. He twists them, starts it up and taxis the Wrangler to the open door of the ranch's garage. He parks it inside, gets out, and then pulls the folding garage door down. Slamming it shut.

FIFTY-NINE

DETECTIVES GATES AND MURPHY BOTH STEP INTO the whitewashed walls of Interview Room One. Peter's gaze comes away from his own reflection and follows the men as they sit down on the opposite side of the table. The one that Peter is chained to. His hands laid flat, palms down.

"Shall I call you Peter?" Gates asks.

"Call me anything you like."

"How about pedophile?" Murphy adds.

Peter swivels to eyeball him. When his gaze takes in the ripped hole in Murphy's shirt, the patch of blood, he asks, "What happened to your shoulder?"

"I met your Mother," Murphy explains. "Real nice lady."

"I wouldn't call her nice," Peter replies in a deadpan.

"I'm sure your upbringing was a wonderfully warm affair," Gates remarks. "Now tell us how you got to be in possession of Michael Henderson?"

"Do you have automatic weapons in this building?"

"What kind of answer is that?" Murphy blurts out.

"Curve balls from the weirdo," Gates grumbles. "Okay. Then how about this question. Where'd you get all that money we found in your car?"

Peter just stares at him.

"Or, how about: where in the hell did you get all that state-of-the-art surveillance equipment?"

Still nothing.

"Maybe you can tell us where Paul Adams is?"

Instead of answering, Peter rises ever so slowly from the chair, the chain clicking against the loop he's attached to. He leans over the table. Both detectives ease back in their chairs.

His eyes burn into Gates.

"Someone is coming," he tells the detective. "Someone who will kill anyone that stands in his way."

Both detectives narrow their eyes.

"You got a rescue party coming?"

"No. Not rescue. More like a hit man who wants my Mother for whatever reason. But he *is* coming."

"Is this the same guy you were with on the freeway? The one who killed four troopers?"

"I'm not with him. He was after us."

"Who? Paul Adams?"

Peter breathes in, then out. Sits back down. "Look," he says calmly, "I don't really care if you believe me or not. But I'll tell you anyway. This place isn't safe. *You* aren't safe. The man who is coming is utterly ruthless. He *will* kill every last person in this building if they get in his way. Not unless you prepare yourselves."

"This bogeyman got a name?"

Peter's eyes glaze over. "They call him the Hunter these days," he says. "But I knew him as Tommy."

SOMEONE PRESSES the buzzer to the front door. The shutters are all down. They clack and bang against their frames as a trooper working the front desk emerges from the lobby to push the button that opens it.

"Okay. Okay," he moans as whoever it is outside presses the buzzer once more.

The shutter lifts slowly to reveal a tall figure in a hooded coat. When the screen is high enough, the person steps under it, flicks back the hood, and reveals a pretty face crowned by pure white hair.

She gets an ID out. "I'm Special Agent Anderson," she says, holding it up to the cop. "I've come to see the three people you have in custody. One of them I believe has been identified as Michael Henderson."

"You're early," the trooper says as he closes the shutter. "We were told FBI wouldn't be here for another two hours."

"Well, I'm here now. So you'd better take me to whoever is in charge."

Several corridors later, they come across a large man with a wide, square jaw and hair the color of fire. He is standing outside Interview Room One, gazing through the window.

Agent Anderson stops at the one-way and studies Peter's dead eyes. The vacant, almost featureless face is the type that could be described as anyone in a police report. Providing barely enough information for a lineup of nothing more than nondescript handsome white men.

The big man in the corridor is Chief Daniels. He turns his considerable bulk to face her.

"Who are you?" he grunts.

She doesn't turn from the window. Instead, she holds her ID up sideways and says in a nonchalant wheeze, "Special Agent Lynnette Anderson. I take it you're the chief."

"I am."

"And those two in there are your detectives?"

"They are."

His eyes narrow on her. "How come you got here so quick?"

"I was in town. He said much yet?"

"Not really."

"What about the kid?"

"Reckons they been living out in the country on some farm. Apart from that, the social worker can't get squat outta him."

"The old woman?"

Chief Daniels points a finger at the one-way. "You see that blood on the detective's ripped shirt and the sore complexion of his face?"

"Uh-huh."

"Well, she did that to him for the kindness of giving her a cup of coffee. Since then, we've left her well alone."

"You mind if I try speaking with her?"

The chief looks surprised. He was expecting her to pull his two detectives out and take over the interview with Peter. As it goes, he is more than happy to have her waste time with the old woman.

Giving a dry laugh, he tells her, "Be my guest."

Mother doesn't look up from the table when Special

Agent Anderson walks into the interview room. Not until the woman is sitting dead opposite.

When she does look up, Mother's blank expression begins to slowly crease into one of surprise. Her eyes brighten and she drops the dumb act.

"You remember me, don't you?" Anderson says as they stare at each other.

"Catherine," the old woman breathes.

"That's right, Mother," Ibliss says. "It's Catherine."

SIXTY

Headlights emanate from the dark storm. The grille of a Ford pickup follows, as if manifesting from the swirling, frozen air itself. Four men line the front seats, all squashed together.

Semyon waits for them at the front of the house. Bruno the Alsatian sitting dutifully at his side. The Ford Raptor comes to a stop. The four men get out and soon they are lined up before him, their faces poking from the hoods of white coveralls.

For the sake of the mission each man has been named with a number. Number One is team leader. He is of average build with a scar running down the left side of his face like a jagged crack. Number Two is a short diminutive man with mean little eyes. Number Three, who is built like a rake, has long blond hair tied in a ponytail. The last, Number Four, is formidable. He is built like a wrestler and towers over the others.

"You are the Hunter?" Number One asks in Russian.

"I am."

"I worked with you in Georgia eight years ago."

"I remember."

"Let's hope this one goes as well as that did."

"Let's hope."

Number Two, who has been looking at the dog the whole time, asks Semyon, "May I pet your dog?"

The short man inches toward the Alsatian. It immediately begins snarling. Semyon looks down at Bruno, then back at Two as the wet-boy freezes midway.

"Better not," Semyon warns. Then addressing the whole group, he says, "We'll go inside. I have a plan already."

"Parfyon said you have guns?" Three asks.

"I do."

"Assault rifles?"

"And a whole lot more. Come in. I'll show you."

And with that Semyon leads them into the house, the dog following behind. Growling back over its shoulder at the wet-boys when they get too close to its new master.

SIXTY-ONE

"COME ON, MAN. WHO THE HELL *ARE* YOU?"

Detective Gates shouts it at Peter in exasperation. Stood up out of his chair, hands planted on the table, he sweats profusely. His shirt covered in dark patches.

"I told you," Peter says coolly. "I'm no one. It's Tommy you need to worry about."

Gates ignores him. "No prints. No ID. Nothing but a name the kid gave us. Peter. But you must have come from somewhere."

"I come from nowhere."

Murphy is shaking his head. Gates, who still stands, turns to his partner and gives a face that says, *"You try."*

Murphy leans forwards. In a low, ominous whisper, he asks Peter, "You get all that money we found in your car from trading kids?"

Peter swivels to meet Detective Murphy with cold eyes.

"I'm not a trafficker," he says with some force.

"Yeah. Then how'd you end up with the kid and a trunk containing ten million dollars?"

Peter stares at him.

"Where were you taking him? The docks at Anchorage? Put him on a ship heading to the Middle East or Asia? Some rich Arab prince that likes kids, huh?"

"You want the truth?"

"I'm all ears."

"He's my son."

Both detectives make faces.

"Wow," Murphy snuffs. "You hear that?"

"I sure did," Gates says. "Sounds like we got ourselves a real deluded son-of-a-bitch. Thinks the kid he bought off a kidnapper is his own."

Peter sighs. "You know what?"

"What?"

"None of this matters."

"And why's that?"

"Because soon *he* will be here. And when that happens, nothing will matter."

"You mean this bogeyman you keep talking about? Your accomplice Tommy. The one who murdered four state troopers and a pilot out in Fairbanks?"

"And he'll murder a whole lot more pretty soon," Peter assures him. "My advice is that you go to the arsenal and unlock the strongest guns you have. Arm every single trooper here and keep the shutters down. Because there's a whole lot more coming this way than just a storm."

. . .

"I don't understand, Mother," Ibliss says. "Who is Misha?"

"My husband," the old woman tells her.

"You were married?"

"Yes. We were supposed to defect together." Her face goes sad, pensive. "But he never made it. I waited for him until there was no more time. We had to leave." She looks up at Ibliss. Her eyes brighten. "And now he has come to take me back to Russia."

"But the man you were with isn't Misha. He is a man we know as the Hunter. Too young to be your husband."

Mother narrows her eyes on the assassin. "You are confusing me, Catherine."

"I am sorry for that, Mother. But you have to understand that the one you think is Misha is actually an enemy. He was going to hand you over to a man named Parfyon Rogozhin."

Mother's gray eyes enflame. Her hands tug on the handcuff chain.

"Parfyon!" the old woman practically spits. "Misha told me he was dead."

"He lied. He's not Misha. And Parfyon Rogozhin is very much alive. The Hunter was taking you to him. They have a rendezvous. I need to know where that is."

Mother's eyes go blank. She looks deeply confused and Ibliss almost feels sad for her.

"I don't understand," the old woman whispers.

"He was tricking you. Pretending to be Misha so that you'd come peacefully."

Mother muses over it. Ibliss lets her. Stays silent as the

old woman's eyes stare into the middle distance and her expression slowly changes from bewilderment to a half-light realization. Tears begin to fall gently down her cheeks. She comes alive and look directly at Ibliss.

"He's dead, isn't he?"

"Who?"

"My Misha. The one I left behind."

"I'm afraid so, Mother."

The gray eyes narrow, the tears spill out. "Then who was...?" She squints. Searches her mind. Then her voice is no more than a whisper. "I get so confused, Catherine. Sometimes it is like I'm in another place. Somewhere else, but at the same time, I'm still here. In two places at once."

The old woman feels something warm on top of her hand and looks down. Ibliss has slipped her own hand across the table. Mother trembles underneath it.

"I'm so scared, Catherine," she confesses. "This... This confusion. It scares me. More than anything I have ever experienced."

"I'm so sorry for that, Mother," Ibliss says softly while squeezing the hand. "But I need you to think."

"About what?"

"About what the Hunter talked to you about. You must've talked, right?"

"Yes."

"Then did he ever tell you why Parfyon Rogozhin would want you back in Russia alive?"

Mother tries to think. But before long she is clenching her eyelids shut and shaking her head. "I don't know," she gasps. "I don't know."

. . .

"When can I see him?"

It is the innumerable time he has asked, and for the innumerable time the social worker tells Michael, "I'm afraid you can't."

"But why not?"

They're walking through the precinct, on their way back to the Detectives' Office. Candy having taken the kid on a guided tour of the building after he'd begged her. "I've always dreamed of being a cop," he'd said. "Can't you show me around? What's the Evidence Room like?"

Candy had cheerfully agreed. Anything to get the kid to open up.

They'd visited every room in the place except for the interview rooms. A tour that had lasted a total time of twenty seven minutes, thirteen seconds. Wasilla Police Department not exactly big.

The feeble tour was sufficient, though. The kid believing he's gathered enough intel from it.

Candy changes the subject.

"Are you looking forward to seeing your grandparents?"

"I asked you why I can't see him," Michael says dryly.

"They should be here by tomorrow afternoon if the storm passes. Coming all the way up from—"

"I want to see him," the kid interrupts.

Candy sighs. "You can't, Michael. Okay. He's being questioned."

"Then take me to Mother."

"I can't do that either."

They are standing at the door to the Detectives' Office. Staring at each other.

"Look, Michael," the social worker says in a soft voice, "I know you've had it rough. I mean, you're a darn hero for being so with it after what you've been through. But there's things that have happened to you that you just can't understand right now. Not until later when you've had a chance to think about it all."

Michael steps right up to her, never breaking eye contact.

"I want to see him," the kid seethes.

THE DETECTIVES SPILL out of Interview Room One.

"Chief, we can't get no sense outta him," Gates says.

Chief Daniels shakes his fat head at them both. "You disappoint me, boys."

Murphy goes to add to his partner's assessment when the door to Room Two opens and Ibliss strolls out.

"I need you to place her in your most secure cell," she tells the chief.

"And why's that, Special Agent Anderson?" Daniels asks.

"FBI already?" Gates interjects, a bemused expression wrinkling his nose.

"Says she was in town," Daniels informs him.

"I think someone very dangerous is coming. I need you to lock the station down. No one is to come in or out."

"Now hang on," the chief says. "We can't do that in the middle of a storm. There could be people stranded out there. We'd be letting them die."

"If you let this person in even more people will die."

"Who in the hell's coming?"

Gates and Murphy are frowning at each other.

"Wait," Detective Gates says. "You mean *he* was telling the truth?"

He's pointing at the one-way: at Peter.

"There's no time to explain," Ibliss tells him. "Whoever is coming will be heavily armed. He may have help. Where is your arsenal?"

The chief looks at her with a dumb expression. "Hold up," he stammers. "I don't get it. What the hell is happening here? Who in the hell is gonna attack my police department?"

"The Hunter."

"The Hunter?"

"Yes. And we need to act now. Before it is too late."

BLUSTERING wind rattles the hell out of the backdoor shutter. The K9 unit is close by and the dogs howl and bark in their cages.

On duty is Trooper Lee. He sits at the booking counter, his boots rested up on top, chair leaned back on its hind legs.

Reading a Jack Reacher book while picking his nose, he uses the same finger that he stuffs up his nostril to turn the pages.

Right behind him are the bars of the drunk tank. Inside is a single occupant. An old hobo by the name of Mac. He sits on the bench at the back, scraping dead skin off the balls of his feet with long dirty fingernails.

A telephone stands on a wall close by. When it starts bleating, Trooper Lee swears, folds his page, and answers it.

"What's that, Chief?" he says after a short while. "Lock-down the back door? No one else allowed in? But what if... Okay okay, Chief. I hear ya. No backchat. Okay, I'll get it done."

He places the phone back and walks to the shutter.

"What is it, Lee?" asks the tramp from inside the tank, having wandered up to the bars.

"It's nothing, Mac. Just sit yourself back down."

Trooper Lee reaches the shutter, but right at the moment his hand hovers above the isolation switch, it jolts into action and begins moving upwards. Someone having pressed the outside button.

Lee stands back and waits. The storm billows in through the opening. Two men are slowly revealed. The first he recognizes as Trooper Beatty, his uniform coated in snow. The second he doesn't recognize.

Trooper Beatty leads the other man into the precinct by a set of handcuffed wrists.

"Phew!" he says, taking his hat off and shaking the snow out of his hair. "I thought my dick was gonna freeze off!"

"Who in the heck is that?" Lee asks, looking the prisoner up and down.

The man that's been brought in is very tall and very skinny with long blond hair. But it isn't his physical state that most alarms Lee. It is his clothing. He stands there in white hooded coveralls, dripping all over the linoleum floor tiles, swaying from side to side on a pair of long feet, red eyes glazed over.

"This joker," Beatty says, "was just hanging out in the storm. Wasted by the looks of things."

"Well, you're lucky," Lee tells Beatty. "Daniels just called. Wants me to lock the back door. No one in or out, he says."

"Really?"

"Yeah."

"Why?"

"Not a clue. He told me not to ask questions."

Beatty makes a face. Shakes his head. "Whatever. I'll just shove him in the tank with old Mac. We'll book him when he's sober."

"You searched him?"

"Yeah. He's clean. Just the clothes he's standing in." Trooper Beatty turns to the drunk. "Okay, Bozo. Let's go."

Lee opens the door to the barred cage for him. As the prisoner steps through, Beatty stops him and removes the cuffs. Old Mac sits at the end, eyeing the stranger with a dubious look. One drunk sussing another.

Once the cuffs are off, Lee closes the door on him and the drunk takes a seat at the other end of the bench from Mac. Sitting forwards, his hands rested on his thighs, he doesn't make a sound. Just stares into space. As if he's waiting for something.

WASILLA POLICE DEPARTMENT's arsenal isn't much more than a locked cabinet. It contains nothing heavier than two Colt M4 carbines, five Remington Model 870 pump action shotguns, and some flares for whatever reason. There are no rifles, and only the sidearms the troopers have. Many of which are privately owned by the officers themselves.

Slim pickings.

It is while Ibliss passes one of the Remington 870s down a line of troopers that the voice of Chief Daniels erupts behind the mass of people blocking the hallway.

"Hold it there!" the chief shouts.

Ibliss thought she'd escaped him. That he'd gone off and left her to it. But he hadn't. He's been in his office making enquiries.

Everyone turns as the chief's wide body waddles through the crowd.

"Put those weapons back," he says red-faced. "That's an order."

"What's going on, Chief?" one of the troopers asks.

"*She*," Daniels spits, pointing a fat finger at Ibliss, "is an imposter."

"What the hell are you talking about?" Ibliss says.

"I just spoke to a friend of mine at the FBI's Anchorage office. Agent Cooper. He tells me he's never heard of a Special Agent Anderson in Alaska. Says that the team he sent out got caught in the storm. Won't be with us till the morning. Says there's nothing about any one else coming early."

"I'm not with Anchorage," Ibliss replies confidently. "I'm from Washington. I told you. I was in the area."

Chief Daniels steps right up to her.

"But that don't make no sense," he growls. "'Cause Coop tells me that no one should have arrived yet." He turns to the troopers. "Now put those guns away. I want every one of them back in there and accounted for. Trudy?"

"Yes, Chief?" Trooper Trudy Kelly says as she comes before him.

"Put handcuffs on *Special Agent Anderson* and escort her to the cells. Hand her over to Trooper Lee. She can wait the storm out there."

"You're making a terrible mistake," Ibliss says as Trooper Kelly comes toward her.

"Trudy, take her away."

"I'm sorry, ma'am," the curly haired trooper says, coming toward Ibliss with her handcuffs drawn.

"Till we find out who you really are," Chief Daniels says when the cuffs click over her wrists, "I want you away from my gun cabinet."

As Trooper Kelly escorts her away, Ibliss calls out, "He's coming. And if you're not ready, he's going to kill you all."

Candy of Child Services walks sheepishly up the corridor towards the interview rooms. Gates doesn't notice her at first. He is too busy sipping coffee from a Styrofoam cup, gazing through the one-way, eyes fixed on the blank stare of the stranger in Room One.

"I'm sorry to bother you, Detective," the social worker says, catching his attention and making him turn.

"What is it, ma'am?"

"The boy insists on seeing the, eh, suspect."

Gates frowns. It sends a shiver up his spine.

"He said why?"

"No. Just that he wants to see him."

Gates turns back to the one-way. Not to Peter, though. No. He fastens his gaze to the CCTV camera in the corner of the room that films everything.

"Maybe we should let him," he says.

Candy looks astonished. "I don't think that's healthy. Or ethical. If, as we suspect, the boy has been abused by this man, it may trigger him."

"Yeah. But they also might say something to each other that lets on exactly what the hell went on six months ago down in California. Explain who the hell that son-of-a-bitch is."

Gates is pointing across the hallway. Right at Peter.

WHEN TROOPER KELLY reaches the cell block with Ibliss, she finds Trooper Lee nowhere to be seen.

"Where the hell is he?" she mutters under her breath as they stand at the abandoned counter. "Hey, Mac?" she calls into the tank.

The old tramp looks like he's snoozing. Sitting on the bench with his head hanging between his shoulders, hands rested on his knees. She calls him again and he snuffs and shakes himself like a waking dog.

"Where's Lee?" she asks when his sore eyes look their way.

"He went off with Ned."

"You mean Trooper Beatty?"

"Yup. Ned Beatty." The tramp shows off the few front teeth he still has, impressed at his own joke. "It was him what brung the other guy in," he adds.

"The other guy?" Kelly puts to him, wrinkling her nose.

Mac appears to be all alone inside the tank.

"Yeah," the drunk snorted. "He showed me a trick."

"Okay, Mac." Turning to Ibliss, she rolls her eyes. "Whatever you say."

The assassin stands there patiently. Waiting for her moment.

A set of swing doors open outwards and Troopers Beatty and Lee emerge.

"Hey, Lee," Kelly says in a sharp tone, standing with Ibliss at the counter. "Where've you been?"

Lee is about to answer when he spots Ibliss. He swallows, glances back over his shoulder to his friend, whose own eyes are stuck on the atomic blonde, then begins strolling toward the counter like he's John Travolta in *Saturday Night Fever*.

"What's up?" he asks Trooper Kelly in as cool a manner as he can.

Trooper Kelly frowns. Turns sharply to Trooper Beatty. "I don't need *you*."

Beatty shakes himself, smiles at Ibliss, leaves.

"I need you to book her in," Kelly tells Lee.

"What for?" he asks while taking a seat behind the counter.

Kelly has a finger to her bottom lip as she thinks.

"I'm not sure," she says after a while.

"Look," Ibliss butts in, "can we hurry this up?"

"I guess," Kelly says, "it'll have to be for impersonating an officer."

Lee wrinkles his brow. "Impersonating an officer?"

"Yeah. Chief says she was pretending to be FBI."

Lee's brow creases up even more. "O-k-a-y."

He begins typing it into the computer that sits atop the counter. The whole procedure doesn't take long. Less than five minutes later, Trooper Kelly is handing the prisoner over to Trooper Lee and he, sweating profusely by now, takes her by the elbow.

"This way," he says.

It is then, as he begins guiding her past the tank toward the single cells, that Trooper Lee stops sharp.

"What the hell?"

He stands frozen, eyes staring into the tank. It is the first time he's looked into it since coming through those doors. Too busy looking at Ibliss.

"Where's the other guy?" he asks, turning to Kelly.

"What other guy?"

"The one in the boiler suit."

"How in the hell should I know?"

"See!" Mac exclaims with a toothless grin, rocking back and forth on the bench. "I told you there was another guy."

"Mac," Trooper Lee says, "who took him?"

"No one did. He done a trick."

"A trick?"

"Yeah. He said I had to close my eyes and count to fifty. When I opened them, he was gone. Probably used that key I saw him pull outta hisself when I peeked."

"What key?"

The tramp's grin grows all the way up his whiskers. "He pulled the darn thing right outta his ass!"

Mac slaps his thigh as he bursts into laughter.

Frustrated, Lee asks, "What are you talking about, Mac?"

"Said it was his magic key that he pulled right outta his ass!"

"Shit!" Lee says in a panic.

"Who is he talking about?"

He turns to Ibliss. It was she who had asked.

"Some drunk dressed up in a boiler suit. No ID. Nothing."

"And now he's loose?"

"It looks like it."

Ibliss goes pale. "It has begun," she says. "Do you hear me? The attack has begun."

SIXTY-TWO

Candy guides Michael to Interview Room One. Detective Gates is standing across the hallway from it.

"You good, kid?" he asks Michael when they reach him.

The kid says nothing.

Gates turns to the social worker. "So we're all good?"

"Yeah," Candy replies nervously. "But I still don't think this is right. I could get into trouble."

Gates leans into the social worker and keeps his voice down. "Just think. There could be other kids this sick bastard has stashed away. Think about them."

While they talk Michael stands right beside them, staring at Peter, their eyes meeting across the one-way.

"You ready, Michael?"

The kid faces Candy. She is smiling. It is so fake the kid finds it irritating and can't help smirking at her a little.

"Sure," he says.

They move to the door. As she opens it, the social worker glances over her shoulder at Detective Gates.

He winks confidentially at her.

Peter turns to the door the second it opens. When he sees Michael, the blank look drops. His expression becomes benevolent yet sad.

"Take a seat, Michael," the social worker tells the kid.

"Why they got him chained to the table like that?" he asks her.

"Because he's dangerous."

"He ain't dangerous. So long as you're not."

Candy smiles nervously.

Michael takes a seat across the table.

Peter asks, "How they treating you?"

"They think you and Mother have been abusing me."

"What have you told them?"

"Nada."

Michael stares into Peter's eye, then looks downwards. Without anyone except Peter noticing, the kid makes a couple of quick hand signals. Peter, in turn, makes a reply with his own. It is all so quick that not even the watching Gates sees any of the secret conversation.

"Now, Michael," Candy says, standing at the open door. "You are not to move from that chair, you hear?"

"Yes, ma'am," the kid replies obediently, sitting perfectly still and staring into Peter's eyes.

"You're not to pass him anything."

"Yes, ma'am."

"You cannot touch him."

"I won't."

"Okay. I'm going to leave now. Just remember that we're right outside the room. And will be watching. There's no need to be scared."

"Goodbye, Candy," the kid says in a nonchalant tone as she removes herself from the room.

She pauses at the doorway, glances back at Michael, goes to says something, doesn't, so leaves. She is walking across the hallway to Detective Gates when the kid gets up from the chair and rushes to the door.

"Hey, what the...?!" Gate says as he does.

By the time the detective has rushed across the hallway and is gripping the doorknob, Michael has already used a key to lock it from the other side. Gates goes to grab his own and it's at that point that he realizes the kid must've pickpocketed it a moment ago while he was busy speaking to the social worker.

Gates moves to the one-way. Michael is using a paperclip he stole from one of the offices to pick open Peter's handcuffs.

"Hey!" Gates cries out, hammering on the one-way.

Michael turns sharply to it. Runs up to the mirror. Pulls the blind down over it.

"Little shit!" Gates cries out as he beats his hands against the pane.

"What's going on?"

It's Detective Murphy.

"John, help me bust this door down," Gates cries at him.

Murphy moves his considerable bulge as quickly as it will shuffle. The two men then stand back from the door and ready their shoulders.

"On three," Gates says. "One, two, three!"

They rush at the door. It bends inwards, creaks, but doesn't give way.

They hit it again.

By the fifth time it bursts inwards, the bolt ripping the keep and the jamb out of the frame.

Both men pull up and scowl the second they clamber into the room.

It's empty.

"Look," Murphy says, pointing at the ceiling tiles.

Like most of the ceilings in the building, Interview Room One has a drop-down ceiling, made up of light tiles balancing on metal racks that hang down about two feet from the actual ceiling.

Several of the tiles are out of place. Right where there's a gap of about a foot between the wall and the permanent ceiling. Giving access to the adjoining room.

"THAT'S RIGHT," Trooper Lee barks into his radio. "We got a prisoner escaped from the tank."

He and Trooper Beatty are barreling along a corridor that bisects the building. Rounding a corner, they almost bump straight into the beer-pregnant belly of Chief Daniels. He stands with a whole bunch of troopers, their faces turned earnestly to their commander.

"Chief?" Lee says. "Chief, we got an escaped prisoner."

"You what?"

"God darn drunk has got out of the tank somehow."

"Now how in the hell—"

"Chief?"

The big man turns. Detectives Gates, Murphy and the social worker are jogging up to them.

"The Henderson suspect has gone," Gates tells him.

"The boy, too," Candy adds.

The chief goes red. "What in the hell is going on in this place?"

And then, as if to answer him, the lights go out and the building is drenched in black, until the emergency lighting comes on, drenching them alternately in red.

"Okay. Okay," the chief barks. "It's just the power. Probably the storm. Someone go check it out. Switch over to the generators. The rest of y'all split up and find these missing prisoners."

PETER AND MICHAEL are already in the parking lot.

After crawling through the gap, the two had traveled into and out of several rooms via similar gaps above the false ceilings, before emerging into a stationary cupboard. From there they had made their way through the building, avoiding the confused troopers that wandered about. In the abandoned canteen, they had climbed atop some tables and escaped via a skylight.

Their entire getaway had been based on reconnaissance work Michael had completed during Candy's tour. It was in the breaker room that he had spotted the gaps at the tops of the walls where the ventilation shafts went through. At least a foot gap on one side of the metal chute. Enough to fit through.

"Can I take a look?" he'd asked. Candy had shrugged and replied, "I don't see why not." The social worker had even footed the stepladder while he'd gazed all the way along the cavities to Interview Room One.

Peter and Michael make a beeline for the flashing orange indicator lights that illuminate the fog when the kid presses the key fob he stole from one of the rooms earlier.

"We're not leaving her, are we?" Michael asks when they reach the police cruiser.

Peter says nothing as he opens the driver's door.

"Get in," he tells the kid. Then, right before he closes the door on him, he adds, "Wait here."

"You're going back for her?"

"Just keep hidden and wait."

And with that, Peter turns on his heels and marches back toward the precinct. Michael watching all the way up to the point when he's swallowed by the storm.

TROOPER BEATTY VOLUNTEERED to check the electricity. As he gets closer to the breaker room, an ominous smell reaches his nostrils: burning plastic. Like the type used for insulating electrical wires.

The room fizzes and hums. His right hand is already rested on his sidearm. As he moves around a cabinet that blocks his view of the terminal, he lifts his radio slowly to his mouth, then freezes.

Sparks and smoke trail from the fuse board where a fire axe pokes out, the head buried deep.

Trooper Beatty is about to call it in when something moves to his left. He twists that way, pistol drawn. Trains it on the man standing at the far end of the room.

"So this is where you've got to," Beatty says. "How in the hell did you get outta that tank?"

Number Three initially wears a blank look. But when

Trooper Beatty steps toward him, a high-cheeked grin slowly creeps its way up his face, until it is spread across most of it.

Beatty stops. Frowns.

Not at the grin.

At the AK-74 hanging on a leather strap from Three's neck.

"Where in the hell'd you get that?" the trooper asks.

"*He* gave it to me."

"Who?"

"Him."

The tall man points over Beatty's shoulder.

The trooper slowly swivels around to find a truck of a man standing right behind him. He is as wide as the other is thin. A sinister grin similar to his friend's stretches across his brutal face.

Before Beatty can move, the hunting knife is through his chest plate and buried in his heart. Number Four then snatches the gun from his hand as though he were snatching a rattle from a baby and pushes the trooper off the blade.

As Trooper Beatty lands on the floor, Four states into his comms, "West point clear."

THE SECOND TROOPER LEE enters the cell block through the swing doors, he knows it's not good. Cold wind billows down the hallway. Snowflakes float in the air. At the end the back door is wide open. The shutter all the way up. The blizzard billowing inwards.

Lee already has his gun out.

"What the...?" he breathes when he spots that the single

cell he had locked Ibliss in only minutes earlier is now empty.

"That you, Lee?"

The trooper turns to face the tank. Old Mac pokes his head out of the bars.

"Any chance you can close that door?" the old man asks.

"Who opened it?"

"The guy opened it. Let his friends in."

"His friends?"

"Yeah. Whole bunch of guys."

Lee gazes into the storm. Without power, they won't be able to close it back up again. Then another thought slowly creeps over him. He turns left to the double doors that lead to the K9 Unit. The dogs have been making noise since the start of the storm.

Now they are strangely silent.

Gripping his Glock, Trooper Lee begins making his way toward the doors. He pushes one side. It swings in with ease.

Within the red light, he immediately notices the open cage doors. Then spots the dogs. Three Alsatians standing at the opposite end of the room. Growling in guttural undertones. Eyes honed on the trooper as he approaches.

Trooper Lee puts the Glock away and is about to give a command when a man emerges from behind a stack of cages to his right. He's dressed like a trooper. But, the thing is, Lee has never seen him before in Wasilla.

"Who are you?"

"I'm the dog handler," the man says in a cool tone. "Wanna see me handle the dogs?"

Lee frowns.

The man whistles. The guttural growls turn into snarls. The dogs leap forward, jaws wide open, each grabbing a part of the trooper, mauling and wrestling him down onto the ground.

While they rip the trooper apart, Semyon stands there, watching. A sly smile creeping its way up the sides of his mouth as the man screams beneath the dogs.

CHIEF DANIELS and at least half of all the troopers clog up a corridor.

"It's like that FBI agent was saying," one of the troopers is blurting out. "We're under attack."

"She weren't no FBI agent," Daniels insists.

"But where in the hell has Beatty got to?"

"He probably don't have his radio on him. Troopers Bradley and Sanchez will soon find him."

It is then that Trooper Bradley calls on the radio.

"*We just found Beatty dead,*" comes his crackling voice. "*Some son-of-a-bitch has stabbed him in the heart. What in the hell's going on, Chief?*"

Chief Daniels doesn't say anything for a while. Just stands there slack-jawed and staring blankly ahead.

"Chief?"

"Hey, Chief?"

"Chief, what'll we do?"

"*Chief, did you hear me?*" the radio exclaims.

Chief Daniels shakes himself. Comes alive. "Okay. Fuck it," he says as a bead of sweat runs down the side of his face. "Let's empty the arsenal."

"Yeah!" several troopers yip.

The gang march off. Fire in their bellies. But before they get farther than a few yards, every one of them freezes.

A short man stands at the end of the hall, his cold-eyed face poking from the hood of his white coveralls. Holding what looks like a can of soup.

It's not. It's a flashbang.

He tosses it at them and the thing goes off, illuminating the corridor in strobing light.

Temporarily blinded, the troopers turn the other way.

That's when they spot the second man.

He throws a smoke grenade into their group. As it hisses fumes into the air, making everyone cough, the AK-74s begin barking.

Panic erupts in the troopers. Some run. Some draw pistols. Some don't get the chance, mown down by a hail of bullets that cuts through the group from both ends. Chief Daniels thinks only of himself. Insulated in the middle, he dashes for the door of an office and throws himself into the room. Abandoning his troopers as they're gunned down.

"I need every available trooper to meet me at the arsenal," he whispers into his radio, marching across the room and leaving it via a rear door. "Now!"

Mac sits in the tank, a blanket wrapped around him, teeth chattering. He is staring at the open backdoor when a figure emerges from the storm.

The old drunk says nothing. Merely watches the figure keenly with his bloodshot eyes.

Peter stops in front of the tank. Takes a few seconds to look at the old man. Then he turns his eyes to the rest of the room. Spotting a row of thick winter coats hanging from a rack, he takes one and hands it through the bars to the tramp.

"Here," he says, holding it out.

Mac gets up from the bench. Wanders over, reaches a trembling hand out and grabs the coat.

"You with the others?" the tramp asks as he steps back to the other side of the tank and places it over his frail body.

Peter shakes his head.

"Son-of-a-bitch killed Lee," Mac whimpers. "Set the dogs on him."

He points a bony finger past Peter at a set of double doors with the words "K9 Unit" written above them on a plaque.

"Is the man still there?" he asks.

"No. He left. Bastard was dressed like a cop. But I ain't ever seen him in Wasilla. And I know every cop from here to Anchorage."

Peter makes his way slowly toward the double doors. Pushes one side gently. Enough so he can see through the two-inches gap he makes.

The dogs are back in their cages. Blood matts their muzzles. In the red emergency lighting it looks black. Like engine oil.

They begin growling the second Peter enters the room. By the time he is reaching the splayed feet of Trooper Lee, the snarling has increased to a crescendo of vicious barks.

The assassin freezes. Turns to them. Makes eye contact with each dog individually, one after the other, until the dogs gradually settle down.

Peter's attention turns back to the dead man.

Trooper Lee no longer has a face. It is all exposed bone.

Ignoring the horrific wounds, he crouches beside the body and removes Lee's Glock 43X from its holster. Checking the magazine, he is glad to find it fully loaded.

THE WALLS of Interview Room Two tremble. The whole station is at war. Machine-gun fire. Pop-pop of pistols. Flash-bangs exploding. The thud of feet pounding the floor as people rampage past.

Men's screams.

Someone begging for his life.

A rat-a-tat-tat of automatic gunfire bringing an end to the pleading.

Mother sits consumed by hazy thoughts. Chained to the table and humming Irving Berlin, she is not sure if it is the Americans or the Armenians who have captured her. Or perhaps she is in Afghanistan. No. The room is too cold for that and the furniture too neat. This has to be Western Europe. But where?

France?

While her mind meanders in circles, the door handle begins flipping up and down. The lock clicks and the door bursts open.

Mother turns to it. Smiles.

"Catherine."

Ibliss comes into the room, heeling the door shut behind her.

"Keep your hands still," she says taking a pick and approaching the handcuffs. "We haven't got a lot of time."

They leave the interview room and Ibliss guides Mother

away from the shooting and explosions, the ground vibrating beneath their feet.

"Hey!" a familiar voice shouts behind them. "Stop right there!"

They freeze. Spin around to find the bear-like Daniels lumbering toward them with his pistol trained on Ibliss. Detective Gates isn't far behind, his own weapon drawn and pointed at the assassin.

"Put your hands in the air," Chief Daniels barks. "Both of you."

Ibliss stands with Mother directly behind her. She slowly raises her hands. So, too, does Mother. All the time gazing at the back of Ibliss's trousers. At the Beretta M9 tucked in the waistband.

"Cuff the old woman," Daniels tells Gates.

The detective tucks his pistol in its holster, removes his handcuffs, and cautiously moves toward them.

It is when he is blocking the way between Ibliss and Daniels that Mother strikes. She snatches the Beretta and fires three rapid shots.

One hits Chief Daniels in the hand, sending the pistol spinning. The second hits his left knee. The third his right. His legs buckling underneath him.

Within a matter of seconds the smoking gun is trained on Gates. The detective stands there paralyzed from fear, a hand frozen over his holstered gun.

"Don't even think about it," Mother growls.

Ibliss marches up to Detective Gates and snatches the handcuffs from him, grabs his arm, spins him around, and snaps them over his wrists.

"Who the hell are you people?" he asks.

Her answer is brutal.

She removes his pistol, raises it high, and brings it crashing down on his crown. The blow knocking the detective out cold.

Just like he has planned, all the action is happening around the arsenal at the opposite end of the building. And, as planned, it gives Semyon a relatively clear path to the interview rooms.

He is disappointed to find them both empty.

This he hadn't planned.

While he stands inside Room One pondering his next move, a trooper jogs past the open door and stops when he notices Semyon.

"Hey," the trooper calls inside the room from the hallway. "We need to get to the others and help them."

Semyon has his back to the door. The trooper only sees the uniform he's wearing. Without turning around, the Hunter asks, "Where's the old woman?"

"I don't know. I think the chief moved her. Come on, we need to help the others."

Semyon, yet to look, raises his Margolin MCM and sends several bullets into the guy's chest. He then turns to the door, walks out the room and stands over the still breathing trooper. The guy looks up at him from the floor with terror burning in his eyes. A thread of blood pours from the edge of his mouth.

Staring right back into his eyes, Semyon aims the pistol and puts another two bullets in him.

Around the next corner, Chief Daniels has managed to

sit himself up against a wall. He is holding his bust hand with his good, his legs stretched out before him, bleeding and useless.

"Hey! Trooper," he blurts as Semyon reaches him. "Get me out of here. That old bitch shot me."

Semyon crouches before him. It is then, as he makes eye contact, that the chief frowns. Realizing for the first time that he doesn't recognize the man reaching a hand out and grabbing him by the scruff of his shirt collar.

The chief shudders as the cold steel of Semyon's Margolin is pressed to his fat chin.

"Where is the old woman?" Semyon growls.

"She took her."

"*Who* took her?"

"The FBI agent."

Semyon narrows his eyes. "Is she pretty, athletic, plump lips you'd give your life to kiss?"

The chief gently nods.

"Where'd they go?"

"That way."

Daniels is pointing down the corridor with his good hand.

"Thank you," Semyon says before pulling the trigger and blowing the chief's brains all the way up the wall.

SIXTY-THREE

Ibliss guides Mother to the edge of the building's flat roof. The pair of them have just emerged through a skylight in much the same way as Peter and Michael earlier.

At the edge, the assassin kneels, takes the old woman by the hands, and lowers her down to the ground one story below. She drops her the last two feet, the thick snow cushioning the fall.

Ibliss jumps down. Upon landing, she grabs ahold of Mother and goes to guide her onwards when the old woman staggers and has to stop.

"What's the matter?"

"I feel... dizzy," Mother tells her breathlessly. "All this... is making my head rush."

"We can rest a little further on. But not now. They'll be coming."

Mother gazes at her. As she does, her winkled brow furrows. She reaches a hand out and touches Ibliss's cheek.

"Catherine," she breathes, "what did we do to you?"

Ibliss goes to answer but doesn't get the chance. She can hear running feet across the roof, coming quick on their position.

"Come on," she says, hauling Mother forwards.

THE HALLWAY on the eastern side ricochets with a pyrotechnic explosion of sounds. Smoke clogs the narrow L-shaped corridor. Everyone wears gas masks. They can hardly see. The troopers fire blindly, their muzzle flashes lighting up the gray, swirling air, a full-on Fourth of July parade right inside the building.

Number Three and Number Four hold one end of the hallway. Number Two holds the other. This pins the majority of the cops at the arsenal.

Semyon's voice comes over their comms. In Russian he says, "*I need you all outside. Ibliss and the old woman are on the western edge of the building.*"

"Copy that," Three says.

The beanpole turns sideways to the alcove on the opposite side where his much broader partner hides in cover. They nod at each other and shoulder their weapons. Four takes a smoke grenade. Three grabs a flashbang. They toss them toward the troopers.

More smoke. More flashes. More confusion.

The two men leave their cover, spraying the hallway with suppressive fire as they beat a retreat toward the back door.

. . .

Having followed the same route as the women, Semyon marches across the parking lot, eyes concentrated on the two indefinite shadows that amble onwards through the hazy air about twenty yards in front. It is a shame that he cannot tell between the two in such low visibility. Otherwise he could terminate Ibliss without fear of it being Mother.

"Katya Igorevna," he calls into the storm. "It is me. Misha. Your husband. Where are you, my love?"

It doesn't take long for a reply.

"Misha?!" Mother's voice calls from the blinding snowstorm.

One of the shadows has stopped and is looking his way. The other grabs her.

Semyon knows who is who.

He raises his pistol. Readies the shot. The movement of air and the fact that they have begun running makes it harder, as well as the two women being so close together. His finger strokes the trigger, he goes to fire—doesn't get the chance.

He spots something in the corner of his eye.

Muzzle flash. Pop pop.

Semyon is already diving. He rolls along the ground. One of the bullets grazes his body armor. Emerging from the roll, he sends three blasts of the Margolin at a figure that moves rapidly within the storm. The shots miss. The shadow gets low, lunges inside his reach. A hand bursts from the blizzard. Grabs the Margolin. Semyon uses his free hand to block the figure's rising pistol. They become locked up, holding each other's wrist, their guns pointing off elsewhere, Semyon face to face with the figure.

His lips purse into a smirk.

"Hey, Pete," he says. "Long time."

Peter has one question that's been bugging him all day.

"How'd you get out of those woods with a broken leg?"

"Long story. Maybe I'll tell it to you one day."

Semyon yanks the trigger of his gun. The report, so close to Peter's head, fills his skull. Peter jerks back. Semyon hammers him with a headbutt. Spinning his body away, Peter loses grip of his pistol, the Glock skittling off into the storm.

Semyon's eyes glint as he raises the Margolin for the kill shot. But Peter is too skilled a gymnast to let it go down like that. Going along with his momentum, he pivots and brings a sweeping high kick around that smashes the gun out of the Hunter's hand before he can unleash its fury.

Peter then shifts his weight. Pushes himself away from Semyon, gets a two-feet break between them, and comes at him with a series of open palm strikes.

Semyon expects them. He blocks each one as it comes. Before countering with a leg sweep that forces Peter into a retreat.

The fight is on.

MICHAEL HAS the engine running and the headlights aimed at the churning air. Nervously tapping his foot up and down, he spots two indistinct figures staggering through the thrashing snow.

Jumping out of the police cruiser, the kid shouts, "Mother?! Mother?!"

The figures pause in the thick air. Turn in his direction.

Fear begins to fill the kid. He considers that this might

not be who he thinks it is. He starts to back up toward the cruiser, eyes fixed on the silhouettes as they begin making their way toward him.

"Peter?"

Michael recognizes the voice of Mother and instant relief floods him. He rushes toward them, hoping that the other figure is Peter.

Mother holds her arms out to him. "Peter," she breathes as Michael plunges into them.

It is then that the kid spots Ibliss.

"Who's she?"

"Her name is Catherine. She's here to help."

"You're Michael Henderson, right?" Ibliss puts to the kid.

"No no," Mother interjects. "His name is Peter. He lives with me and Magda now."

"You mean you're still training—"

"I'm not part of the program," Michael butts in.

"Whatever," Ibliss says, turning her attention to the burning headlights of the police cruiser. "We don't have time. Is that your vehicle?"

"Yeah."

"Then we need to leave."

"Not without Peter."

"I thought *you* were Peter."

"No. The other Peter."

THE *OTHER* PETER is just that second caught in a blistering tornado of moves and counter moves.

The two fighters part. Only a few feet of blustering air between them.

Semyon reaches to his belt. Takes the Finka knife from it. Holds it in his fist, the blade glinting from the edge of his closed hand.

He comes at Peter.

Azrael parries the knife with an X block, crossing his wrists in front of him. The blade slices his forearm. The risk was worth it. Despite the cut, he gets leverage on the hand holding the knife and forces it upwards. He tries to grab Semyon at the wrist, but the Hunter twists and slips away from him.

For a while Semyon comes after him with the knife, Peter vaulting off parked cars, running along the roofs, maneuvering and shaping his body so that he avoids every stab and slash, Semyon doing the same to deflect the kicks and punches that come his way through counters.

In the seventeen years since they first met, both men have hardened and grown. Their bodies, lean and taut, trained and disciplined, are meant for this. Like two grey-hounds bred over hundreds of generations for the job of catching the hare, every sinew of every muscle in both men's bodies moves precisely to the task of fighting.

"You remember Venice?" Semyon asks when they part to regain their breaths.

Peter says nothing.

"Of course you do," Semyon goes on. "You remember me waving at you from the rooftop, don't you?"

"I also remember the bullet that flew over my head."

"That wasn't for you, Pete."

"Then who was it for?"

"That bullet was meant for Walter Smith. That's who we were there to kill. Not you. You, we were there to save."

Peter narrows his eyes at him.

"Smith was the target. Azrael was to be captured. *Alive*."

It is Peter's turn to shake his head. He points a finger at him.

"You killed all those other assets in the program."

"As your program would have killed me and my men. But *you*, you were to be taken with us. To my commander Parfyon Rogozhin. He was so looking forward to meeting you."

Peter's face stretches into confusion.

"Who is Parfyon Rogozhin?"

"The man who wants the old woman."

"Why?"

"They have an old score to settle."

"But why alive?"

"Who cares. She won't remain alive for long. I'm sure Parfyon has got something terrible planned for her."

Stepping forwards, Peter says, "I can't let that happen, Tommy."

"It's not Tommy anymore. It hasn't been ever since you left me for *dead*."

"You left me no choice."

"There was a choice," Semyon retorts. "Remember? All you had to do was kill them and join me."

"Despite what you think, they didn't deserve it. Magda didn't deserve you killing her like that. Mother doesn't deserve whatever is awaiting her with your boss."

"That's always been your problem, Pete. *Her*."

"I can't let you take her."

"Then you'll have to die."

Semyon attacks. Coming at Peter, he moves him backwards across the open space of the parking lot, the knife glittering in quick arcs and jabs.

"LOOK, KID," Ibliss pleads with Michael, "we have to move. There are five of them. They are armed with assault rifles. They are trained and deadly. They will not hesitate to kill us. And here we are sitting in this darn car waiting. We need to move and then reengage the enemy when we're not sitting ducks."

She sits facing him from the passenger seat. Michael in the driver's, hands on the wheel, staring forwards into the storm.

"No," the kid says firmly. "We have to wait for Peter. He'll be here soon."

"Peter," Mother says softly into Michael's ear from the backseat, "we have to go."

"Not without him," the kid insists.

"Look," Ibliss says sternly, "very soon I'm gonna stop asking. You get me?"

She's glaring at the thirteen-year-old.

His eyes suddenly brighten.

"Look!" he announces, pointing out the windshield.

A shadow grows larger in the blizzard. Coming towards the cruiser. Ibliss sits forward trying to guess who it is.

A man.

She's at least sure of that. Average build, average height. As he grows larger, she spots another shape. Something in his hands.

An assault rifle.

"Get down!"

They throw themselves into the footwells as the air ignites. They expect the windshield to be hit. But the hail of bullets is instead aimed for the tires and the engine.

From his low position, the kid reaches up and twists the keys in the ignition. Taking it out of park, he pushes the gas pedal all the way down with his hand. The screaming wheels skid on the frozen ground.

Then gain traction.

The cruiser leaps forward. One dives out of the way. The vehicle continues onwards across the lot, until it smashes into a line of parked cars.

Number One lifts himself from the snow. Just as he spots two more shadows approaching his position. One of them is bulky. The other is not.

"I found them," he tells his companions through the comms.

SEMYON COMES at Peter full force. But not with anger. No.

Neither Semyon nor Peter are fighting with anger. Rather, they fight with precision and meaning. Anger, for what it's worth, blinds the fighter, makes him too hasty, too impatient. He loses his most important weapon: timing.

For a split second, Semyon overextends a slash, his body leaning too far forward with the knife. Peter manages to slip underneath it and hit Semyon's wrist. The Hunter does well to keep hold of his weapon. Drawing back, the blade catches

Peter across the palm, a deep cut that pours instantly with crimson.

Once more they stop. Step apart. Both men are now panting. Their breaths stretching into the frozen air.

"Back in Venice," Semyon says, "what happened once you and Smith got away?"

"I ditched him. After all, if you and the rest of the GRU were after me, I was better off not carrying baggage."

Semyon smirks. "And once again, Peter Black, you showed the most amazing of all your talents. *Luck.*"

Peter's eyes cut at his opponent.

Semyon explains. "Smith wasn't there to rescue you."

He pauses. Letting this sink in. Before going on.

"He was taking you to be terminated, Pete. If you hadn't given him the slip, you would have been taken to a secure location. One occupied by a wet team sitting around until you and Smith got there so they could execute you the moment you walked in. You see, the GRU never had an agent inside the program. We'd tried for years, but never managed it."

"Then who gave the codes to our trackers?"

The smirk grows large. "None other than Walter Smith."

Peter stares at him, saying nothing.

"Don't you get it?" Semyon continues. "They sold their own program out. Got us to do their dirty work after Smith decided to pull the plug."

"But why?" floats weakly from Peter's lips.

"Congress began asking too many questions at CIA briefings. A committee was set up. There was going to be an enquiry. A lot of powerful people felt exposed. Deputy

Director Walter Smith amongst them. That was when they chose to get rid of the whole thing."

Peter's brow is wrinkled. "By handing us over to the GRU?"

"Yes. We thought it was a genuine leak from some rogue CIA officer. Turns out it was the sons-of-bitches at the top. Management."

Peter's eyes come alive. "What happened to the recruits?"

Semyon's expression becomes serious. "They euthanized them," his voice echoes inside Peter's head. "Nine farms. Nine kids. All shot in the head and buried in the woods."

Peter now knows why he had felt strange when considering the date of death on the seventh file. Asset 172. The boy who had been shot after turning on Mother. That is a lie. He hadn't turned on anyone. She had killed him because it had been ordered by men protecting their careers. He knows this for sure because the day it had happened was the same day he'd been attacked in Venice. The day the program had fallen.

"An executive decision," Semyon says. "Taken by men with families. Children of their own. But able to order things like that to be done to other people's children in the blink of an eye."

"Mother," Peter begins before swallowing and going silent.

"Yes, your dear old Mother. You know what she—"

Before he can finish Peter unleashes a flurry of strikes, as fast and light as the storm itself. Semyon finds himself on the defensive, using the knife to deflect his opponent, unable to get anything away.

Peter opens up his opponent's block, launches himself into the air, catches Semyon in the chin with a Wushu jumping front kick. It sends the Hunter reeling back. Peter comes flying at him as he staggers and before Semyon can adjust his feet, Peter has hold of his wrist and is pushing him backwards, locking the arm up.

Semyon crashes into a car. Peter presses him into it, the knife trapped between them. The other arm comes around and Peter grabs that too. With the knife pointing at Semyon's chin, Peter begins forcing the arm upwards. It is at that moment Semyon's comms crackle in his ear. "*We've located the old woman,*" Number One tells him in Russian. "*She's at the far end of the parking lot with Ibliss and some boy.*"

It distracts Semyon long enough for Peter to get the upper hand in the struggle. He gains control of the knife and sends it rising toward Semyon's throat. The Hunter flexes his muscles, slows the blade, uses all his strength to keep his arms from being pushed any farther.

Except Peter has him in such a way that Semyon begins to lose the battle. Strength leaks out of him like air from a puncture.

For the first time since he was a child, Semyon feels fear. Just a tinge. But enough to worry him that he won't be leaving this place. That he will die here in the same godforsaken land that brutally formed him all those years ago.

Except that's not what happens.

As the tip of the blade presses into the flesh where the neck meets the chin, that devilish grin reappears on the Hunter's face and Peter sees something reflected in his eyes.

But it is too late.

Pain paralyzes Peter and all his strength ebbs away as

Number Two's knife passes into his side, just below the ribs. His grip on Semyon's wrist, and therefore the Hunter's knife, loosens, until he is falling away from him.

Number Two tugs the knife out as Peter goes down.

On all fours in the snow, he tries to get up, but slips straight back down. In his futility, all he can think about is getting to the kid.

Mikey!

The dwarfish Russian stalks up behind him, raises the knife and is about to plunge it into the back of Azrael, when Semyon stops him, placing a hand across his chest.

Turning his spiteful eyes to the Hunter, Number Two finds him gently shaking his head.

"Leave him," Semyon says in Russian. "Go get the car."

The other man nods. Wipes the knife on his coveralls, places it back on his belt. He takes one last look at Peter, spits onto the snow and walks off.

Azrael is trying to turn over, blood dribbling out of the stab wound. Once he gets himself into a sitting position, Semyon crouches before him.

The assassins lock eyes across the snowflakes. Peter's display caution. The eyes of a dying wolf.

"You left me alive in those woods all those years ago," Semyon tells him. "So now I'm returning the favor. But I warn you, Pete. Don't bother to call me back. As I learned all too well, no one is coming. You are all on your own."

"STAY DOWN THERE, PETER," Mother warns Michael.

The kid is crouched beside her. The two of them hiding behind the cover of a Ford Police Interceptor Utility.

"Give me a gun," he cries.

Mother ignores him as she sends a three-shot burst in the direction of the bulky wet-boy, Number Four. The wrestler. He hides in cover on the corner of the police building. The burst sends him further into hiding as the concrete chips and explodes close to his wide face.

His skinny colleague Number Three is about forty yards to the left of his larger friend, edging his way along the backs of cars on the other side of the lot. Using the support of a sedan's rooftop, he fires off a volley from his AK.

It does exactly what he intended it to. Sending Mother into hiding.

"Let's hit them from both sides," he says into his comms to Number Four. "Keep them pinned down."

The large man lines his eye up with the sight of his AK.

Steps out of cover.

Never gets to pull the trigger.

"Alexei!" his partner cries out when he spots Ibliss creeping up behind Number Four. Shoving a Beretta to the back of his neck. Blowing a hole through his spine and out his throat. Spraying the snow red.

Three stands there frozen. Eyes trapped on the man he's known for twenty-five years. First in the army. Then special forces. Now together in the GRU. All his emotions hit him at once and he allows anger to cloud his judgement.

It is a mistake. A terrible one.

The rakish wet-boy turns his attention on Ibliss. She is running back into the sightless storm. A stitch of bullets chase her along the wall of the police department. She dives behind a row of dumpsters, the things sparking and pinging with ricocheting bullets.

This first mistake leads to a second.

Losing sight of her, Three makes the fatal error of rushing out of cover, AK cinched between shoulder and cheek. He gets a few yards across the expanse of snow, the gun shaking in his arms, and stops. Totters sideways as if he's lost his balance. Falls flat onto his face.

The AK has stopped firing.

The bullet Mother sent into the side of his head has blown the skull away at the back of the right ear. Blood pours from the cavity like wine from a fallen bottle. His legs twitch jittery snow angels on the frozen ground of the parking lot.

Mother stands behind the cab of the Ford Interceptor. The Beretta smokes in her hand. Her gray eyes scan the snow. At the beginning of this there had been three of them. She can't help wondering where the other one is when she spots a scarred face reflected in the Ford's bodywork.

She turns and he's right there.

It isn't much of a struggle. She's seventy-six, after all. Number One grabs her wrist and bashes it against the Ford. It forces her to drop the gun, the arthritic limb going numb with pain. She looks for Michael and is thankful that the kid is nowhere to be seen. She goes to strike her attacker with her free hand but he easily catches it.

He folds her arms down and twists her around roughly like a cop arresting a drunk driver, pushing her face into the SUV. She goes to struggle, but her old body does what you'd expect: overexerts itself to no avail.

Number One takes a set of plastic zip-ties strung together to resemble a pair of handcuffs. He slips the loops over her fingers and pulls them tight when they reach her wrists. So tight the plastic cuts into the skin. She attempts a headbutt. Flipping her head back at him. But he's all too familiar with this. In Syria he had been placed in charge of a facility the Russians used to "interrogate" rebels. At any one time he had been entrusted with over a hundred and twenty prisoners. With so many angry men being handcuffed and moved about each day, you got used to standing far enough back to avoid having your front teeth knocked out.

Number One pulls out a syringe filled with tranquilizer. He is plucking the plastic point protector off the end of the needle with his teeth when Michael appears from under the Ford.

The kid sends an uppercut sailing right between the guy's legs. Just like Mother taught, it keeps on going as if the punch is intended for his heart. Number One lets out a stifled scream as his testicles flatten against his groin. The scar on his face changes shape. The punch instantly winds him. Sends pain stabbing through his body, his crotch burning. Gut-twisting nausea. He loses his grip of Mother and she tugs herself away.

"Peter!" she shouts. "RUN!"

Michael pulls himself along on his stomach underneath the Ford. Climbing out the other side, he sprints into the blizzard.

Number One pulls himself together. He unshoulders his AK-74 and rests it on the roof of the Ford, trains it on the kid as Michael slowly fades into the storm. Gets set to fire. To kill a thirteen-year-old boy. The crosshairs of the scope stuck to the kid's back. Right between the shoulder blades.

He pulls the trigger.

But the spray of bullets never reaches.

They trace an arc through the air that moves away from the kid. Mother leans all her weight against the wet-boy, having shoved him sideways. He pushes her away, sweeps the old woman's feet from under her with a hook kick. She tumbles over with a thud that knocks the air out of her.

Number One trains his gun back on the snow. But the kid is gone.

The Russian turns to Mother, who tries but fails to lift herself from the ground. Enraged, he swings a boot and kicks the old woman in the stomach.

Mother groans. Keels over. An old woman kicked hard by a grown man. She can do nothing as the wet-boy comes over her and injects the tranquilizer straight into her neck.

She lets out a sigh that gradually turns into a hiss. Her gray eyes gradually glazing over, before finally closing.

SIXTY-FOUR

THE KNIFE WOUND IS DEEP. PETER IS SURE THAT IT has punctured his stomach. Possibly wounded his liver.

The pain is hell.

Still sitting in the middle of the lot, he can hear the cops at the back door. Hear their low chatter as they cautiously fan out of the building. He watches their shadows move slowly through the blustering snow. Toward the position of the most recent gunfire.

They walk right past him.

For about the fifth time, Peter attempts to raise himself onto his feet. The wound parts. Opening like a mouth taking a breath. Blood spurts against his shirt, the fabric clinging to his flesh. The screaming pain merges with a droning ring that pounds his ears. It feels like his skull is filling with blood.

At last, he gets himself upright and staggers on, a hand clinging to the warmth spilling out of him with every step.

The ringing in his skull distorts all sound, cutting him off from the world.

All he can think about is the kid. He has to reach the kid.

Peter fumbles onwards, picking his way through the storm. Going in the same direction the cops are wandering in. The direction Semyon had headed. The diminutive Number Two, as well.

He comes across the body of Number Four at the corner of the precinct. Lying in a glossy puddle of his own blood. Peter lets out a gasp of pain as he crouches down to take his AK-74 one-handed.

He continues onwards. Shadows flicker across the storm. He's not sure if it's the cops or the Russians. About thirty yards on, he spots the crashed police cruiser and the shot-up Ford Interceptor.

Drag marks lead away from it in the snow.

He goes to follow, but his legs buckle underneath him and he drops to his knees. He can feel himself sinking into unconsciousness. The world around him is white noise and fuzz. The sound of the storm begins to fill him and he starts to forget just why he happens to be here in this gray place.

His mind is slowly shutting down.

He fights it. Focuses. Anchors his breathing.

Everything rushes back.

The kid.

Peter's eyes snap open. He cries out in pain as he rises once more to his feet. Each step, he draws in air, one breath at a time, the AK dangling from an arm, the muzzle trickling along the ground and leaving a childish scrawl in the snow.

Breathe.

He focuses on each individual step, pushing back the burning pain that stretches through him.

Breathe.

The drag marks lead him out of the lot. Toward the shadow of a man.

Breathe.

The man isn't moving. Like he is waiting for Peter.

Breathe.

Peter uses his left forearm as a crossbeam, settling the AK on it.

Breathe.

He promises himself that there will be no more pain beyond now.

Breathe.

The shadow slowly comes into focus within the icy debris.

Breathe.

It is Semyon.

Breathe.

He has the kid.

Breathe.

But the breath doesn't come.

Peter freezes, lowers the AK. Michael's terrified eyes shine. Semyon stands behind him, the cold metal of his Margolin pressed to the kid's temple, an arm clamped across his chest. If it wasn't for the gun and the kid's horrified expression, this could be the pose of an uncle and his nephew getting ready for a holiday snapshot.

"He's yours, isn't he?" Semyon shouts over the wind.

Peter says nothing.

"Looks just like you did at his age."

Semyon glances down at Michael. Ruffles his hair. The kid trembling in his arms.

Turning back to Peter, Semyon adds, "You shouldn't have come back for her. You've cost your boy his life."

"No!" Peter shouts.

He lurches forward. Doesn't get far. The weakness dropping him once more to his knees. The pain and futility making him cry out like an injured wolf.

"I'm glad this all hurts you, Pete," Semyon growls. "Now you know how hurt I was that day you left me in those fucking woods. Having to reset my own leg. Trek four hundred miles to the nearest hunting lodge through bear and wolf infested woods. Almost starving to death. Dying of exposure. Cutting the dead flesh off my toes. Working my way back to civilization. All the time knowing that the person I thought was my brother was responsible for it. I was glad when Parfyon gave me this job because I had the chance to get *her*. But now, with you here too, it's like the stars have aligned to give me my revenge."

He cocks the weapon. Michael closes his eyes. The kid doesn't expect to live. Semyon focuses on Peter. He doesn't want to miss the look of horror on his face when Michael's brains get scattered across the snow.

Except no shot is fired. The snow around them remains white.

Semyon is frozen. Because something cold has been pressed into the back of *his* head.

A Beretta M9.

A pair of lips, the type you'd give your life to kiss, move close to his ear. "Let the kid go," Ibliss whispers.

Semyon smiles. Weighs it up.

"Okay," he says, removing the pistol from Michael.

After that, he slowly retracts the arm from across the teen's chest.

The kid runs the second he's free. Throwing his arms around Peter and burying his head in the assassin's shoulder.

"Drop the gun," Ibliss orders Semyon.

Semyon obeys. Drops the gun into the snow.

Ibliss is quick. The pistol whip hits the back of the Hunter's head before he has a chance to wheel around, the blow knocking him out cold.

Filled with pain, Peter reaches for the AK. But when his blood sticky fingers touch it, there is a foot on top of the gun, clamping it to the icy ground.

He follows the leg all the way up to Ibliss's face. She is gently shaking her head.

"Take your boy, Azrael. This one is mine."

"You're taking him alive?"

"Those were my orders."

NUMBER ONE IS thankful that the old woman is light.

Folded over his shoulder, he carries her through the wind and snow toward the warm lights of a Toyota Land Cruiser. The engine is running. Steam trails from the hood and its headlights face the road. Number Two sits in the driver's seat.

One opens the trunk and lays the old woman inside. Then he gets in the front passenger seat.

"Where's Semyon?" Two asks.

"He couldn't make it. Now let's go."

"We're leaving him?"

"Those are the orders."

Two shrugs, crunches the Toyota into gear and they're off, hauling ass through the snow toward the main road.

THE VAGUE OUTLINES of Cops move about the blizzard. Michael does his best to plot a path through them while Peter leans heavier on him than he'd like to.

The two of them have a series of very real and immediate problems. Firstly, if they stay in the storm, they'll freeze to death.

That's problem number one.

Problem number two is the fact that Peter is bleeding out. He knows it. Even the kid knows it. Medical attention is a priority.

Three. Having crashed the only cruiser they had keys for, they don't have a vehicle, and neither of them have the type of tools required to jack one. That's why they are heading toward the police department building and not away from it.

Reaching a row of parked cars, the kid sits Peter down in the space between two of them. Azrael sits heavily against the driver's door of a cruiser.

"I need to steal some keys again," Michael tells him.

He goes to leave but Peter stops him.

When he turns back, Peter says in a breathless voice, "You have a good memory, right?"

Michael nods.

"You need to remember this address. You ready?"

Another nod.

"Evergreen Ranch, number fifty-three Eagle River Drive, South Fork Falls. It's south on route one. Say it back?"

The kid repeats it perfectly.

"Good. That's where you take me. But not if I die. If that happens, you go to the nearest police precinct and turn yourself in. *Do not* go to that address if I am dead. Okay?"

For a third time, the kid nods.

Then he dashes off. Leaving Peter to stare at his own jaded reflection in the chrome of the car door opposite.

WHEN MICHAEL RETURNS NOT ten minutes later, Peter is mumbling incoherently.

"Tommy... Tommy..."

The kid goes to lift him but it's impossible.

"Peter, I can't move you without help."

He takes a handful of snow and rubs it over the assassin's pale face.

When that doesn't work, he slaps him.

The assassin gradually opens his eyes. For a second he stares blankly at Michael. Like he's not sure if it's the kid or someone else.

"Mikey," he eventually breathes.

"I got us a car. So you need to get up."

With Michael's help, Peter stands, screaming into the back of his teeth. The wound pulling apart. His stomach pulling apart.

They shuffle off, taking a direct line to a black Ford F-150 pickup.

"What's in bag?" Peter asks, spotting the rucksack on Michael's shoulder.

"It's ours. I found it in the office I got the keys from."

Michael helps Peter into the passenger seat of the Ford,

closes the door, gets in the driver's side. When he starts the pickup, the fog lights startle a nearby trooper. But by the time his vision is clear, the Ford is racing past him out of the lot and hitting the main road.

Inside the pickup, Peter sinks in and out of consciousness.

"Mikey?" he says weakly.

"What?"

"I might not make it."

"Of course you will. You always do."

"If I don't, then I need you to know something before I lose my chance to tell you."

Michael says nothing, eyes fixed on the beating field of snow.

"Before she died, your mother told me something."

Michael still says nothing.

"She told me you were my son."

For a moment the kid doesn't speak. Then. "I know."

Peter's sweat-frosted forehead furrows. "You know?"

"Yeah. And not just because your old roommate said so. I figured it pretty soon after that night. They never pretended that Carl was my biological dad. I always knew my real father was someone else. Probably the same asshole who left my mom all those years ago. Ergo: *You*."

Peter manages a smile. Turns back to the storm.

So the kid knew all along is the last thought to run through his head before everything sinks into darkness.

SIXTY-FIVE

SEA OF OKHOTSK, 2021

FOR HIS LIFE'S FINAL TASK, THE PRESIDENT himself has given Parfyon Rogozhin the use of the Russian Navy's flagship submarine. The *Knyaz Vladimir*—or *Prince Vladimir* if you prefer English.

Named after Vladimir the Great, who reigned Rus for thirty-five years from 980 AD and is credited with introducing Christianity to the Slavic people, the vessel is one of only three Project 955 Borei-class submarines. It carries twelve Bulava submarine-launched ballistic missiles, which in turn carry six 100-kiloton warheads. That's enough yield to create a blast range of about ten miles. You set twelve of them off, you could wipe a country off the map.

It is why the honor of being given the nuclear submarine for his own personal use is not lost on Parfyon Rogozhin. A last present from a man he met many years ago when the young president was a lieutenant colonel in the KGB and

Parfyon was a Main Directorate chief. Back in those days, the two had schemed together in ways which had turned out profitable to their careers later on. The president never forgetting his old boss when he became the ultimate boss himself.

Captain Stepan Dubrovsky knows neither the president nor Parfyon. He finds himself involved in this episode purely because his Borei Class submarine was the only Borei Class submarine available. Only three days ago he had received orders that his annual leave was over effective immediately and he was to return to the *Prince Vladimir*. Two days had then been taken getting the vessel up to scratch, as it had spent the last month in Vladivostok taking repairs to its hull after an overenthusiastic planesman had steered them through too narrow a trench during training operations in the Pacific.

Once the *Prince Vladimir* was ready, Captain Dubrovsky had been given a mission. Top secret and exceptionally strange. Escort a dying man to international waters off of northern Alaska, where they will be receiving a "cargo."

That was it.

Captain Dubrovsky hates being left in the cold. Especially when his officers begin asking questions he really should have the answers to. Like: why are we sailing a nuclear-warhead armed submarine within miles of the coast of a country we share a certain element of *hostility* with?

"Stop worrying," he had told his officers during discussions in his cabin shortly before they'd set off. "This isn't a code red situation. We will not be engaging with anyone from the US Navy."

But he didn't know that.

He should. But he didn't. After all, no one has brought this many warheads this close to American territory since the Cuban Missile Crisis.

A knock at his cabin door makes the captain look up.

"It's Surov, sir," a voice says on the other side.

Surov is the communications officer.

"Enter, Surov. The door is unlocked."

The officer walks in, closes the door behind him and salutes his commanding officer. He is young. Mid-twenties with a smooth face and boyish rosy cheeks. Somewhere, Dubrovsky thinks, there is a *babushka* pining for his safe return.

"Sir, I just received this message."

He hands a piece of paper over.

"Have you read it?" Dubrovsky asks as he takes his reading glasses from the nightstand beside his bunk.

The officer swallows as the captain begins reading.

"Well, have you?" Dubrovsky asks once more, glancing up at him from the note.

"Yes, sir. Sorry."

"It's okay," Dubrovsky says as he reads it himself. "I can't blame you for curiosity. I'm as in the dark as you are, petty officer."

The captain reads on.

It is once he's finished that Surov asks, "Who is the 'knight,' sir?"

"I have no idea," Captain Dubrovsky replies, holding the note in his hand and gazing at the junior officer. "Neither do I know what the package is or who the king could be. But then this note isn't for us, Surov. It is for our passenger."

Dubrovsky puts his cap on and makes his way down a narrow walkway to the cabin they've placed the dying man in. A doctor sits in there with him. A morose man with black hair and a thin, high cheeked face.

He is checking Parfyon's vitals when Captain Dubrovsky knocks. Both patient and doctor turn their eyes to the door. Then at each other. Parfyon nods and the doctor opens it.

He says nothing to Dubrovsky. Instead, he glances back at Parfyon and nods once more, before stepping past the captain and leaving them.

"My communications officer just brought me a message from above," Dubrovsky says as he enters the cabin and closes the door behind him.

Parfyon lies on his back, propped up on pillows, an oxygen mask grasping what's left of his thin face.

"You'll have to, huh, read it to me, I'm afraid," Parfyon wheezes.

Dubrovsky reads off the paper. "Everything has gone as planned. The package is aboard. The knight is with their king." Looking at the old man, he adds, "That is all."

"That is all it needs to be," Parfyon says, a grin riding his frail cheeks. "Everything is falling into place."

SIXTY-SIX

A WAREHOUSE IN ANCHORAGE, 2021

"Oh good," a man's voice says. "You're awake."

The hood is ripped from Semyon's head. Light burns his eyes. They slowly focus. He is sitting in a chair, arms secured behind his back. Halogen lamps shine brightly at him. The silhouette of a man steps in front of them.

The owner of the voice.

It is Walter Smith. Looking much older than the six years that have passed since Semyon last locked eyes on him in Venice through the crosshairs of a scope.

Smith's hair is completely white. His skin jaundiced. He looks frantic. Eyes bulging. Jaw taut. Holding something in his right hand. Semyon knows what it is. And he'll know how high it is set soon enough.

Smith brings his face right up to Semyon's and snarls, "You remember me, you piece of shit?"

He doesn't wait for an answer. He merely jabs the

Knightro stun baton into Semyon's chest, right above the heart. Sending 30,000 volts through him.

Semyon goes into spasms, every sinew clenching. It is now that he figures Smith has it about halfway. Five more settings to go until it is on maximum. When it won't just electrocute him. It will start to burn his flesh.

SIXTY-SEVEN

EVERGREEN RANCH, ABOUT TWELVE MILES NORTH OF ANCHORAGE, 2021

PETER'S EYES OPEN SLOWLY. HE ACHES ALL OVER, and when he attempts to lift his hands, they feel so heavy he can't manage it.

The room is a blur. Static on an untuned television set. He squints to bring it into focus, and when it is, he finds himself in what he surmises is a guest bedroom. It's not very big and there aren't any photographs or other decorations. The furniture consists of several items made from a dark wood. There's a huge wardrobe that stands over the bed like a sentinel on guard, a nightstand, and a chest of drawers. A single window looks out onto a vast hill of snow-covered grassland that ends in trees. The storm has subsided and only a gentle flurry of flakes beats the windowpane.

There's also the kid.

Michael is asleep beside the bed, sitting in a big green

leather armchair. Leaned back, mouth wide open, snoring. An IV line runs out of his upper arm and leads all the way to Peter's own forearm, a movement of blood coming down the plastic tube.

"You needed it," a voice at the far end of the room says. "And the kid said you were the same type."

Peter turns to face the doorway. There is a tall, slightly overweight man in thick-lensed glasses standing there. His round head is bald on top. Curly black hair sticks out at the sides and his thick beard carries a shock of gray that runs down his chin.

"Hello, Peter," he says, holding a palm up to his patient. "Long time no see."

His name is Charles Green. He's a horse surgeon now, but, back in the day, he was part of Pat Hughes's network. Performing surgery on non-equestrian patients out in southern California.

After the fall, he moved up here to Alaska and opened a horse surgery. Peter has kept tabs on him ever since. Just in case.

The assassin's eyes follow Green all the way as he moves toward the bed. Michael starts to wake up. He splutters, leans forwards, wipes sleep from his eyes. Turns sharply to Green.

The surgeon has come to a stop at the foot of the bed.

Peter notes the edgy look on the kid's face. He goes to talk but his mouth is too dry. Michael takes a glass of water from the nightstand and presses it to his lips. Peter takes a few sips.

"How long have I been out?" he asks Michael when the cup is removed.

It is Green who answers.

"Only four hours," he says. "The surgery was pretty minor. You had a small laceration to your liver. Puncture to the stomach. It took two hours to clean it up. You've slept another two. The kid wouldn't let me sedate you any further. Otherwise you could have gotten a good eight hours."

"I'm good," Peter says. Before turning to Michael and telling him, "Get the car ready."

He goes to get up but his weak arms aren't up to the task, so he collapses back into the bed.

"You're not going anywhere," Green tells him. "At least not for a few more hours. You lost a lot of blood. If the kid hadn't had the same blood type as you, your life would have been finished. Now get some rest. You and your boy can stay as long as you want."

Peter stares at him. He feels helpless. He has only ever met this man twice. Once when he'd been shot during a hit on a mafia boss in LA. Another time when he'd broken an arm falling from a Las Vegas hotel balcony whilst evading an Arab prince's security detail. One that was dead set on avenging their murdered master.

Both times it had all been arranged by Pat. Peter and Green had hardly spoken. The crux of it had been that he was fixed up and left. Easy.

He wishes he can do that now.

Charles Green lays both hands on the metal railing at the foot of the bed. The springs creak as he applies his weight.

"I see you've kept your propensity for danger," he says with a gentle smirk.

"We won't take up much more of your time," Peter assures him. "Thank you for helping us."

"No need to thank me. It was quite a joy to work on a human again." He turns to Michael. "You can remove the line. I think your father has enough blood now."

As Michael plucks the long needle from his arm, Green adds, "Once you've said your good mornings, come to the kitchen. I've made you breakfast. You've lost about a pint and a half of blood yourself. You need to regain your strength."

Green removes his hands, the bed rising. He turns and leaves the room. Peter keeping his eyes on him all the way.

When he's gone, Peter turns his attention on the kid.

"You can't trust him," he whispers.

"He seems okay."

"Well he's not. Keep an eye on him. Okay?"

Michael nods.

Green calls from the kitchen. "Hey, kid, how do you like your eggs?"

"Sunny side up," Michael shouts back.

"Watch him," Peter reiterates.

SIXTY-EIGHT

A WAREHOUSE IN ANCHORAGE, 2021

Ibliss sits behind the wheel of a black Hummer. Through the veil of gently falling snowflakes, she watches a brick warehouse that sits across a vacant lot. An earpiece hums in her ear as she listens to Smith beat into the Hunter, knowing that it hardly bothers the assassin. That it's more about Smith than it is about inflicting pain.

"That your boss in there?"

Ibliss looks up into the rearview.

Clive the pilot sits in the back. Hands bound on his lap. A sleepy, disheveled look to him.

"Shut up," she says.

The pilot rolls his eyes.

Ibliss's phone vibrates on top of the dashboard. She grabs it. Instinctively looks up at the mirror, at Clive.

"I know," he says. "Keep my mouth shut."

Ibliss removes the earpiece, the slapping thud of fist against flesh diminishing as she places it on the dash.

"Sara?" Harry says immediately when she answers the call.

She is Sara to him. Catherine to Mother. Ibliss to Smith.

"Yes."

"Sara, where are you?"

His voice sounds broken. A pang clenches her stomach.

"I'm down here in Vermont."

"No. You're not."

Everything goes cold. Her head throbs. The warehouse becomes fuzzy.

"Why would you say that?" The words tremble from her mouth.

"I bumped into Greg Fisher in a Starbucks earlier today."

Ibliss feels like she is fading. Like her whole body is turning to water. Greg Fisher works for the same company she does.

"He asked how your mother was," Harry goes on, every sentence a new blow. "And, see, that confused me. Because I've been married to you for five years and I always thought your parents died in a car accident when you were eighteen."

Tears fill Ibliss's eyes. The lies unraveling.

"So I ask Greg," her husband's voice goes on in her head, "why he says that, and he tells me it's because you took two weeks' emergency vacation to go down to Ohio to care for your mother after she had a stroke."

"Harry, I can explain."

He doesn't give her a chance to speak. "What is it?" he butts in. "An affair? You're seeing someone else?"

"No. It's nothing like that."

"Then what the hell is it, Sara? Because in all the time we've known each other I've told you everything about me. Yet you—you I know practically nothing about. Sure you told me it was hard growing up. Your upbringing difficult. So I backed off. But I've never met so much as a friend of yours, let alone family. And now you disappearing like this. Please, Sara, for the love of our little girl, tell me what is going on."

Ibliss can't help glancing up at the rearview mirror. Clive wears a fatherly look.

The assassin breathes in and then out. "Harry, you're right," she says in a defeated tone. "I'm not in Vermont. As for my parents, I never knew them. I was found outside a hospital when I was two days old. I was suffering opioid withdrawal. I told you they died in a car accident because it was the easiest way to explain their absence without you constantly asking questions."

Harry doesn't speak for a moment. All she can hear is his breathing. Then he says, "What happened to you after that?"

"After that, I spent time in a series of children's homes until I ran away at the age of eleven and started living on the streets. At the age of thirteen I killed a man who was pimping me out after I couldn't take his abuse anymore. I was sent to..."

SIXTY-NINE

EVERGREEN RANCH, 2021

MICHAEL FINISHES BREAKFAST ALONE IN THE kitchen. From the window is a view of snow-swept wooden stables. They appear absent of horses. Business must be slow.

Beyond that is an endless field of pine. In between, a lot of white and not much else.

Michael places his dirty dishes in the sink, then leaves the room. Green had been with him in the kitchen till just a moment ago. The kid wonders where he is.

He finds him in the bedroom. With Peter.

The vet is bent over the patient. Michael spots the syringe in his hand. The needle going into Peter's forearm. The assassin already asleep, having dozed off naturally.

"What are you doing?" Michael says from the doorway.

Green twists around to him. "Oh, hey kid," he says, before turning back to Peter and pressing the plunger.

"What is that?"

"Just a little something to help him sleep."

Green pulls the needle from the arm and dabs the puncture wound with cottonwool.

"He said he doesn't want anything like that," Michael tells him. "He wants to leave here as soon as possible."

Green faces Michael. "Look, kid. He's got a lot of stitches in him. Had one hell of an injury. Lost a lot of blood. I know he may come off as superhuman sometimes, but he needs rest. Lots of it. No one ever tell you the human body heals much faster when it's asleep?"

Michael just looks at him.

"Come on, kid," Green says, placing the syringe in his pocket. "Let your old man have a snooze."

He comes across the room to Michael. Places a hand on the teen's shoulder. Says, "Let's go sit in the lounge."

SEVENTY

A WAREHOUSE IN ANCHORAGE, 2021

THE LIGHT FROM THE HALOGEN LAMPS MOVES IN and out of focus. His head hangs between his shoulders. Blood dribbles down his chin from his cut mouth. He feels along his shattered teeth with his tongue. To the left canine.

It's a little loose.

Soon, Semyon thinks.

Overall, the pain is no more than a dull echo in the darkness. Only the daze of being hit in the head over and over affects him.

Smith puts all his weight into a punch that almost pulls the old man over with it. The right hook smashes into the left side of Semyon's mouth, almost snapping the canine off its root.

Smith staggers after the fist. Does well to keep himself upright. Spends the next few seconds panting into the cold air of the empty warehouse.

"You look tired, old man," Semyon remarks dryly.

Smith turns over his shoulder. Eyes narrowing on the man in the chair. He snatches the stun baton from the wet concrete. Comes at him. It's already on full. Has been for a while.

He jams it into the assassin. Sends him into convulsions. Holds it there till he can taste the stench of burning flesh on his tongue.

The whole time, Semyon never loses eye contact or makes a single satisfactory sound that allows the old CIA man to know he's getting to him. To know that he's actually hurting him.

Smith leaves off. Steps back. His shirt is off and his pink flesh glistens with sweat. Steams rises off him. He takes a pack of smokes from the pocket of his pants. Taps it against his palm. Shoves the pack to his mouth and drags one out with his teeth.

After lighting it, he holds the pack of Camels out to Semyon. "You want one?"

Semyon gives a gentle grin. "Smoking is bad for your health."

Smith coughs a dry laugh. "I admire a man who can be cocky so close to death."

"I've been close to death my entire life."

Pointing his smoldering cigarette at Semyon, Smith says, "You know I've spent the last six years learning everything I could about you."

"I am honored."

"You should be."

"What did you find?"

"I found out you're an American for one."

Semyon shakes his head. "Oh no. You have it wrong. I was never American. Your Constitution never protected me and your government saw nothing except meat."

Smith takes in a big drag, before letting out a single word along with the smoke. "*Thomas.*"

Semyon says nothing.

"That's your name, isn't it?" Smith proposes. "Thomas Reed. Born eighth of March 1990. Youngest of five along with his deformed twin. Got left behind in a shit-covered crib by his meth-cook parents during a drug bust. Lucky, though. Because two years later Daddy had a psychotic breakdown and murdered the whole stinking lot of them. Wife and four brats. Including your disabled twin. Shame they left you behind. Would've saved a lot of bother if Daddy had butchered kid number five."

Smith blows smoke right at Semyon.

The Hunter smiles. "I guess that means we have something in common."

"Oh, yeah?"

"Yeah. Both our families were massacred."

Smith's top lip curls. He resembles a snarling dog.

Visions move through his mind like film through a camera.

Visions of *that day*. Venice.

Having lost Azrael at Fusina Dock, he had looked for him amongst the crowds for a while before realizing the danger inherent in sticking around too long. After all, the Hunter was still out there.

So he had left the dock and gone straight to the rendezvous. The family holiday scenario had been true. He really had been on vacation when they intercepted messages that the Russians planned to take alive their most valuable asset: Azrael.

Having informed the four highly trained special forces assassins waiting at the "safe house" that he had lost their quarry, Smith had returned under guard to his family.

However, in all his planning he had not had the foresight to protect them. He'd merely kissed them goodbye that morning as they'd prepared for a day of sightseeing and arranged to meet back up with them that evening. Excusing his absence as some "work thing" that needed his immediate attention.

Never had he imagined that when he walked through the door of his hotel suite later that day he'd find them gagged, bound, and shot in the back execution style.

"You and your colleagues," Semyon says, "sent orders that day to kill nine children. What makes you think your own children deserved any better?"

"You killed Coby's kids, too," murmurs out of Smith's mouth.

"Yes. I knew you'd recognize the scene. Did it remind you of your own children's deaths?"

Smith says nothing. Instead he shoves the smoke in his mouth, drains it off. Then flicks it at Semyon, the thing exploding in sparks as it hits his face. The GRU's top assassin unmoved.

Gripping the Knightro in his fist, Smith marches right up to him, lashes out, bringing the pins of the taser into the Hunter's cheek in a stabbing motion.

The jolt of electricity makes Semyon urinate himself for the innumerable time, but the assassin is glad. The left canine took the brunt of the blow. The tooth is almost out.

SEVENTY-ONE

EVERGREEN RANCH, 2021

THE LIVING ROOM WINDOWS ARE COVERED WITH venetian blinds. Closed almost all the way, Michael can't see out of them. Thin blades of light cut through the dusty air. Charles Green is a single man who doesn't bring women back to his place. Michael can tell by the mess and general uncleanliness of the place. First off, there is a distinct aroma of horse dung. Then there is the beaten-up furniture. Two brown leather chesterfields, worn and split, looking like a couple of overfed pigs. A coffee table stands between them, covered in half read books, open and facedown.

"You wanna drink?" Green asks as Michael takes a seat on one of the fat chesterfields.

"I'm good."

Green sits down on the opposite chesterfield.

"You wanna watch TV?"

"I don't watch TV."

It is true. Michael hasn't watched television since the night his world fell apart. When he'd been sitting watching a movie with his family one moment. Getting shot at the next.

"Suit yourself," Green says. Leaning back in his chair. "So where do *you* come from? I mean, I never heard your father mention a son."

Looking him dead in the eyes, the kid replies in a deadpan, "Why would he mention me to you? Aren't you the guy who performs surgery on criminals so that they're not questioned at hospital about all the bullet wounds? That's you, right?"

Green smiles. Pushes his glasses up the bridge of his nose.

"Smart, kid," he says. "I guess you're right. It wasn't exactly the kinda gig where you went around showing off pictures of your family to each other."

"I wouldn't have thought so. Not when you were working for a man like Pat Hughes."

"You knew Pat?"

"No. I didn't know him. But he knew me. Enough to send men to kill my family."

"Well, I wouldn't know about that. I just did a little contract work for him from time to time."

Green smiles. Then gets fidgety. He gets up from the chair and wanders to a drink's cabinet. It's already open and he plucks a well-used bottle of Kentucky bourbon from it. He pours one. Glugs it down. Pours another. Carries it back to the worn leather of the chesterfield.

"Yeah," he says as he sits down. "Kind of screwed a lot of people that."

"What?"

"Your old man going up against Hughes."

"Pat Hughes wanted him to kill an innocent woman and let her kid end up in some pedophile's dungeon."

"I guess," Green says before taking a sip. Then. "But didn't she end up dying anyway? And isn't said kid now nowhere to be found?"

He cocks an eye over his whiskey. Takes another sip.

"Peter did what he had to do," Michael states.

"Didn't he just," Green says, hardly able to control his angered tone. "Went and brought the whole damn house down on us in the process. I had to give up my practice in California to come move up here in the middle of nowhere. Forced to leave everything behind because of the feds hanging around me. Bringing me in for questioning. Watching me. Waiting for me to come for the money I got hidden in a safety deposit box down in Amarillo. All my ill-gotten gains—seven hundred grand—all sitting there doing nothing but being watched by bastards waiting for me to come get it. All because of your *daddy*."

The vet presses the glass to his lips and drains off the remains of the whiskey. As he then uses a hand to wipe the drips from his hairy chin, the doorbell chimes.

"Ah," he says. "That'll be my friends."

"Your friends?"

"Yeah. Stay right here."

Green lifts himself from the couch and leaves the room.

Michael waits until he is walking off down the hallway. When he is, the kid dashes across the room to the door. Green had heeled it shut, but it hasn't closed. There is an inch gap.

Michael places an eye to it. Watches the vet answer the

front door to two men. One of them is average build with a scar running down the left of his face. The other is practically a dwarf.

They walk in without a word. The short one carries a hold-all.

"That the money?" Green asks in a hushed voice, nodding at the bag.

"Yes," Number One replies. "Where are they?"

"The kid's in the living room. Azrael is fast asleep in the guest bedroom. It's at the end of the hallway. I can't believe you didn't let me do it myself. I could have made this a lot easier."

"We prefer to do these things ourselves."

Number Two places the hold-all on a round side table. Green is straight on it.

"A hundred thousand, right?" he says, snatching at the zip. "Used bills?"

"Sure," Number One says coolly as he opens his coat partway and pulls a silenced Glock 17 from it.

Green pulls the bag open. Frowns.

"It's filled with shredded newspaper," he complains.

He doesn't get the chance to turn. The gun is already an inch from the back of his head. When One pulls the trigger, it sends Green's brains all over the hold-all of ripped paper.

SEVENTY-TWO

A WAREHOUSE IN ANCHORAGE, 2021

"So you're doing one last job for your old CIA commander?"

Harry's voice vibrates in Ibliss's ear. She's right at the end of her entire history as she knows it. She has told him *everything*. Even recalling details she thought she'd forgotten. Memories buried so deep she's only now acknowledging that they happened.

"I am," she says after a few seconds, wiping a tear from her cheek with the back of a hand.

"And he's threatening to expose you if you don't help this last time?"

"Uh-huh."

Harry takes a few seconds. Then. "Holy crap. This is a real mind fuck. Sorry."

"It's okay, honey."

"The government training orphans. Sending them out to kill. Then turning on them. Killing *them*."

"But, Harry, it's nearly over. He's got the guy now. He's gonna kill him and then let me go."

"You should go *now*. Honestly. Fuck this Smith guy. You're not Ibliss anymore. You're a wife and mother. You're the love of my life. Of my child's life. These people turned you into a killer and then came after you. Fuck them. You owe them nothing. If it comes to it, we'll expose it all. Go to the Canadian government. To the United Nations. They can't do this."

"They can. And they do."

"No, baby. Come home now. Please. Come home to *your family*."

These final words sink in deeper than anything else he's said so far. Her resolve softens completely. Without even thinking about it, she starts the engine.

In the back, Clive is smiling.

"Okay, Harry," she says. "I'll leave."

It sounds like he's crying when he says, "Oh baby, I love you so much."

The Hummer is already reversing, the back end swinging around, the headlights sweeping across the trees that crowd the warehouse.

"I'll be home soon, Harry," she says, shifting the Hummer into first. "But I have one last thing I've got to do first."

"What?"

"The woman who trained me."

"Mother?"

"Yeah. She's in danger. I have to help her."

SEVENTY-THREE

EVERGREEN RANCH, 2021

"*RAZ, DVAH, TREE*," NUMBER ONE AND NUMBER Two say in unison, shaking their fists with each count.

They're still standing in Charles Green's hallway. The dead vet lying on the floor next to their feet, leaking blood into the thick scrub of the carpet.

They open their fists.

One wins with paper over Two's rock.

The Russian smirks at his diminutive comrade, kinking the scar on his face, before making his way down the hallway toward the guest room.

Two sighs. Like he did in the parking lot, he has once again lost the chance to kill the great Azrael. Turning to the living room door, he feels that the man's son is scant consolation. He takes his Glock from his jacket and pushes the door the rest of the way. Keeping the gun hidden behind his back.

Disappointment floods him a second time in quick succession. The living room is empty.

In the far corner a set of venetian blinds flap in the wind. Reaching the window, Two leans out and eyes the snowy ground below. Boot prints, small enough to be a thirteen-year-old's, lead along the edge of the house.

The GRU man climbs out and begins following them.

IN THE MEANTIME Number One stands at the foot of Peter's bed. He is now the angel of death. The shadow he casts across the unconscious man is reimagined in his mind as a great horned creature with giant bat wings.

Curtains billow in from the open window. The air is crisp. One breathes it in. He wants to remember every sensation of this. It will make him a legend back home. The man who killed Azrael.

One could retire on that.

"The great Azrael," he says. "What an honor it is to be the one to do this. Even if it's in this cowardly way."

He stretches his arm out, the pistol on its end. Stares at the sleeping face. At the man they all fear. So helpless now.

He breathes in.

Swallows.

Freezes.

An oval dressing mirror adorns the wall next to the bed. In it, he spots someone crouched on top of the wardrobe behind him.

Number One twists around as Michael pounces. Lands on him before One can bring the gun around. Pushes the paring knife he stole earlier from the kitchen into the Russian's neck.

His falling weight pushes One over. The wet-boy lands on his back. Michael on top. The kid using the momentum to drive the knife all the way in. One loses his grip of the gun as his hand strikes the nightstand. Then, just like Mother taught him, Michael moves the knife rapidly from side to side, cutting the windpipe and opening up the arteries.

The Russian lets out a gurgling scream, coughing blood at the kid, more of it squirting from the wound, covering Michael as he continues to lever the knife.

The gurgling turns to a wet hiss and the wet-boy's chest decompresses one last time.

Michael collapses on him, pushing the last of the air out of the Russian's lungs.

For a while, he remains there, lying on top, the warm blood of his victim seeping into his clothing. It is beginning to feel sticky when a voice in his head screams at him to *GET UP!*

Michael springs into action. Peels himself from the dead man. His face and clothing coated in blood. Grabbing ahold of One's feet, he drags him to the bed. Rolls him underneath.

That done, he takes the Glock from the floor and scrambles back up the wardrobe like a cat. Once there, he waits, the pistol trained on the billowing curtains. The end of it trembling mercilessly. Michael doing his best not to sink into total panic. He hums Irving Berlin until he hears the crunch of feet on snow.

Michael holds his breath.

Hears nothing but the beat of his heart inside his head.

The wedge of the white snow he can see through the open window goes in and out of focus. Static begins to fill the edges of his vision. The gun pulls heavy on his hand. It becomes hard to keep his aim on the open window.

A shadow seeps across the snow. Stops. Seems to stay there for what Michael thinks must be minutes, but is actually seconds.

Moves.

Comes closer.

Reaches the window.

Leans his head inside.

Michael pulls the trigger.

The .22 bullet hits Number Two in the crown. He collapses over the sill. It is like he has been hit with a brick. His top end hangs in the room. His feet begin jittering and kicking at the snow outside. The convulsions rise up his body, along his arms, his whole body. The bullet hasn't killed him outright. It's just destroyed his brain.

Michael sends another two into him to make it stop.

When the body goes limp, he stares at it for half a minute.

Then he vomits.

SEVENTY-FOUR

A WAREHOUSE IN ANCHORAGE, 2021

The taser smolders in Walter Smith's iron grip. An aroma of sweat, urine and cooked flesh hangs in the air. Jamming the Knightro into the Hunter's spasming torso, it makes a sudden pop and goes dead.

Smith grasps the triggers to no avail.

"I think... you broke it," Semyon wheezes, grinning weakly.

His face looks like a slab of meat that's spent a long afternoon with the tenderizer.

"I think... you're right," Smith says breathlessly.

He drops the baton to the ground. The hollow echo of it hitting the concrete fills the empty warehouse. He snatches his Beretta from his belt.

"I never was one for torture," he says, aiming it at Semyon. "All I wanted was to get some of that anger out of me."

"Did it work?" the assassin asks.

Smith thinks about it. Shakes his head. "Not really."

He comes right up to the Hunter. Stands over him. Presses the cold metal of the Beretta into his skull. But before he gets the chance to pull the trigger, Semyon says something that catches him off guard.

"You know your daughter called out for you right before I pulled the trigger."

Smith freezes. His eyes stare into oblivion.

"*Daddy?!*" Semyon imitates.

Smith's expression changes. His lips curl into a scowl. Leaning back like a pitcher about to send a powerful curveball, he throws all his weight forwards, the Beretta whipping through the air.

The Russian offers up the left of his face. The blow rips the flesh. Fills his skull with ringing pain. But it does something else, too.

It snaps the left canine off at the root.

At last, Semyon thinks as he wedges the broken tooth under his tongue.

He begins laughing manically.

Smith pierces his eyes at him. "What the fuck are you laughing at?"

"Don't you want to know why I let Ibliss capture me?"

Smith frowns.

The deep purple, split lips of the Hunter purse into a smirk.

Semyon hisses, "You're not the only one with vengeance on his mind, Smith."

"What are you talking about?"

"Parfyon Rogozhin has given me a message to give to you."

"Parfyon Rogozhin?" The frown on Smith's face is threatening to consume it.

"The message is simple. He told me to tell you: *Shoyna, 1980.*"

Walter Smith's eyes open wide. "This is all about *that*? This is why he's come for the woman? Because of her defection?"

"Yes. And because of you double-crossing him back then."

"Double-crossing him? But I gave Parfyon the husband."

"He wanted the woman. Now he has sent me to get her back, kill the traitor smuggler Kirilov, and, finally, get *you*."

"Me? And how are you..."

Walter Smith stops speaking. Realization is dawning on him. There's a sound outside the warehouse. A low humming. He's only just guessed what it is, but it's been there for some time.

A moment ago it began getting closer.

Now it is above them.

"Ibliss?!" Smith shrieks into his comms. "Come in. There's a drone. The Russians have sent a drone!"

While a full-body panic sweat attacks the CIA man, Semyon spits the tooth at him, before throwing himself backwards off the chair. Scrambling to his feet, he runs across the wet concrete.

"*Do-svidaniya*, Smith," he cries out over his shoulder, his voice picked up by the drone's recognition software. The launch code having been spoken.

Smith looks down at the bloodied tooth that's skittled to his feet. It's false. But not filled with a cyanide capsule. No. Filled, instead, with a GPS locator.

Smith only has time to lift his eyes to the roof of the warehouse before he is vaporized.

SEVENTY-FIVE

SHOYNA, 1980

"We cannot wait for him any longer, Katya," Magda said into her ear as they stood on a bank of sand.

Her shimmering eyes stared back at a wooden house that stuck up out of the marsh grass. Hoping for the sight of a figure arriving late.

A frozen wind rasped across the vacant beach, throwing sand in their faces. Black waves crashed behind them, the wind carrying the spray to them. The sound of the sea hissed and boomed in their ears. The trafficker, Josep Kirilov, stood knee-deep in water ahead of them, plotting a route through the waves to open sea.

"Come on!" he shouted. "The rendezvous time is now. If we miss it, the boat will leave and we'll die in the water."

"Please, Katya," Magda begged.

"Where is he?"

Her eyes refused to leave the house.

"Maybe he'll find another way," Magda insisted. "Please. We have to go."

With tears falling, she reluctantly turned to the foaming sea and began making her way through the lashing water.

Never would Katya Igorevna forget that terrible day in that godforsaken place. Shoyna. A fishing village of three hundred souls stuck one end of the Kanin peninsula on the coast of the Barents Sea. Nothing else for hundreds of miles. Just wooden houses bleached gray by the sun, looking like tombstones from a distance. The heavy winds moving the sand dunes down the streets.

So much sand.

And all she could think as she slipped into the freezing water was what had happened to Misha. Why had he missed his chance?

Why?

SEVENTY-SIX

THE NASTASYA FILIPPOVNA CARGO SHIP, BERING SEA, 2021

MOTHER IS THINKING IT NOW. *WHY, MISHA? Why?* Her meandering mind having decided to settle on that terrible day in that terrible place. Shoyna. 1980. The day something died inside of her.

Before heading off on Charles Green's tipoff, Number One and Number Two had dropped her off at the dock in Anchorage. She'd been further sedated and taken onboard a Russian cargo ship named the *Nastasya Filippovna*.

Now she is awake. Locked inside a cabin deep within the ship. Strapped to a chair at the wrists and ankles. Listening to the sounds of the waves crashing onto the deserted beach at Shoyna.

A knock at the door makes her turn. A burly Russian who has been guarding her since her arrival answers it. A short and hushed conversation follows and the guard steps outside. In walks Semyon Mikhailovich. His beaten face practically unrecognizable.

He takes hold of a chair and brings it around her front. Takes a seat in it. Stares right into her.

"You're not Misha," she says.

"You've figured that at least."

She doesn't reply.

"So," Semyon says, "if I'm not Misha, *who* am I, *Mother*?"

"Your eyes are familiar," she tells him. "The eyes of a killer. But I have seen so many killers in my life that you all look the same. *Dead*."

Her defiant tone makes him smile. Then. "Do you know how your Misha died?"

She says nothing.

"He was shot in Shoyna."

Her wrinkled brow furrows. "He made it to the rendezvous?"

"Yes. He did. Arrived eight hours after you'd been pulled from the freezing water into a Norwegian fishing boat."

Confusion fills her. "He was late?"

"Not late. He arrived exactly when Smith told him to."

"But why?"

A malevolent smile appears on Semyon's face. "Because the Americans only ever wanted you. Not your husband. Walter Smith gave him up to the KGB. By the time your beloved Misha arrived, Parfyon Rogozhin was waiting for him. He shot Misha as a traitor there and then."

Mother's eyes glaze over. Then come alive. "Where's Magda?"

Semyon leans forward. Meets those eyes. "Dead."

Tears begin to trickle down the old woman's cheeks. "How?"

"*I* killed her."

"But why?"

"I did it on behalf of all those poor children you and she brutalized on that farm. Including *ME!*"

"You?"

Semyon is shaking his head. "I cannot believe you don't recognize me. You made me shoot the fucking dog for Christ's sake."

Mother takes in a deep breath, before confessing, "I made many children shoot dogs."

"But did they all try to kill you for it?"

Only now does recognition hit Mother. "Tommy?"

"That's right," Semyon says, leaning back. "Tommy. Hey, Mother. How are you doing?"

She is frowning. "How did you survive?"

"With the skills you taught me."

"And how did you end up with the Russians?"

"After surviving rough for a year, I eventually reached Anchorage. There, I took work on a Russian cargo ship. As a matter of fact, this very one. Then, when I reached Vladivostok, I handed myself to the authorities with the intention of helping the Russians expose the Fallen Angel program. However, they offered me something else. They offered me the chance to finish my training. That's when they sent me to a GRU facility in Siberia run by Parfyon Rogozhin. He took a keen interest in me. You know, he used to ask so many questions about you, Katya."

At the second mention of Parfyon's name, Mother's expression darkens.

"What was your history? You and he," Semyon asks, scrutinizing her expression for any sign that he's hitting a nerve. "Was he your lover? I always got the sense that he was your lover. The way his eyes would light up whenever we'd talk about you."

It is her eyes that now light up. They focus on him as she says, "No. Parfyon wasn't my lover. Parfyon never loved anything in his life. Parfyon only ever wanted one thing from me. Possession."

SEVENTY-SEVEN

PARIS, 1979

KATYA WALKED OUT OF THE CHARLES DE GAULLE airport like a catwalk model, catching the stares of all the people she passed. In her orange and red swirl-patterned jumpsuit and burgundy fedora, she looked like the stunningly beautiful wife of some Western diplomat. Not a deadly KGB assassin.

She waited exactly where he had told her to wait. Then, exactly when he said he would be there, a car pulled up at pickup point five on the sunbaked concrete of the airport causeway. Katya got the impression that it had been waiting further back just for her to show up.

The window rolled down and a man stuck his head out. Even though he looked absolutely different to the last time she'd seen him, she knew exactly who it was.

Parfyon Rogozhin. The ghost. The man without a face.

Today he had blond hair and a moustache. He looked

like a German. A dark mole she'd never seen on him before sat on one side of his chin, which was more rounded than last time, and the bridge of his nose seemed more crooked.

Katya got into the Citroën.

Ten minutes later, while they were on the freeway driving southwest into the city, he finally spoke.

"How is my beloved Russia?" came his flat toned voice.

"Still there."

A little red flushed his cheeks and he glanced sideways at her.

"You shouldn't joke about it," he told her. "At least you get to be there. I haven't seen Russia for fourteen years. Stuck out here in the decadence of western Europe."

You could tell, too, that he'd been away from the Motherland a long time. His accent was tinged with English, German, French. He didn't look Russian either. His chameleon appearance changing practically by the month, but never looking like anything other than a Westerner. Always a different one. But always a Westerner. Katya had once heard that he had bases in ten different cities including London, Madrid and Milan. That he was known as a different person in each. That he'd had so much plastic surgery done that his own mother would never recognize him. That even his superiors were unaware of what he looked like now.

In fact, Katya could only be certain it was Parfyon by the fact that he had picked her up from the exact spot he said he would at the exact time he told her he'd be there.

"So I'll ask again," Parfyon says in an angered tone; "how is my beloved Russia?"

"She is fine. Summer in Moscow is hot. And lonely."

"Lonely? Why Lonely?"

"Because for reasons my superiors won't explain to me, I have been kept away from my husband for the past year."

"Haven't you had shared leave?"

"No. Our leaves were arranged separately. When Misha was being redeployed, I was arriving in Moscow."

"That is strange. Husband and wife should have leave booked together. That's Party policy."

"That's what I told them."

"Oh, well. I'll take a look into it. Contact Sergei. See what's up."

"If you could, please."

"Anything for you, *milaya*."

Ugh, milaya, she thought. A sickly term of endearment. One that made her cringe whenever *he* called her it.

Katya turned to the window. Her eyes traced the stone buildings that passed by. Everything was so old in this part of Europe. Even though they'd occupied Paris, the Germans had gone easy on it compared with the Soviet Union. The French occupation hadn't quite been in the same league as the blitzkrieg that Operation Barbarossa had sent forth. That had flattened the entire village Katya was born in. Today nothing in that place was much older than her. The buildings all haphazardly built after the war in the communist utilitarian style.

Here the buildings were architectural beauties covered in decorative cornices and whimsical designs, meant to please the eye as well as serve their purpose. Aesthetics as well as function. They had color and form that lit something up inside her. Staring at the buildings was her favorite part of working in western Europe. Here there appeared time for art. Whereas back home it was—

Parfyon's hand settled on her knee. It made Katya's blood turn to ice in her veins.

"I hope we can reacquaint ourselves, *milaya*," he said.

His eyes never left the road.

She felt nauseous under that hand. Wanted to pick it up, twist it on itself, break the wrist. Wanted to hold him there while she ripped the crucifix from her neck and tore a hole in his throat with it.

But she didn't.

She merely pushed the feelings into the corners. Along with all the other pain.

SEVENTY-EIGHT

THE PRINCE VLADIMIR, 2021

IT TAKES ALL OF PARFYON'S STRENGTH TO STAND. Sweat slides down his bony face. His arm trembles as he holds on for dear life to a handrail that sticks out of the metal wall of his tiny cabin. He gazes in a dress mirror that had been brought aboard with him.

His eyes study the emaciated, eaten-away body that faces him. As a young man he had been athletic. But now the muscle of his youth has ebbed away and only the loose skin remains. His bone-thin legs fill him with fear. To look at them is to think that they will suddenly collapse underneath him like two bamboo canes holding up a house.

"Lift your left leg, Parfyon," the doctor says.

He is crouched beside him holding a pair of slate gray trousers. Acting as his dresser.

Leaning heavily against the rail, Parfyon lifts the leg. The doctor is quick. He hooks the trousers over the foot and up the limb in seconds. Achieves the next leg just as quick.

The suit has been taken in by a tailor, specially for today. It was once much larger to match its once much larger owner. Made for him by a Party tailor in Leningrad in 1975, it doesn't exactly look stylish; the shoulders too square, the material too coarse; but the sentimental value of it is through the roof.

Parfyon wants to be wearing this suit when Katya Igorevna comes through the door to his cabin.

He buttons the shirt himself, sitting on the bed for the job. Even that produces a breathlessness that upsets him.

Parfyon is sick of it. Sick of being *sick*. He has been this ill, this weak, for six months. Right from when the oncologist told him there was no more treatment that would put off the inevitable.

Go home and plan for the end.

With the suit jacket on, he takes a crumpled photograph from his pocket. A woman with bright eyes and a beautiful smile. So joyous as she poses for the taker.

"Soon, Katya Igorevna," Parfyon says to the face in the picture. "Soon." Turning to the doctor, who stands at his side, he asks, "Is everything else ready?"

"Yes, Parfyon. It is all ready."

Parfyon responds to this with a gentle smile. The effort causing him to break into a fit of coughing. Coughing that makes him scared he'll crack himself in half.

SEVENTY-NINE

EVERGREEN RANCH, 2021

Prizing open his heavy eyelids, Peter realizes immediately he has been drugged. A residual dullness rings in his head. His body is weak and practically paralyzed. His vision falters, going in and out of focus, head pinned to the pillows by its own weight. He smells the blood before he sees it.

Then he sees it.

Dripping out the cavity in the top of Number Two's head as he lies slumped over the windowsill, his top half hanging inside the room.

Peter is still alive. *But the hit man is dead.*

How in the hell did that happen?

It doesn't take long to get his answer.

Turning his head slowly to the left, he finds Michael collapsed forwards from the chair, his torso lying across Peter's legs. He is covered in blood. His hair matted.

"Mikey?" Peter says weakly. "Mikey?"

He does well to raise a hand and grab the kid's shirt in his fingers, shaking the teen gently. Hoping to God he's not hurt.

Michael slowly rouses. He swivels his head to face Peter. His eyes are red and swollen. Blood spatter covers him and dry vomit sits at the edges of his mouth.

The kid bursts into tears.

Peter stretches an arm out to him. The two have never hugged. Not in all the six months they've lived together. But the last vestiges of animosity drift away. The thirteen-year-old gets up from the bed and throws himself into his father's warm embrace.

"Oh, Mikey," Peter breathes as the kid lets it all out. "I never wanted this for you. *Not you.*"

AN HOUR LATER, Peter dresses in some of Charles Green's clothes. A pair of tan Levi's and a plaid shirt. He looks like a rancher.

The whole of his right side aches and he's still weak from the effects of the drugs. He walks with a slight limp. But other than that, he feels as good as can be expected for a man who's recently had major surgery and lost almost two pints of blood.

Michael is in the shower. His clothing is in the dryer.

As he stands up from the bed to zip the jeans, Peter spots a silenced Glock 17 on top of the wardrobe. It is the gun the kid used to kill the Russian. The one with half his head missing and now lying under the bed next to Charles Green and the other one, the three dead men attracting a sizable cloud of houseflies to the room.

Peter unscrews the suppressor and tosses it along with the Glock into a black hold-all he found in a cupboard. Then he moves into the kitchen.

Charles Green wasn't much of a shopper. The cupboards are pretty bare. Nevertheless, Peter does find shoeboxes filled with cash underneath the sink. A further inspection finds a loose floorboard. More rolls of fifty-dollar bills stuffed in the cavity.

By the time Michael is emerging from the bathroom, Peter has twenty-three-thousand dollars in used bills loaded inside the hold-all.

"He got much food?" the kid asks from the doorway, a towel wrapped around his waist.

Peter stares at the teen for a moment. Michael has put on a lot of muscle in the six months he's been with him. There was nothing to the kid when they first arrived in Alaska. Now he is toned.

"No," Peter says in answer to the question about food. "I think the breakfast he fed you consisted of practically everything he had. But I did find this."

He lifts a wad of cash from the bag.

"That'll do," Michael says.

He goes to smile but it's flat. There is a shimmer in his eyes.

"Your clothes are done," Peter tells him. "Get dressed and we'll leave. Get away from this place."

Minutes later, both are making their way across the hallway when Peter spots something beside the front door. A black rucksack.

"Is that what I think it is?"

"Oh yeah," Michael says when he spots what he's looking at. "I picked it up from the station house when I stole the car keys. It was on one of the desks."

Peter picks the rucksack up.

"Is everything still in it?" he asks as he unzips it.

"Yeah. Why?"

IT IS dark when they leave. The clouds are closed over them like a dome, and only the snow and ice give off any type of light.

Michael and Peter are in the front of Charles Green's black Chevy Tahoe. The engine idling. Peter sits in the passenger seat, the laptop open on his thighs. On the dashboard sits the StingRay's antenna.

The windows are open and a scent of gasoline wafts into the Chevy.

"So *is* it?" Michael asks.

A grin works its way up Peter's face. He turns to Michael, flipping the laptop around so that the screen faces him.

"Yes it is," he beams. "The burner phone Tommy was using on the train is still active."

Michael gazes at the electronic map: at the red dot working its way up the coast of Alaska.

"What's he doing out at sea?" the kid asks.

"Ibliss must've lost him or he killed her," Peter surmises. "Whatever it is, he's somehow gotten away and is now heading toward a rendezvous point."

"A rendezvous point?"

"Yeah. Airports and other routes are far too dangerous. My bet is that he's on a commercial ship and that they'll be picked up in the middle of the sea by a submarine."

"Then Mother will be there, too?"

"I would have thought so."

Michael is looking at him. "What are you gonna do?"

"What do *you* want me to do?"

He has turned to meet the kid's look.

Without hesitation, Michael says, "Go after her. One way or the other, it's Mother. If there's any chance of saving her from whatever they have planned, then I vote to save her. Because no matter how dangerous, it's the right thing to do."

Peter breathes in, then out.

"Okay," he says, facing the open window. "Save her it is. But first we have to clear up here."

Peter leans out the open window with the Beretta he found in Green's gun cabinet (along with two Ruger M77 Mark II bolt action hunting rifles). Aiming at the ground, at the melted trail that leads through the snow, he sends a bullet into it.

The gasoline ignites and a narrow column of fire meanders along the ground toward the single-story ranch home. The wooden building goes up quickly, especially with the amount of gasoline they poured all over it, and by the time Michael is driving them toward the main road, Charles Green's horse surgery is a huge fireball in their rearview mirror.

EIGHTY

THE NASTASYA FILIPPOVNA, 2021

DAWN APPROACHES AS THE SHIP MOVES UPON FAR calmer seas than it has enjoyed all trip. The gods, or whatever controls the weather, appear to have decided to give them peace for this day.

However, Semyon Mikhailovich doesn't want peace. He wants war.

Inside his cabin, he sits with eyes closed, meditating on his enemy. Envisioning Peter's face. Chanting over and over: "Come find me."

He is like a witch invoking the devil.

In his clenched fist is his burner phone. Switched on and communicating with the nearest cell towers. Giving Peter something to follow.

A knock at the door interrupts the conjuring.

Semyon's eyes open as the door does, and the burly guard in charge of Mother steps inside.

He wears a solemn expression.

"You set?" he asks.

He doesn't really need to. Semyon is already dressed. His kit packed up beside him on the bed.

"As I'll ever be," comes the answer.

"Good. You have two minutes."

The door closes and Semyon closes his eyes once more.

Visions of Peter bubble to the surface.

Clenching his fists and speaking into his teeth, the Hunter hisses, "Come find me, Pete. I repaid the debt. Left you alive. Now come find me. Because next time you die."

EIGHTY-ONE

PETER AND MICHAEL HEAD NORTH TOWARD THE nearest airfield in the hope that they'll be able to commission a helicopter. Or at least steal one.

Heavy wind sweeps snow and ice across the Tahoe's windshield. Michael concentrates on the endless band of gray, the road bending like a serpent through grassland and mountains.

In the passenger seat Peter redresses the wound. The thick stitches and the pursed-together six-inch cut look like a tight-lipped smile. The flesh around it purple.

"You sure you're gonna be up to it?" Michael asks.

"I think so. I'm a quick healer. Plus, for all his other obvious bad qualities, Charles Green is actually a very good surgeon."

"Then why didn't he just get a license and perform it on people without the whole criminal element?"

"Because," Peter replies dryly, "while Charles Green was

studying medicine at John Hopkins, he got caught dealing drugs from his dormitory."

"Wow."

"Yep. He's a felon. And they don't give medical licenses to felons. A veterinary license to perform on horses, okay. But not one for humans."

"What an idiot. He could have been a real surgeon and he threw it away to deal drugs at college."

"In my time amongst society, Mikey," Peter tells him as he uses superglue to waterproof the wound, "I've often found that some people just like crime. No matter if they need to commit it or not. They're just primed for it."

"What about you?" the kid puts to him. "Are you primed to kill?"

Peter thinks about it. "Good question. I'm not sure. Maybe I'm..."

Peter stops talking. His eyes fix to the sky in front. His hand automatically reaches into the glovebox and retrieves the Beretta. He checks it. Chambers a round.

"What is it?" Michael asks.

"Twelve o'clock. Coming straight for us."

Michael looks up. Sees it. Two lights meandering through the black air toward them. Red and green. The types of lights you see on a helicopter.

"Stop the car," Peter tells the kid, "and park it across both lanes."

Michael does as he says. Bringing the Tahoe to a stop in the middle of the deserted highway so that it is side on to the approaching helicopter.

The chopper pulls up about two hundred yards in front before gradually landing on the snow swept asphalt. By the time Ibliss is getting out, Michael and Peter are ducked in cover behind the Chevy. Each holding one of the Ruger Mark IIs they took from Green's place, the barrels rested on the pickup's roof.

"So Tommy didn't kill her, then?" Michael puts to Peter as they watch her through their scopes.

"It would appear not."

She walks toward them, seemingly unarmed, hips swaying from side to side in that catsuit of hers. About fifty yards away, she stops. Takes something from her belt. Begins waving a white handkerchief.

"At Wasilla," Michael remarks, "she seemed to be on friendly terms with Mother."

Peter thinks about it. Breathes slowly out through his nose, the steam clouding the lens of the scope. Groaning, he comes away from the rifle.

"Stay here and keep your crosshairs on her," Peter says as he shoulders the Mark II and leaves the cover of the Tahoe.

Peter makes his way down the cold road, his boots crunching in the frozen snow. He can't help thinking that he's never met another angel except for Tommy. They were always kept far apart from each other. Especially in the field. If ever they needed assistance, it would come in the form of special forces, or, if it was intelligence gathering, a stooge from the CIA. Never another Fallen Angel.

Peter always gathered that the reason for this was paranoia; that if two angels were to form a bond, it could prove deadly.

"Lucky I placed an AirTag on your boy's clothing," Ibliss says when he comes to a stop four yards from her. "And lucky you didn't check."

Peter groans inwardly at the oversight. "What do you want?"

"Are you going for the old woman?"

"What's it to you?"

"You'll need my help." She gestures toward the chopper with a backwards nod. "I got us air power. Wanna join teams?"

"Why do you want to help?"

"Not for you and your boy. For her."

Peter's eyes narrow. "What is she to you?"

Ibliss says one word. "Mother."

Peter feels better now. He turns over his shoulder. Makes a discreet hand signal to the watching kid.

Stand down.

EIGHTY-TWO

BERING SEA, 2021

A THIN, FIERY WEDGE OF SUN RISES ABOVE THE horizon, casting the sky blood red over the black sea. The *Nastasya Filippovna* has its engines switched off and floats idly on the water. The sea is choppy. Driven on by a brisk wind that comes down from the Arctic to the north.

Semyon and Mother stand on the starboard side of the vessel. The ship's captain stands with them. Only he has been invited. The rest of the crew are to remain in the mess hall until the captain fetches them.

Semyon and the captain stand at the edge of the ship, holding onto the railing and staring down at the water twenty feet below. Mother merely watches the crimson sky, hands secured behind her back, waiting for her end.

About sixty yards away, a long, narrow section of water begins to foam and bubble as if the sea is boiling. A giant, black tower bursts out of the waves, rising to the height of the *Nastasya Filippovna*'s deck. It is followed by the topside, or dorsal, of the *Prince Vladimir* in all its nuclear armed glory.

The submarine resembles the black leathery back of a whale.

"Let's get to the boat," Semyon says.

They make their way to a black rubber dinghy that hangs from the side of the ship via a boat winch. Placing the prisoner in first, Semyon follows, taking a place behind her. Next, the captain releases the crank arm and lowers them into the sea. A minute later they are chugging across the short distance to the submarine.

"Soon, old woman," Semyon hisses into her ear, "you will meet your terrible fate."

"Looks like you'll be meeting yours as well."

Mother is looking off to the horizon. When Semyon follows the direction of her gaze, he spots the silhouette of a chopper moving towards them.

The captain of the *Prince Vladimir*, Dubrovsky, has just been alerted to its presence by his sonar technician. He throws open the hatch and climbs out onto the topside, plucking his MP-443 Grach pistol from his belt.

"Hurry!" he shouts at Semyon, coming to the edge of the sub and waving his arms about.

Semyon is already hurrying, but the dinghy's motor isn't that quick. The chopper is almost upon them. Coming from the east, it blocks the emerging sun. All the light, therefore, is concentrated at the edges of the craft. Making it almost impossible for the Russians to focus their eyes on it.

An asterisk of muzzle flash ignites from one side of the cockpit. Someone is hanging out the door with a machine gun. Dubrovsky takes cover behind the sail. The helicopter too far for the Grach.

Two Russian marines emerge next from the hatch. They join their captain behind the cover of the sail. Using AK-74Ms, they send bursts of covering fire at their attacker.

The helicopter pulls up and keeps its distance, hovering about fifty yards from the bow of the *Prince Vladimir*. A searchlight hangs between the chopper's landing skids. Light explodes from it, blinding the Russians and forcing them to shield their eyes.

It is within this dazzling incandescence that the dinghy reaches the submarine. Semyon gets out first. He lifts Mother and uses her as a shield while he makes his way to Dubrovsky and the marines, practically dragging the old woman with him.

"Why don't you send a missile at it?" Semyon asks the captain once they've reached them.

"This close to American waters would be conceived as an act of war," Dubrovsky shouts back.

Semyon shrugs. Acts of war are what he's all about.

From the cover of the sail, he lifts his own AK and joins the men in firing at the helicopter. The chopper swings and moves to avoid the hail of bullets.

Then it does something strange.

It retreats.

The pilot pulls off a maneuver that turns the craft 180 degrees, the searchlight beam sweeping in an arc across the water, and soon it is shrinking into the distant sun.

. . .

FROM INSIDE THE Ultramarine's cockpit, Ibliss gazes down at the dark water. There is something in it. Something that dived from the helicopter not long after she'd blinded the Russians with the searchlight.

Dressed in a wet suit and carrying Ibliss's Heckler & Koch G36 assault rifle on his back and her Ruger LCP on his hip is Azrael. The assassin swimming rapidly towards the submarine.

Reaching the *Prince Vladimir*, Peter climbs onboard and runs along the wet back. While the Russians are too busy gazing after the chopper, he sneaks into the hatch and descends into the vessel before the men hiding behind the sail are any the wiser.

"WAS THAT CIA?" Dubrovsky asks Semyon.

"No."

"Then who was it?"

"A hopeless fool working on his own."

"Not Americans?"

"Not anymore."

"Good. I aim to get my submarine back to Russia without starting World War Three."

They drop below into the tight realms of the nuclear submarine. Once the hatch above is closed, Dubrovsky plucks a bridge telephone from the wall and speaks into it.

"This is Captain Dubrovsky. Take her down."

The alert sounds and everyone clings on to something as the floor tips and feels like it is dropping away from their feet. The metal walkway they stand on vibrates mercilessly. A terrible creak runs through the entire length of the vessel. Rushing up, it clangs in their ears when it reaches them.

Mother is the only one not clinging on. Semyon has to grab ahold of her before she falls.

"I wouldn't want Parfyon's prize spoiling," he growls in her ear.

Once the *Prince Vladimir* is far enough below the scalp of the sea, the submarine rights itself and everything becomes still. The metal walkway is once more firm beneath their feet.

An ensign joins them. A round-faced guy with paper-white skin.

"I'm Ensign Borisov," he says to the guests. "I will be taking care of you during your journey."

Captain Dubrovsky is already gone. On his way back to the confined spaces of the bridge. Like a spilled fish eager to get back to its tank.

Semyon says one word. "Parfyon?"

"Right this way."

The ensign leads them through the cluttered mass of exposed wiring, pipes and metalwork that makes up the internals of the *Prince Vladimir*. Sailors back up against the walls as they pass along the tight corridors.

Reaching the cabin deck, the ensign stops and gestures to his left with a hand.

"You are to stay here, sir," he says specifically to Semyon. "This is your cabin."

"But I'm going to see Parfyon."

"Mr. Rogozhin will send for you shortly. But at this moment he only wishes to see the package. Now I understand you have the key to her handcuffs."

With a disappointed look, Semyon hooks it out of his pocket and hands it over.

"Thank you, sir."

The ensign takes Mother by the elbow.

"When will I see him?" Semyon asks like a son denied a visit to his father after a long absence.

"Shortly, sir. He merely wishes to see the package alone at first. Then he will call for you. Be patient."

The ensign leaves with Mother. Semyon's eyes trail them until they turn a corner and disappear out of sight. Sighing, he goes inside the tiny cabin to wait.

THE ENSIGN ARRIVES at Parfyon's cabin with Mother in tow. His knock is answered by the doctor. The ghoulish looking man nods and the ensign leaves Mother with him.

"So this is the great Katya Igorevna," the doctor says when they are alone. "I've heard so much about you."

Mother doesn't give any indication that she's even heard what he said. She merely looks right through him. Coming around the back of her, the doctor gently pushes Mother through the open door into the cabin. Now is the time she will meet fate head-on.

She half stumbles into the room and comes to a stop in the middle. The doctor climbs in there with her and shuts the hatch door behind him.

Parfyon sits in a leather armchair that must have been brought onboard with him specially. He looks like someone has laid a suit out on the chair and placed a head on top. His gray skin is so tight to his skull that you see the contours of the bones. His blue eyes look huge in their pink sockets.

What hair there is on his head is white and patchy. Four bouts of chemotherapy will do that. An oxygen line feeds air into his nose and an intravenous line sticks out the top of one of his feeble little hands.

Those big eyes fix to Katya, the whole of his emaciated body shaking as he watches her stand in the center of the cabin. A single tear slips down his cheek.

"Never," he says in a voice crackling with emotion, "did I think that I would ever set eyes on you again, *milaya*."

Mother stares at him. Her eyes slowly narrowing.

Turning to the doctor, Parfyon says, "Get our guest a chair."

Nodding, the stringy man takes a folded chair from the corner of the room and places it opposite Parfyon.

"Take the handcuffs off her," Parfyon says next.

The doctor gives him a dubious look. But Parfyon isn't looking. He is fixated by Katya Igorevna.

The doctor removes them and Mother takes a seat, rubbing her sore wrists, her gaze never leaving the sick man opposite.

There is a table between them. On it stands a bottle of cabernet sauvignon and two glasses.

"Could you pour the wine?" he asks her. "I'm afraid I don't have the strength."

He smiles crookedly.

For the first time, she speaks. "You don't look like Parfyon."

"Did Parfyon ever look like Parfyon?" he remarks. "What with all the surgery."

"You don't have his eyes. They can't change eyes."

With every bit of ebbing strength left in his body,

Parfyon leans his frail body from the chair and deftly reaches a hand out to touch her face.

As it moves slowly towards her, she concentrates on his blue eyes. She sees something there. Not Parfyon. Someone else.

"Whose eyes do I have, love?" he asks.

Her lip quivers and she begins to cry.

Taking hold of the hand, she kisses it and breathes, "Misha."

EIGHTY-THREE

SHOYNA, 1980

Misha arrived a full fifteen minutes before he was supposed to. Before the time Walter Smith had specifically given him. It was nighttime and the overbearing clouds made it a pitch black one. In the headlight beams the bones of old fishing boats stuck up out of the long salt grass like the ribcages of long deceased whales. Wooden houses occupied the sandy coastline, ill kept and looking abandoned.

The place they were meeting looked like it was sinking into the sand. The wind having sent half the beach into town, and everywhere there were drifts.

Misha was glad to find Katya and Magda's car already parked in front. The howling wind hit him with sand the second he got out the car. At the rickety door he knocked and a muffled voice told him to come in. Blindly, in need of getting out of that caustic wind, Misha stepped into the house.

He went cold the second he saw Parfyon Rogozhin sitting on the other side of a table with a Markov pistol aimed for his head.

"Take a seat, Misha," the man without a face hissed like a snake. "All is over."

"Where is Katya?"

A disappointed look flooded Parfyon's face. "I'm afraid we've both missed her. Now sit down."

Misha felt like he'd been shot. He practically staggered to the table. There was a steaming kettle on it and some tea glasses.

"May I have one of those?" he asked meekly, moving toward the glasses.

"Of course. One last drink."

Misha paused as his hand hovered over a glass. "Last?"

"Yes. No gulag for you, Mikhail. I get the feeling you'd only escape and come find me. No. Tonight, you die."

Misha finished pouring the scorching hot tea from the kettle.

"More sugar, I think," he said afterwards.

He began spooning it in, one after the other. Practically filling the glass half fall with sugar, before stirring it into the hot drink.

"What happened to Katya?" he asked when he'd finished.

"I got here too late for her. Looks like Smith double-crossed us both in a way. Wanted the wife but not the husband, I guess."

"You mean she made it?"

"Yes. She should be halfway to the West by now."

Misha began laughing. "The American bastard," he guffawed, "he told us two different times. Ha!"

He hammered the table with a palm.

It made Parfyon wince.

Misha met him with his eyes, stopped laughing.

His face going pensive, he asked, "How does it feel to be back in your homeland?"

"I spent a nice night in Moscow," Parfyon replied cordially. "But apart from that, I'm not really here on holiday. I came especially for you and her. Even snuck in on a fake Hungarian passport so no one knows I'm in Russia."

Misha's eyes narrowed within the steam of his tea. "No one knows you're here?"

"I wanted this for myself," Parfyon replied. "Didn't want the Party taking it from me. Wanted to be the one who put a bullet in you."

"So you're here all alone?"

"Yes. Just me. The way I like it."

Taking ahold of his glass, Misha told him, "That was pretty stupid, Parfyon."

It was the KGB man's turn to frown. "I'm stupid? I'm not the one—Ahh!"

The burning hot tea was across the table and in Parfyon's face before he could think. He began clawing away the molten sugary cocktail from his scolded eyes. When he could, he opened them onto the blurry room.

Misha was right there.

Before Parfyon could stop him, he had snatched the pistol, turned it on its owner, and put two bullets into his head.

EIGHTY-FOUR

THE PRINCE VLADMIMIR, 2021

FORTY-ONE YEARS LATER MOTHER ASKS HIM HOW he became the other man. How he went on living as Parfyon Rogozhin.

"Parfyon kept extensive diaries," Misha explains. "One of them was amongst the belongings I found in the trunk of his car. It seemed that even though the KGB forbade it, Parfyon wrote everything down. *Everything*. It would have been a dream for a CIA agent. It *was* a dream for me. In those belongings I found all the details to his safe houses, his personas, the banks in which he stored the money the KGB sent him. All the account details. Then, when I arrived at his main home in Zurich, I discovered a stack of journals hidden under floorboards that detailed every part of his life and history. It was like he was preparing it for a publisher. Perfect for someone who wants to take the place of a man no one recognizes anymore. Not even his mother."

Mother's eyes have misted over. Her lips tremble.

"You pretended to be Parfyon all these years?" she mutters.

"I had to. The Americans had burned me. I only had the Motherland, and, as Misha, I was a wanted man. A traitor. All I could do was return to western Europe. Continue taking missions as Parfyon. Do my best to imitate his voice when I spoke to superiors over the telephone."

Mother smiles. "You always were good at impressions."

"I didn't really need to be. Mostly they only cared that I repeated the passwords correctly. Then in 1989 everything changed. Orders came in. They wanted Parfyon back in Moscow. I almost didn't go. But by then, I was locked into it. There was no other way. I came back and, thankful no one realized who I really was, continued being Parfyon. I even accepted a promotion from Yeltsin to be one of the architects of the KGB's reorganization. I then helped train recruits for the GRU until I retired a year ago from sickness."

The smile drops from Mother's face. She gazes at him with a solemn expression. "What is wrong with you?"

"Cancer, I'm afraid."

"How long have you got?"

"Weeks. Maybe days."

She shivers, leans forward and places her head against his bony chest. His thin arms close around her and she begins crying.

"That's why," he whispers down to her, "I had to find you. I couldn't wait any longer. Even if I risked exposure, I had to see you one last time."

"IT MAKES NO SENSE," Engineer Strakovsky says to his shipmate as they stroll along a stretch of walkway on their way to the Engine Room.

"So you've already said," Engineer Dolgen mutters.

"We come this close. Breach the surface. Then turn straight back for Russia?"

"I told you. It was some stupid training exercise. That was all."

They reach the electronic doors of the Engine Room and stop. Dolgen steps forward and places a thumb on the fingerprint scanner, holding it there while a line of light flashes up and down the glass panel. The doors part and the two men move off without realizing that something has dropped silently from the ceiling behind them and, as the men enter the room, moves up quickly.

The blade is around Engineer Strakovsky and across his throat before he even knows it. The first clue he has is the spew of blood that sprays across the metal walkway. Engineer Dolgen half turns. Only to see Peter flip the knife around and bring it stabbing forwards into his forehead.

As Peter retrieves the knife from the Russian sailor's skull, he spots a third engineer inside the room. The man stands watching him with wide eyes.

He makes a run for the bridge telephone.

Gets within a couple of inches of it when he stops.

Peter's throw was perfect. The knife spinning in an arc all the way to the engineer's side. Sinking to the hilt just below the left armpit.

The sailor lands on his side. The blade has severed the

main coronary artery. He's not dead. Yet. His first thought is to grab the handle of the knife. He tries to pull it out. But before it's even an inch, Peter has sent a bullet from the Ruger into him. The suppressor cushioning the sound.

Placing the pistol back on his belt, Peter begins searching for what he's looking for. The air purification system. It sits in a corner; a great big block of metal with pipes going in and out of it.

There's a grated cover he has to remove.

Once it's off, the pipes are exposed, giving him access to the airflow. He places several incendiary devices inside the unit.

Peter runs back to the door, and, from there, detonates them.

The explosion shakes the *Prince Vladimir*. No damage is done to the integrity of her hull, but the incendiary devises create a spark which causes the oxygen in the filtration unit to catch fire.

The electronic doors slam shut as the whole of the Engine Room erupts into a giant fireball that climbs through the room.

Outside in the corridor, Peter places a gas mask over his face just as smoke begins to pour through the ventilation, filling the air.

Unshouldering the G36 assault rifle, he lines himself up with the sight and begins stalking through the gray smog.

THE SECOND THE ALARM SOUNDS, Semyon leaves the cabin and heads to Parfyon's. He finds the doctor standing outside the door.

"You can't go in there," he says when he spots Semyon's approach.

"The submarine is under attack," the Hunter tells him. "It must be Azrael."

"It doesn't matter. Parfyon is not to be disturbed.

Semyon frowns at him. Places a hand on his bony shoulder.

Squeezes.

The doctor's long legs buckle underneath him. Semyon having hit a nerve.

Pushing him out of the way, Semyon opens the door and walks into the cabin.

"Parfyon, we need to…"

His words fade to nothing when he sees the two of them embraced like old lovers.

"What's going on?" he asks.

Parfyon and Mother part.

"Semyon," Parfyon says, "there is something I must explain."

A minute later, Semyon is shaking all over. His fists screwed up at his sides, the fingernails pressing into the flesh of his palms. The man he saw as a father only a moment ago has just done telling him that everything was a lie. That he is in fact this woman's husband and that instead of the fate Semyon expected for her—the fate he believes she deserves—he has once again been betrayed for this *woman*.

First Peter. Now Parfyon. Or Misha. Or whoever he is.

Semyon's eyes burn at Parfyon.

"You lied to me."

"I couldn't tell you the truth."

"I used to think you asked all those questions about her

because you hated her like me. But all along it was because she was your missing love. This... *bitch*."

Parfyon goes to speak when the lights go out and everything is drenched in red. Captain Dubrovsky's tinny voice then fills the cabin through a speaker.

"*This is your captain. There is a fire in the air filtration system. All crewmen are to find access to a gas mask and to get ready for surfacing.*"

"He's here," Semyon hisses. Then, looking directly at Mother, he adds, "Your boy is here to save you. What a shame he is too late."

The idea comes to him in the moment. Like a wolf, he acts on instinct alone.

"Semyon," Parfyon cautions with wide eyes as the Hunter's shadow begins to swallow him up. "Semyon, don't do anything stupid."

"You betrayed me."

Mother stands up and comes between them. Semyon backhands her, swatting the old woman away like a fly. She tumbles into the wall, and when she tries to get back up, she collapses onto the floor breathless.

Semyon's hands reach forwards. Misha can do nothing. His body failing to muster the requisite strength to even move out of the man's way. Semyon takes hold of his head, the whole of it fitting into his hands, his thumbs coming over the eyes. Parfyon takes ahold of his arms. So weakly that the Hunter doesn't even feel the press of his fingers.

Parfyon begins to scream as Semyon pushes his thumbs into the sockets.

. . .

THE FIRE IS SPREADING through the submarine. Black smoke fills the cramped aisles. The *Prince Vladimir* is heading for the surface. The walkways tipping and creaking beneath their feet.

Officers shout at crewmen as they help them evacuate. The sailors all clambering up the stairwells to the top deck.

Close to the Engine Room an officer reaches into the billowing smoke from the bottom of a stairwell. He is taking hold of people's hands and pulling them out. Pointing them up the stairs.

A strange thing happens when the next hand grabs *him*. Pulls *him* into the smoke. He is flipped around and the cold end of a pistol is pressed to the bottom of his chin.

"Where is the old woman?" a man asks in perfect Russian, his voice muffled by the gas mask.

"Top deck," the guy shivers. "Officers' cabins."

Peter knocks him out cold with a smash to the head from the Ruger. Stepping over the body, he makes his way up the stairwell, through the smoke, meandering in between and around the crewmen that file up the stairs, their hands linked, officers pointing them onwards.

No one bothers about the armed man in the wetsuit. Assuming that he must be part of those GRU guys they have onboard.

At the top deck Peter heads toward the aft while the crewmen all head to the bow. That's where the emergency hatches are. Peter wants the cabin section.

But no sooner is he walking into it than Semyon's voice fills his ears.

"Pete?!" he shouts. "Oh, Peter! Come and watch beloved Mother get her throat cut!"

SEMYON'S EYES search the smoke. It isn't as bad here as it is on the lower decks and he doesn't yet need a mask. The old woman stands in front of him, a knife to her throat, an arm across her chest.

A shadow grows larger and so too does the grin on Semyon's face.

"I'm gonna make him watch you die," he hisses in the old woman's ear. "Just like I made you watch your beloved Misha."

She doesn't make any sign that she has even registered what he said. Since he lifted her off the floor, Mother hasn't spoken or made a single sound. She hangs there in front of him, his arm doing most of the work to keep her upright.

"You wanna hear something fucked up?" Semyon calls to the shadow coming toward him. "The old man didn't want her dead. He just wanted to see her."

A man emerges from the smoke. His face distorted behind a gas mask. He is holding a pistol. He comes toward Semyon and doesn't stop. Unsure, Semyon throws the knife at him in a whip-snap movement.

Captain Dubrovsky was only coming to guide them to the emergency hatches. And for that, he gets a knife through the jugular. Nevertheless, it also means there is no longer one at Mother's throat.

She comes alive. Flips around. Faces him. Stabs the pencil she snuck from the cabin into his eye.

It breaks off in her hand. A broken end sticking out of the socket as he cries out, his voice filling the entire corridor. Staggering back, he grabs ahold of the pencil. Pulls. Feels every millimeter tug from his destroyed eyeball until it is released.

Blinded in one eye, he watches the old woman stagger off.

Fury explodes in him.

He dives for the captain's pistol, snatches it from the deadman, and aims it. The smoke has swallowed her up. He fires blindly. Letting off four shots.

Number four hits.

Mother cries out.

Semyon removes the knife from Dubrovsky. Wipes the blood off on his thigh. Begins marching toward her. Eager to do terrible things to her with this knife. Terrible, terrible things.

But as he reaches her slumped up against the railing of the stairwell, his lack of a left eye causes him to miss the person dashing at him from across the corridor.

The ferocity of his opponent and the speed of the attack catch Semyon off guard. A hand grabs his arm and smashes it repeatedly against a pipe that sticks from the uneven wall. A gun goes off. It isn't the one he's holding. Once. Twice. Three times. He feels every shot ripple through his leg like a bomb detonating inside it. The thigh bone shatters. The muscles tear apart. He loses focus as his hand is repeatedly slammed against the railing until his wrist shatters and he's dropping the gun, the thing skittling off down the steps of the stairwell, disappearing into smoke.

Semyon swipes left with the knife. A blind, hopeless swing that is more anger than skill. Peter isn't even there. He comes underneath it and plants a headbutt on Semyon that breaks his nose into his face. Really mushes it in. Before the

Hunter can react with the knife, Peter has hold of that hand. Drives it into the wall. Smashes the blade from his fingers.

As this goes on, Mother, wounded in the lower back from the gunshot, pulls herself up off the deck with the help of the rails, her old body screaming out in pain.

When she is finally on her feet, she moves to the pair. Semyon's arm flails about as Peter lands more punches and kicks on him. Mother takes him by a wrist with every ounce of her ebbing strength.

As well as the pencil, she has swiped the handcuffs used to bring her here. She now snaps one end over a pipe and the other over the wrist.

Semyon goes to move, but can't. He is fastened to the submarine. Peter steps back, avoiding the lashes that come his way. He then joins Mother and she instantly collapses into his arms.

Peter throws her over his shoulder, and, without looking behind him, starts making his way toward the emergency hatches, leaving Semyon trapped. Flames begin to lick the air of the stairwell, igniting the oxygen. The smoke gets thicker and, as Peter and Mother begin to disappear, Semyon starts to choke.

Like a wild animal, he tugs on the handcuffs, his bust leg hanging from him.

"Peter?!" he cries out. "Peter, come back! Don't leave me!"

THE HATCH they use is abandoned. When they climb up top, all the crewmen are gathered at the aft. They do nothing more than watch the American and the dissident emerge from the hatch. None of them approach and none of them stop the two climbing aboard the helicopter that comes to pick them up. Continuing to watch as it dissolves into the red sky.

"She okay?" Ibliss asks from the front of the Ultramarine.

"No," Peter replies.

Peter cradles Mother in the back. She lies in his arms, gazing up with shimmering eyes. The bullet hole in her lower back is pouring with blood. Semyon has hit an artery.

Peter knows that there will be no saving her unless they get her to a surgeon within the next ten minutes. Something that is absolutely impossible.

Peter feels cold all over. His throat aches and tears begin to fall from his eyes.

"It is okay," she says weakly. "Don't be sacred."

She reaches a hand up to his face and touches it.

"I'm so sorry, Peter," she says, her gaze never leaving his. "So sorry for what I did to you. For what I did to all the children that came to the farm."

"It's okay," he sobs. "You were the only mother I ever knew."

Her hand upon his face feels so cold.

"I always loved you, you know," she tells him. "Even when I made you think I didn't. I always felt it in my..."

The hand falls from his face and her eyes go blank.

Bringing his lips to her forehead, he whispers, "Goodbye, Mother."

EIGHTY-FIVE

ALASKA, 2021

THE NEXT DAY, PETER, MICHAEL AND IBLISS STAND before a funeral pyre. They are at the farm. The one they grew up on. The pyre takes up the center of the living room. Right there in the middle of the floor. A stack of wood and kindling.

On top of it lie the bodies of Mother and Magda. They are both wrapped in cloth. No one has come to the farm to see what is up. When the three of them returned, they found it pretty much untouched apart from the deer they found inside the house. The one that had stumbled around knocking things over until it managed to fly out of the kitchen door and bolt into the woods.

Magda's body had still been in the freezer.

Peter lights his torch then leans toward Michael, lights his, before lighting Ibliss's. Following that, the three of them approach the pyre and set fire to it.

Before long the whole building is a flaming wreck.

"So what now for you and your boy?" Ibliss asks.

She and Peter stand side by side in front of the burning farm, the flames licking the evening dusk. Michael is behind them. Sitting inside Charles Green's Tahoe.

"I don't know," Peter replies. "He's got a decision to make."

Ibliss glances over her shoulder at the kid. "Shame he had to kill," she says. "Innocence lost. You're never the same."

Peter sighs. Looks back at Michael.

The kid stares at the flaming farm. Peter has noticed a difference in him since they left Evergreen Ranch. The light that existed in his eyes only a few days ago, the crackle of joy in his tone, his enthusiasm for play, these things have become lesser in him since he became a killer.

Turning back to the fire, Peter tells Ibliss, "In a way, I would have preferred it if he had of let me die. Had of just run away into those woods."

"But he didn't," Ibliss points out.

"No he did not."

Peter wishes they could go back to the day they lay in the frozen woods hunting deer. The day Michael was unable to kill the animal with the knife.

That day he had been innocent.

Now he is not.

Now he is a killer.

EIGHTY-SIX

SAN DIEGO, 2021

IT IS A WEEK LATER WHEN THE FATHER AND SON arrive in San Diego. The kid thinks it's because they're meeting up with Marta. It kind of is. But first they need to stop somewhere.

Michael realizes what's up the second they pull off of West Mission and head into Santa Fe Hills. After all, he's spent enough Thanksgivings and Christmasses here.

In the midday Californian sun, they pull up outside a single-story flat-roofed house in the pueblo revival style: adobe-colored stucco walls with rounded edges and projecting wood beams. Peter stops the car at the end of the driveway and turns to Michael.

The kid is watching him with a stern face.

"Peter," he says, his voice almost breaking, "what is this?"

Before he speaks, Peter reaches into the back and pulls

out a rucksack. He lays it on his lap, unzips it, and removes something that is wrapped in black cloth.

Holding it in his hand, he unwraps it with the other.

For a moment neither says anything. The kid just sits there gazing at the Glock 17 that Peter holds.

"This is yours if you choose it," Peter tells him.

The kid raises his eyes to his father. They shimmer.

"There," Peter says next, pointing at the house, "is your grandparents' home. It is also your home. If you choose to leave this car, you will have a normal life with them. And please believe me, Mikey, when I tell you that if I was you, that would be my choice."

Peter and the kid stare at each other from across the car.

"I will not lie to you," Peter goes on. "If you choose the gun, there will not be much out there for you except more of the same pain you've already experienced while with me. The way of the assassin is a lonely, cold road." Peter pauses. Stares hard at the kid, looking for any sign. "But for however long I survive it," he adds, "I will be there, traveling that road with you."

Michael stares at the Glock. Then at his grandparents' house.

"Now choose," Peter says lastly. "The gun or the home."

Don't miss UNPUNISHED DEEDS. The riveting sequel in the Peter Black Thriller series.

Scan the QR code below to purchase UNPUNISHED DEEDS.

Or go to: righthouse.com/unpunished-deeds

NOTE: flip to the very end to read an exclusive sneak peak...

DON'T MISS ANYTHING!

If you want to stay up to date on all new releases in this series, with these authors, or with any of our new deals, you can do so by joining our newsletters below.

In addition, you will immediately gain access to our entire *Right House VIP Library*, which includes many riveting Mystery and Thriller novels for your enjoyment.

righthouse.com/email

(Easy to unsubscribe. No spam. Ever.)

ALSO BY DAVID ARCHER

Up to date books can be found at:
www.righthouse.com/david-archer

ROGUE THRILLERS
Gates of Hell (Book 1)
Hell's Fury (Book 2)

JACOB HUNTER THRILLERS
The Kyiv File (Book 1)
The Bogota File (Book 2)

PETER BLACK THRILLERS
Burden of the Assassin (Book 1)
The Man Without A Face (Book 2)
Unpunished Deeds (Book 3)
Hunter Killer (Book 4)
Silent Shadows (Book 5)
The Last Run (Book 6)
Dark Corners (Book 7)
Ghost Operative (Book 8)

ALEX MASON THRILLERS
Odin (Book 1)
Ice Cold Spy (Book 2)
Mason's Law (Book 3)
Assets and Liabilities (Book 4)
Russian Roulette (Book 5)

Executive Order (Book 6)
Dead Man Talking (Book 7)
All The King's Men (Book 8)
Flashpoint (Book 9)
Brotherhood of the Goat (Book 10)
Dead Hot (Book 11)
Blood on Megiddo (Book 12)
Son of Hell (Book 13)

NOAH WOLF THRILLERS
Code Name Camelot (Book 1)
Lone Wolf (Book 2)
In Sheep's Clothing (Book 3)
Hit for Hire (Book 4)
The Wolf's Bite (Book 5)
Black Sheep (Book 6)
Balance of Power (Book 7)
Time to Hunt (Book 8)
Red Square (Book 9)
Highest Order (Book 10)
Edge of Anarchy (Book 11)
Unknown Evil (Book 12)
Black Harvest (Book 13)
World Order (Book 14)
Caged Animal (Book 15)
Deep Allegiance (Book 16)
Pack Leader (Book 17)
High Treason (Book 18)
A Wolf Among Men (Book 19)
Rogue Intelligence (Book 20)
Alpha (Book 21)

Rogue Wolf (Book 22)
Shadows of Allegiance (Book 23)
In the Grip of Darkness (Book 24)

SAM PRICHARD MYSTERIES
The Grave Man (Book 1)
Death Sung Softly (Book 2)
Love and War (Book 3)
Framed (Book 4)
The Kill List (Book 5)
Drifter: Part One (Book 6)
Drifter: Part Two (Book 7)
Drifter: Part Three (Book 8)
The Last Song (Book 9)
Ghost (Book 10)
Hidden Agenda (Book 11)

SAM AND INDIE MYSTERIES
Aces and Eights (Book 1)
Fact or Fiction (Book 2)
Close to Home (Book 3)
Brave New World (Book 4)
Innocent Conspiracy (Book 5)
Unfinished Business (Book 6)
Live Bait (Book 7)
Alter Ego (Book 8)
More Than It Seems (Book 9)
Moving On (Book 10)
Worst Nightmare (Book 11)
Chasing Ghosts (Book 12)
Serial Superstition (Book 13)

CHANCE REDDICK THRILLERS
Innocent Injustice (Book 1)
Angel of Justice (Book 2)
High Stakes Hunting (Book 3)
Personal Asset (Book 4)

CASSIE MCGRAW MYSTERIES
What Lies Beneath (Book 1)
Can't Fight Fate (Book 2)
One Last Game (Book 3)
Never Really Gone (Book 4)

ALSO BY VINCE VOGEL

Up to date books can be found at:

www.righthouse.com/vince-vogel

PETER BLACK THRILLERS

Burden of the Assassin (Book 1)

The Man Without A Face (Book 2)

Unpunished Deeds (Book 3)

Hunter Killer (Book 4)

Silent Shadows (Book 5)

The Last Run (Book 6)

Dark Corners (Book 7)

Ghost Operative (Book 8)

JACK SHERIDAN MYSTERIES

A Cross to Bear (Book 1)

The Clay House (Book 2)

Into The Woods (Book 3)

The End is Nigh (Book 4)

A Step Into The Dark (Book 5)

Holier Than Thou (Book 6)

Streetlight City (Book 7)

An Offering for Sin (Book 8)

A Lark on the Wind (Book 9)

A Glass Darkly (Book 10)

Never Came Home (Book 11)

ALEX DORRING THRILLER

Agent 192 (Book 1)

The Hitman's Death (Book 2)

The Wrong Man (Book 3)

Who Dares Wins (Book 4)

The Highwaymen (Book 5)

The Ring (Book 6)

ABOUT US

Right House is an independent publisher created by authors for readers. We specialize in Action, Thriller, Mystery, and Crime novels.

If you enjoyed this novel, then there is a good chance you will like what else we have to offer! Please stay up to date by using any of the links below.

Join our mailing lists to stay up to date -->
righthouse.com/email
Visit our website --> righthouse.com
Contact us --> contact@righthouse.com

 facebook.com/righthousebooks

 x.com/righthousebooks

 instagram.com/righthousebooks

EXCLUSIVE SNEAK PEAK OF...

UNPUNISHED DEEDS

CHAPTER 1

OLENIVKA PRISON COLONY, EAST UKRAINE - RUSSIAN OCCUPIED TERRITORY

VASILY SAVELYEV SITS INSIDE A MIL MI-24 helicopter gunship staring out of the window at its ominous shadow gliding over an expanse of flat grassland. The scenery is relatively peaceful—for a war zone, at least. Along the horizon are low hills, beyond which are the Ukrainians, and the rapidly growing momentum of their counter offensive.

But Savelyev tries not to think about that. Instead he concentrates on the work ahead.

Vasily Savelyev is a commander in the Federal Security Service of the Russian Federation (FSB), the principal security service of Russia and main successor agency to the Soviet Union's KGB. With the Russian state essentially stretching into new territory, it means a widening of responsibilities for men like Savelyev. Chances to be a hero.

The prison colony comes into view. Tall fencing punctuated by gun towers surrounds a compound of rectangular concrete structures. They look like shoeboxes from a distance. Their walls are pitted with tiny, horizontal barred windows, mere slits in the stone. Very little sunlight reaches inside the dark chambers of Olenivka.

Before the war, this was where the Ukrainians would send their very worst. Now the Russians bring captured soldiers here.

The chopper lands at the far end of the compound. The relevant group of soldiers are there to greet Savelyev and check the legitimacy of his identification. All the men here are members of a Chechen unit already infamous in the war.

The one known as Scorpion Team.

Savelyev feels uneasy in their presence. In his early years, during the Second Chechen War, the FSB man had spent so long "disappearing" and torturing young Chechen men that he now felt uneasy around them. Like the ghosts of their ancestors hung from them. *Hell,* he would think whenever in their company, *I may well have once tortured one of these men's fathers or uncles.*

Nevertheless, time rolls over everything. Enemies become friends. Friends enemies.

"Take me to Tagirov," Savelyev says to the officer who hands back his papers.

The officer has gray in his beard and a sunbaked face. It wrinkles into a frown. "You mean the Colonel?"

"Yes."

The man guides him toward one of the concrete blocks. As they get closer, the sounds of men shouting, pleading, screaming, gets louder and louder until they are reaching the entrance to the cellblock and the cacophony rings in Savelyev's skull.

A soldier stands one side of the door. He salutes the officer and opens it for them.

The change in atmosphere is instant. Outside, the air was fresh, the world open. In here it is stifling and oppressive. The air thick with the stench of despairing horror: sweat, blood, feces.

Savelyev almost chokes on it.

"It takes some getting used to," the officer says, holding out a bottle of water.

Savelyev thanks him and takes the bottle, slugging a mouthful down, hoping to wash away the taste of this place. The worst of the screaming comes from behind a closed door at the very end of the corridor. The officer tells him it is where "the Colonel" is.

Of course it is, Savelyev thinks.

The officer leads on. They pass the barred walls of cells. Inside are men. They look barely alive, like the animals of some backwater traveling zoo. Some of them don't even look that good.

A soldier blocks the door. A few words are exchanged between him and the officer and it is opened for them. Savelyev steps into a small red brick chamber with a vaulted ceiling. The acoustics of the room amplify the insane screams to the point that the air shakes.

The door slams shut behind them, closing them in with it. Savelyev stands staring at a badly beaten man tied to an X-shaped rack. Splayed out across it as though he were frozen in the act of performing a jumping jack. His hands and feet are bound to the rack and he is naked except for the black hood over his head.

Two men occupy the room with him. Members of Team Scorpion. Tagirov stands before the hooded man like an artist in front of his work, running a hand down his thick beard.

"Colonel," the officer says to him.

The artist turns. Tagirov is just how Savelyev remembers him—crazy eyed, black bearded. Grinning, the Chechen shows off a set of yellow teeth.

"Savelyev," he hisses. "Long time no see, old friend."

The grin rides up the black hairs of his cheeks.

"Tagirov," Savelyev grunts back.

The two men don't shake hands. Don't hug. They aren't "old friends," despite the Chechen saying it. These men only meet for one reason, and one reason alone.

"The last time you came to see me," Tagirov says, "a lot of people ended up dead."

"They did."

"So what is it now?"

"Two things."

Tagirov goes to speak but Savelyev interrupts him.

"Outside," he says. "Away from your men."

Tagirov turns to the man in there with him. A dead-eyed subordinate with the look of death about him.

"You remember Khodov, don't you?"

The dead-eyed man nods respectfully at Savelyev.

"I do," the FSB commander says. "But I prefer to speak only to you."

"So be it." Tagirov turns to the officer. "Help Khodov with the interrogation."

"Yes, Colonel."

The two men leave the cell and the hooded man recommences with his screaming. When they exit the cellblock and enter sunlight, Savelyev feels himself able to breathe again. Tagirov, on the other hand, squints in it, bringing an arm over his face to protect his eyes. He looks as though he preferred the darkness.

"Wow," he says. "It's been a while since I was outside."

He takes a pair of shades from the breast pocket of his camo shirt and slips them on.

"That's better," he says before turning to Savelyev. "Now what is it you've come to ask?"

"This morning I got word that we are repositioning our defensive line eastwards."

Tagirov frowns. "Another retreat?"

"Not retreat. A strategic repositioning of battle lines."

"I'm sorry. I'm not Russian. I don't have your capacity for state-sponsored bullshit. It is a retreat."

"Call it what you want. In twenty-four hours the Ukrainians will be here. Before you and your unit move on, I need you to cover up what you've been doing in this place. The last thing we need are more pictures of atrocities in the hands of our enemies."

"And then what?"

"I have a new mission for you."

"What new mission?"

"A very important one. Easily the most important mission you've ever been on. One which will go down in history."

"History?"

"Yes. But before I brief you properly, I need you to get rid of this place."

"Count it done."

Tagirov turns to a subordinate and tells him in Chechen to evacuate all buildings of soldiers and to leave the prisoners chained in their cells. Then he asks the guy to get him an RPG-7 shoulder launcher and a crate of GSh-7VT anti-bunker warheads.

CHAPTER 2

SORRENTO, ITALY

THE THRILL OF A GOOD ENGINE. THE ROAD rushing by a few inches below you, gliding on the air itself. The tremble of the wheel beneath your grip. The tiger's roar when you accelerate. The bucket seat surging you forwards.

This is what life is all about, Michael says to himself as he slides the black 1987 Ferrari Testarossa convertible along the sunbaked coast of southern Italy. The road follows the shore and every now and then they pass through little towns —Torre del Greco, Torre Annunciata, Castellammare— until, finally, they are approaching home: Sorrento.

From here on, the road is a narrow ridge cut into the side of the rock cliffs. Peter, who sits in the passenger seat, watches the villages down below at the water's edge slip by, the houses resembling breadcrumbs.

As the landscape rises into Sorrento, they come across a

bolder in the middle of the road that has broken away from the cliff.

Michael dodges it with a nonchalant swerve.

Houses line the rocks above them, straggling up the mountain, and below, the tile roofs of the lower buildings are silhouetted against the blue sea.

It is late afternoon when they arrive at the old stone city on the edge of the cliffs. Michael steers the Ferrari up zigzagging cobbled streets, toward home; a large two-story house with an iron gate that opens onto the road, and a terrace that projects over the cliff's edge, giving them the perfect view of the sea and surrounding streets.

As well as a good sniper's nest. If that is ever needed.

"What are you going to do when we get back?" Michael asks as he taxis through the narrow thoroughfares.

"Probably take another shower. I can still smell blood in my nostrils."

"Oh stop going on about it. I said I was sorry, didn't I?"

"You could try listening to me next time. I told you the M82 was too much. You should have stuck with the SSG 69 using .308 Winchester rounds like I told you."

"But would they have penetrated the glass?"

"Yes. They would have. And they certainly wouldn't have caused the guy's head to explode all over me."

"Yeah yeah yeah," the kid waves away as they reach their street. Then. "Who's that?"

A tall man in a black suit stands in front of their gate. Michael stops the Ferrari a few yards from him. Lays a hand on the grip of the pistol hidden beside his seat.

"It's okay," Peter says. "It's Salvatore."

The long-limbed Salvatore strolls up to Peter's side.

"Can we speak inside?" he asks in a deep voice.

"Sure."

———

MICHAEL MAKES the coffee while Peter and Salvatore sit in the shade of the living-room. The Italian is sixty-three years of age with grayish skin and bloodshot eyes like a bloodhound.

Despite his washed-out look, the man is probably the most socially connected person in this part of the world. Sure, you won't find him attending Puccini operas with politicians or being asked his opinion on news items. He has no presence on social media, let alone a following. He's not an influencer.

But he is still very much connected. Because the circles that Salvatore spends his time in aren't the types to advertise themselves or their activities. The shadows are where men like Salvatore spend their time, and, like a spider with a web, the jaundiced Italian listens out for the vibrations of his people, and for a fee, sells what he finds out to those willing to pay.

Peter and Michael keep him on a retainer. Make sure that they are the first to find out if a hit has been placed on them or if a police investigation is getting to close.

"Two men have been asking around for you," he says once the coffee is served. "They are offering a huge price just for this address."

"Names?"

"No names and I cannot describe them because this information came to me secondhand. Only this morning one of my associates asked if I knew anything about Azrael living in Italy."

"How much are they offering?"

"A million just for this address."

Michael widens his eyes. "Wow." Turning to Peter, he asks him if he knows anyone that would be willing to pay such a high price.

"Many," is the answer he gives the kid.

"Look," Salvatore says, "I take my contract with you seriously. I never break an oath. But others know where you are. And they may be more willing to sell you out, so be careful, Azrael."

He finishes his coffee and leaves after that.

Michael and Peter watch him walk away from an upstairs window.

"What are you going to do?" Michael asks.

Peter takes a deep breath and then lets it out. "I don't know."

They watch Salvatore all the way until he disappears around the curve off the street.

"Come on," Peter then says. "It's your turn to cook."

"I'm not eating at home."

"Oh?"

"No. I'm eating out with Bianca."

"That little girl you've been dating?"

Michael knits his brows. "She's not a little girl. Anyway, there's a pizzeria that she's been raving about. Then, afterwards, we're off to a party."

Right on cue, a moped horn sounds down below in the street.

"That's her now," the kid adds. "Don't wait up."

Michael applies a couple of splashes of expensive eau de cologne and skips out of the house. Peter watches from the window as he climbs onto the back of the girl's scooter and they buzz off.

"So I'll be eating alone," he says to himself. "Again."

CHAPTER 3

TYRRHENIAN SEA, ITALY

FOUR O'CLOCK THE NEXT MORNING, IN THE twilight just before dawn, Peter and Michael sail their small boat the *Mother-Magda* toward a set of tiny islands about eight miles off the Gulf of Naples. A collection of craggy rocks poke from the scalp of the sea and begin to emerge along the horizon with the sun.

Peter is in control of the craft. Michael too busy throwing up over the side.

"I take it you drunk beer at this party," the father says.

All Michael can do is hold a thumb up to him.

A few minutes later the kid comes away and flushes his mouth out with bottled water, washes the dregs from his chin. When he rejoins Peter at the cockpit, his father is holding out a stick of gum.

"Thanks," the kid mumbles as he takes it, before lumping himself down in a seat at the stern.

After a few cups of coffee from a thermos, Michael is more with it. "The wind's coming in from the east," he tells Peter. "If you want to hit the landing spot you need to steer into it. Otherwise we'll sail past and have to go around again."

When they initially bought the *Mother-Magda* Peter didn't have the first clue about sailing. A sailboat wasn't exactly the sort of thing you used in the world of espionage. It was a skill he had never required. If he needed to get around on water, he chose a motorboat every time. Didn't rely on the wind.

Michael, on the other hand, spent much of his summer vacations as a youngster with his stepfather Carl on their yacht. By ten he had learned to sail. Now he was passing that skill upwards to his father.

"How was the party?" Peter asks as he pitches the craft into the wind.

"It was good."

The kid is green.

"It looks it."

"The only reason I'm so ill," Michael attests in a somewhat bitter tone, "is because I'd only managed two hours sleep before my father came crashing into my room, telling me we'd be training today."

"We have to stay alert," Peter tells him. "Training sharpens the senses. Plus, it gives me a chance to hang out with you. You're always with your friends. I hardly see you anymore."

Michael grins. "You miss me?"

"You're my son. Of course I do."

The kid chuckles.

"You find that funny?"

"No," Michael assures him. "I find it sweet."

"Sweet?"

Peter has turned around to him.

"Yeah. That you miss me. Now pay attention or we won't make the spot. We wouldn't want you missing that, too."

———

FANG ISLAND IS a cluster of jagged, rocky islands that poke out the water and resemble teeth. Hence the name the locals have given it. Officially, Fang Island has never had a name, and only shipwrecked fishermen have ever called it home. Well, except for a brief period during World War II when the Nazis built a collection of fortifications on the three largest of the islands and placed armaments there in case the Allies ever invaded from the south. A series of concrete blocks that are partially buried in the excavated clifftops stand as the only testament of that time. The sea has greened much of them now through the perpetual crash of waves, but the bunkers themselves are still relatively intact.

They tie the boat up at the only place you can—a rickety jetty that sticks out from the sheer cliffs—then scale thirty meters of pure vertical rock wall, carrying 100lb loads on their backs.

Like Peter was at his age, Michael is now a sinewed machine adept at physical strain of any type, his body displaying perfect balance.

At the top, they find their usual gap in the barbwire

fencing, ignoring the futile keep-out signs, and make their way into the main hallway of the bunker.

The sounds of the sea echo in the vaulted space. Dawn is here and wedges of sunlight shine in through the horizontal gunner slots that line the walls.

Peter checks over his weapon; a Tavor CTAR-21 bullpup battle weapon. Once he's sure of its tip-top condition, he twists a custom-made suppressor on the end—being that he would prefer it if passing fishermen didn't hear them.

In the meantime, Michael tightens the straps on the body armor covering his torso.

"You know the drill," Peter says in a cool tone. "The flag is on the other side of the island. You have a five-minute head start. You have to get the flag, then double back and bring it here. Place it in that holder." He points to his left, where they've fixed a loop of rope to the wall. "Added to that," Peter says next, pulling back the cocking lever on the side of the Tavor's barrel, "we won't be using paintballs, because..."

"... it doesn't have the same psychological effect as knowing you could really die," Michael says over him. "Yeah yeah."

"There should be consequences," Peter says sternly. "Even in training."

"You're starting to sound like Mother."

"You want me to discipline like her?"

"No."

"Then make sure your helmet's on properly. I wouldn't want it slipping off and you taking one in the head."

The kid thinks about this. Then he asks, "What would you do if you did accidentally kill me?"

Peter spends a second or two pondering it. Then he

answers. "Probably bury you somewhere on the island, go back to the house, pack up what I can carry, leave."

"Cold."

"I keep telling you. It's the life of the assassin. Now run!"

———

Four hours later Michael commands the boat as Fang Island shrinks into the horizon behind them. His shoulder aches where Peter got a hit on his body armor, and from time to time he flexes the arm to relieve it a little. Peter doesn't allow him the use of pharmacological pain relief. Only meditation.

It's now nine o'clock in the morning and many of the other sailing boats are on the water, enjoying the bright and beautiful day.

"Why are we heading back to Sorrento?" Peter asks his son as the mainland looms into view. "I thought we were sailing out to Capri today."

"We are," the kid assures him. "But first we have to pick up Bianca."

Peter groans inwardly.

Fifteen minutes later they arrive at Sorrento harbor. There, at the end of a jetty, stands the pretty Bianca in shorts and polo shirt, a sash of red linen tied around her slender neck. Black hair flows down her back and big Dior sunglasses cover her eyes. A $350 gift from Michael for her birthday.

"Ah, bambino!" she shrieks when Michael jumps out of the boat and takes her in his arms.

It's left to Peter to tie the boat up.

With the help of Michael, who holds her delicate hand as though she were a princess, Bianca steps on board the thirty-foot craft.

"Ciao, Peter," she says with a smile.

"Good morning..."

She doesn't even wait for him to finish.

"... Bianca."

The girl has already turned to Michael, flipped her sunglasses up onto the top of her head, and, showing off her white teeth, throws herself into his arms, the teens necking almost straight away. Peter forced to avert his gaze. Then Michael grimaces when she squeezes his shoulder.

"Oh, baby," she coos, coming away from him. "Are you hurt?"

"It's nothing," he tells her bravely.

"Let me see."

He lets her lift his shirt and when she sees the bruising from the gunshot—purple and shaped like a fist—she cries out tenderly.

"My God! What happened, bambino?"

"I fell while we were rock climbing."

"Again?"

Bruises being a regular occurrence.

"Yes. But not too bad."

"Let me kiss it better."

This is too much for Peter. He has to leave them. Go somewhere else. But it's a small sailboat. All he can do is untie them from the jetty and pilot the *Mother-Magda* back out to sea, doing his best to avert his eyes.

———

DURING THE JOURNEY TO CAPRI, Peter does most of the sailing. The two teenagers spending the time giggling in the cabin. At one point, he decides to be facetious. In a loud voice, he asks Bianca how her father is. To which, Michael walks to the cabin doorway, eyeballs him from within, and unceremoniously closes the doors.

The day in Capri is much the same. The two teenagers practically ignore Peter as they stroll lazily around the narrow thoroughfares and market piazzas, the stalls and the shops. In the end, he leaves the lovebirds to it. Just peels off on his own, the two of them not even noticing his absence until he is long gone.

He simply sends Michael a text that he'll meet them back at the boat at five. To which he gets a thumbs up emoji as a reply.

For the rest of his lonely time on Capri, Peter sits people-watching from the café terraces. As for Michael, there's only one person he has any desire to watch.

Bianca.

The way she smiles with her teeth, eyes shining, the dimples on her cheeks showing, breathes light into him— makes everything taste better, look better, feel better. Not to mention the way anything can trigger that smile. Simple things like finding an ornament in some dusty tourist shop that she thinks quaint—or the low-ceilinged basement rooms at the bottom of an old bookshop that excite her.

There is such joy in her enthusiasm for life that she appears to hog all the light to herself. Like it is drawn to her and everything around her is cast in shadow.

Sometimes this includes Michael. And he can't help

worrying, during these moments, about how she would feel toward him if she knew what he was.

A killer.

The teens spend most of the day on the beach. Sunbathing and swimming. In the afternoon, they swim around the rocky coast to some caves they know. Inside is their own private place, and there they do what most teenagers do in such isolated settings. They make out.

Not that it makes it to sex.

On the occasions it ever gets that far, Bianca reminds Michael that she is Roman Catholic, not bothering to mention the part about sex before marriage, but definitely implying it.

Michael suspects the real reason has nothing to do with religion. That the truth is she's shy. Like Michael is shy. They're both virgins, and their inexperience shows. Each time they get close to the act, they back away. Bianca mentioning about being Roman Catholic, and Michael naturally disengaging, inwardly grateful, whilst at the same time wondering what would happen if she didn't stop him.

He can tell that it's getting close. That eventually the two of them will step over that line—that daunting, fascinating, exciting line. That they will take the plunge into the unknown.

Michael tries not to think of this as the two of them slip into the water and swim back to the beach.

———

"Do you think your papa likes me?" Bianca asks.

They are making their way to the harbor along a cobbled boulevard that runs past various little shops and cafés.

"Of course he does," Michael assures his girlfriend.

"But he never talks to me."

"Peter never talks, period. Don't take it personal."

She waits a little while. Then. "Mikey, why don't you respect your papa?"

"I do respect him."

"Then why do you call him Peter?"

"I told you. I had another father before."

"Yes. Carl. But Carl wasn't your real papa."

"I know. But when you've spent most of your life calling one man dad, it's hard to then call another man the same word."

"I guess. Ah! Gelato."

Bianco shows her teeth and draws in more light.

It makes Michael smile. Her attention so easily won.

And lost.

He buys them both ice cream and they walk off eating them.

"Michael?" Bianca says in the tone she uses when she is about to ask something personal.

"Bianca?" Michael replies in the same tone.

"I know you told me it is business. But what business is it that your papa is into?"

"I told you, he doesn't like me talking about it."

"But what is it?"

"It's a secret," he tells her before taking a lick of his gelato and winking.

She simpers at him. "Oh, Michael. You know how much I like secrets. Please tell me."

He grins at her. Opens his mouth. Looks like he's about to spill the beans. Then teases her with, "No. I can't."

She pouts, her bottom lip sticking out. "Michael, please," she whines. "If you love me, you would."

"You really want to know?"

She claps her hands together. "Yes. Yes."

In an ominous tone, looking left and right before he says it, Michael tells her, "He sells guns."

Her eyes are wide. "To banditos?"

"No no. He trades them legitimately to armed forces. Police. Things like that. We're in Italy because he's contracting for Beretta. Promoting their handguns."

"Really?"

"Yes. He doesn't like me to say because, well, you know, people don't always like guns. They get funny. Especially with those that trade and sell them."

"So your papa is an arms dealer?"

"No," he corrects. "Not an arms dealer. He's a legitimate salesperson working for Beretta."

"That sounds so much more boring."

"Would you prefer it if my father was an arms dealer?"

She smiles. Then her eyes brighten even more. "No. Better than that. I would prefer it if he was a hired killer. An assassin."

Michael blushes. Concentrates on the ice cream.

But then she shakes her head. "No. Not an assassin. Your papa could never be an assassin. He is too... boring."

She laughs loudly and Michael prods her on the nose with his ice cream.

"Michael?!" she squeals, wiping it off.

She goes to get him back, but he sidesteps it and her ice cream falls onto the floor.

"I'll get you!" she says, coming at him, and then tripping on a protruding cobble and falling into his arms, where he catches her and then pulls her up to him. "You saved me, Michael," she says.

"Then you owe me a kiss."

"I do," she says, showing off her white teeth.

Scan the QR code below to purchase UNPUNISHED DEEDS.
Or go to: righthouse.com/unpunished-deeds